THE BABY I STOLE

An unputdownable psychological thriller with an astonishing twist

MCGARVEY BLACK

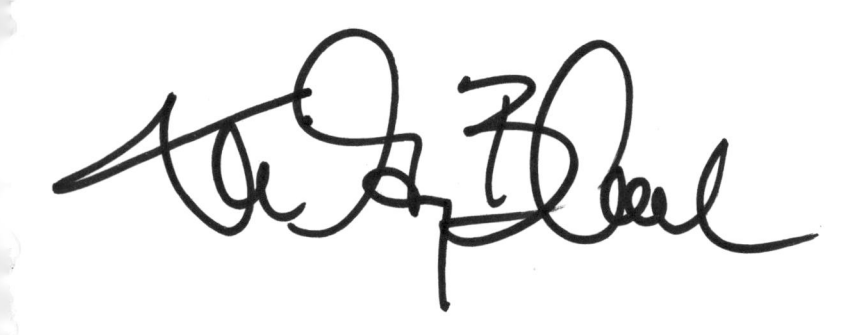

Joffe Books, London
www.joffebooks.com

First published in Great Britain in 2024

© McGarvey Black 2024

This book is a work of fiction. Names, characters, businesses, organizations, places and events are either the product of the author's imagination or are used fictitiously. Any resemblance to actual persons, living or dead, events or locales is entirely coincidental. The spelling used is American English except where fidelity to the author's rendering of accent or dialect supersedes this. The right of McGarvey Black to be identified as author of this work has been asserted in accordance with the Copyright, Designs and Patents Act 1988.

Cover art by Nick Castle

ISBN: 978-1-83526-347-1

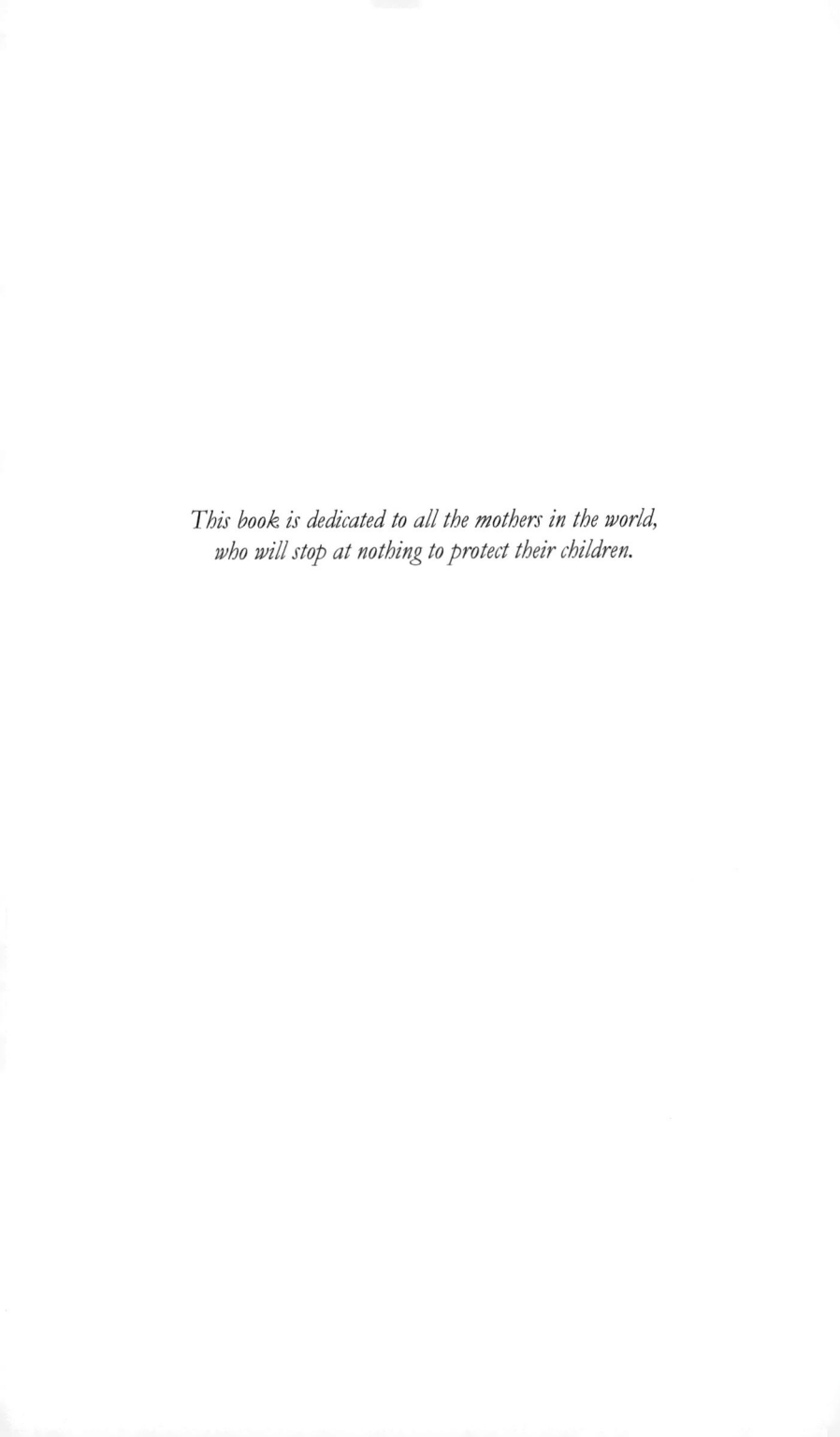

This book is dedicated to all the mothers in the world, who will stop at nothing to protect their children.

PROLOGUE

Rocky Point Beach — The Hamptons
Long Island, New York

The shrill sound of a whistle pierces the air. When I look up, two lifeguards jump down from their tall chair onto the sand. They're waving their arms and signaling for everyone to get out of the ocean. Most of the people on the beach get up and head towards the water. I'm halfway between the shore and the parking lot standing on my towel trying to get a glimpse of what's going on. Several young men run past me. I distinctly hear one of them say the word "shark." I shudder. We've had shark sightings in the Hamptons before.

Out in the water, I see three young lifeguards repeatedly dive under. A crowd forms along the water's edge with everyone talking and pointing at once. Some are taking videos of the chaos in the water. It's bedlam.

Unable to surmise exactly what's happening but desperate to know, I too walk towards the water. On the way, two teenage girls come towards me.

"What's going on?" I shout out to them. "Did somebody get hurt?"

"Some guy said a woman went under," says one. "The rip currents are really bad today."

My pulse quickens as I look out at the chaos erupting in the surf.

"It's not a shark, then?" I say.

"I don't think so," says the other teenager. "Some kid told us a woman's been missing for almost fifteen minutes. Can you live after being under the water that long?"

I shrug my shoulders and shake my head, a sick feeling overtaking me. The sun's in my eyes, but as I get closer to the water's edge, I can clearly see the lifeguards' desperate attempts to find the missing woman.

Sasha's been under for twenty minutes. She can't be alive after all that time.

I watch the sad scene in the surf for a moment before I turn. With my arms full, I walk back up the beach to my towel. That's when I make a snap decision knowing it will change my life forever. Grabbing the beach bags, I fill them as quickly as possible and throw the straps over my shoulders. Then, I pick up the carrier.

Before making my final move, I take one last look around making sure I've left no trace of anything. Everyone is focused on the drama playing out in the water, not on me. After a quick panoramic scan of the beach, I take my first step towards the parking lot with only one thought — get to the car before they find out.

I've not gone far when two police cars, lights flashing, pull in. My heart is pounding and I can literally feel the blood coursing through my veins. I wonder, will this cardiac strain I'm experiencing be that seminal event that does me in? The doctors have all warned me about this.

Four officers leap out of their still-running vehicles and run directly towards me.

They know. They're coming to get me. My husband won't understand. I'm a mother now. A mother will do anything to protect her child, even go to prison or worse.

Fifty yards separate me from the oncoming police. In thirty seconds, they'll be on top of me and it will all be over.

Twenty-nine.

Twenty-eight.

Twenty-seven.

A voice screams inside my head. *Stop and everything will go back to normal.*

Deep down, I know the voice is lying. Some things can never go back to the way they were, no matter how much we want them to.

Thirteen.

Twelve.

Eleven.

I don't listen and keep moving towards my car.

I'll never tell anyone what happened today, not even my husband. This will be my secret alone for the rest of my life.

The cops are so close now, I can practically see the color of their eyes. One has a mole on his left cheek. To avoid eye contact, I look down and fuss with my beach bags before stealing a glance at them. That's when I realize they're not looking at me. They're gazing over my head at the ocean. They're not here for me at all, they're here for her.

Three.

Two.

One.

As the police blast by me, my legs turn into limp noodles barely able to hold my adrenaline-fueled body erect. To ground myself, I dig my toes deeper into the warm sand and try to calmly walk to my car. Easier said than done.

Loading up the back seat as fast as possible, I close the car doors and slide in behind the wheel. Once the car is in drive, I slam my foot on the gas pedal and pull quickly out of the parking lot, my tires spitting up gravel. As I pull out onto the highway, every nerve ending in my body is on fire.

After there's some distance between me and Rocky Point Beach, I look into the rearview. No one's behind me so I slow down, but only a little. I need to get far away from here before anyone sees me or my car.

My parents' beach house is ten minutes away on the other side of the big pond. I turn off the highway a few blocks from their home and pull over to the side of the road to call my husband.

It rings four times before he answers.

"Daniel," I say, unbridled excitement in my voice, "You're not going to believe what happened. I have the most wonderful news . . ."

CHAPTER ONE

THE WIFE

Three Hours Earlier

It's a clear June morning on the East End of Long Island. The car windows are down as I pull into the Rocky Point Beach parking lot and grab the last available space. There are only twenty. Rocky Point is mainly used by the locals. It's never crowded like some of the other beaches. My goal today is to bury myself in a new book for a few hours and maybe take a nap.

As my feet hit the sand, I look around for my special spot on the right-hand side of the beach. There's a lone tree over there that provides shade, but only in the mornings. Whenever my husband and I come here, I insist on setting up camp by that tree. Too much sun will destroy your complexion. One has to take extra care of one's skin after turning forty.

I trudge through the warm sand towards "my spot." As I get closer, I see another woman has the same idea. She's younger than me, with long dark hair and is wearing a large, floppy-brimmed straw hat with a red ribbon. I stop and look around for an alternative location for myself knowing there is none. I've been here hundreds of times and there's only one shady area and that's it. The rest of the beach is virtually empty. Will she think I'm weird for plunking myself down right next to her when there are so many other places I could sit? I have my skin to consider, so I continue walking towards her.

"Excuse me," I say as I approach her, "I hope you don't mind, but this is the only spot on the beach that has any shade and I was wondering if . . ."

"It's a free country. Help yourself," she replies with a smile before pushing her large dark sunglasses up the bridge of her perfectly straight nose. "It's fine with me as long as you don't mind the noise."

Noise? I look down. She's got a baby in a portable car seat.

"Don't worry," she says with a light but distinctly Slavic accent, "he's a very good boy, hardly ever cries."

I smile and lean over to get a look at the sleeping child. When I see his face, he takes my breath away. Soft wisps of light-brown hair, tiny red bow lips and the chubbiest cheeks — he's gorgeous.

"He's beautiful," I say. "How old is he?"

The woman stands up in her one-piece navy-blue swimsuit, stretching her arms across her chest, first one, then the other. She's incredibly fit and I'm a little jealous.

"He's four months old," she says, "and he's the love of my life."

I look down at him again and notice he has a faint strawberry mark between his eyes. She must see me looking at it because she says something.

"It was much darker when he was born. The doctors say his spot will disappear in a few months and everything will be perfect."

"I'm sure the doctors are right. You can barely see it now."

She nods. "I hope so."

"You look amazing, by the way," I say in awe of her physical condition. I work out with a trainer once a week and don't look half as good as she does right after giving birth. Life can be so unfair.

She nods. I smile awkwardly and lay my towel down as far from her as possible while still staying in the shade. Once settled, I lie down and flip over on my back to stretch. Usually, I can lie on a beach for hours, but this day, I'm restless. I wait a few minutes and flip back onto my stomach, pull out my book and try to read. Despite trying, I can't concentrate. Something about this woman with the accent and the baby intrigues me. I catch myself glancing over at them several times while pretending to read.

"I notice you have a slight accent," I shout out. "Where are you from?"

She tips back the brim of her large straw hat, peers at me over the top of her sunglasses and smiles. Now, I can see she's got dark-brown eyes, professionally shaped brows and a small beauty mark near her right eye.

"You have a good ear," she says. "Most people don't notice it. I'm originally from the Czech Republic, but I've been living in the States since I was eleven. Have you ever been to Prague?"

"No. I've heard it's beautiful."

"You should go there in the spring," she says while checking on her baby. She fusses with his blanket and then lays her head back down on her towel.

With nothing left to say, I continue with my book, keeping one eye on the girl from Prague. I finish a chapter and reach for a piece of gum. Still curious or maybe just nosey, I call out to her again. "You want some gum?"

She sits up and smiles. "I would love it. My throat is so dry." Trying not to groan as I stand, I push myself up off the sand, walk over, and hand her a piece. She thanks me and I return to my towel.

"I love this beach," I say loud enough for her to hear as I sit down. "Never too crowded and there's always lifeguards. Better safe than sorry."

"It's my first time," she says. "I just moved here from Chicago a week ago. I'm renting an Airbnb for the summer. Tomorrow, I'll start looking for a job. You live here?"

I shake my head. "I'm staying at my parents' summer house for a few weeks while they're in Europe. My husband and I live in Brooklyn. I work at an art gallery in Manhattan."

"I love art. And your husband?"

I smile. "He's an actor."

"So, you married a movie star," she says with a grin as she stretches her right leg up and arches her foot, pulling it towards her chest with her arms.

I laugh. "Not quite. Daniel's a *struggling* actor. He's had small walk-on parts in a few films and TV series. He's also done some Off-Off-Broadway, but nothing big. He makes most of his money doing modeling jobs for men's clothing and things like that."

"He must be very handsome."

I grin. "I think so."

"You have kids?"

I press my lips together, trying to decide how much of my personal life I want to share with a total stranger. I answer her question honestly because I'm in the mood to talk and she seems nice. Also, I'll probably never see her again.

"Not yet," I say. "We've been trying, but no luck so far." I guess this intrigues her because she flips onto her side, puts her hand under her head and looks directly at me. I've got her full attention, so I keep talking. "I have this stupid heart thing and my doctors want me to focus on that." She nods and I shift the conversation back to her. "Are you out here with your husband?"

"It's only me and my son," she says as she reaches into the baby carrier and strokes her son lovingly. I feel a distinct pang of jealousy as I watch the tender mother/son moment. *I want to be a mother so bad.*

"I'm sorry, I didn't mean to pry," I say hoping I hadn't been too personal. I was enjoying our conversation. I didn't want it to end because I invaded her space or sounded judgmental.

"No worries," she says as she sits up and looks at me. "I met Liam's father at a huge party in Chicago. His name was Jack . . . I think. Never got his last name, and I'm still not a hundred percent sure about his first. We'd been doing shots of tequila at an open bar. He was handsome, and we were both drunk. We left the party early and went to some hotel. He paid cash for the room and I left the next morning while he was still sleeping. I never saw him again. Seven weeks later, I took a test and I was pregnant."

"Liam's father has no idea he has a son?"

The woman in the big floppy hat shakes her head. "He was in town on business. He said something about a friend of a friend had invited him to the party. He could have been married for all I know. I had no way to find him and frankly, I didn't want to."

"What about your family, your parents?"

She laughs in a mocking sort of way. "I haven't talked to them in years. They had different ideas on how I should live my life. I called them once after Liam was born, but before I could tell them they had a grandson, it was clear they didn't want anything to do with me. They hung up before I could tell them about Liam."

I feel so sorry for this young woman and search for the right words. When I finally speak, they come out sounding wooden and clinical. "I'm sorry to hear that. It must have been a very difficult time for you." *Ugh*.

She lets out another sarcastic laugh. "That's the understatement of the century. One does what one has to do in order to get by, right? I'm a survivor."

I nod in solidarity. "Maybe you could try calling them and . . . ?"

"No," she says sharply before I finish my sentence.

I feel so sorry for her. She's got no one. My life is the polar opposite. I get tremendous support from parents and Daniel. I can't imagine being all alone in the world like she is. I honestly don't know what to say, a rarity for me.

"It was partly my fault that things with my family ended badly," she continued. "My father's company transferred him to Ohio when I was eleven and my brother seven. Ohio is very different from the Czech Republic. We all became American citizens. During my senior year of high school, my father's company summoned him back to Prague. By that point, I was totally an American kid and told my parents I wasn't going back. I wanted to party and go out dancing. I liked my life here."

I nod. I get it. I like my life here, too.

"There were many loud arguments," she continues. "Then, one night I came home high and my father hit me — hard. That was the end for me. The next morning, I took off with my boyfriend on his motorcycle and disappeared. There was nothing my parents could do. I was over eighteen. A few months later, I learned my parents and brother had returned to the Czech Republic without me."

It occurs to me that this woman's story is far more compelling than the mediocre romance novel I'd been reading. I stick the book into my bag and face her, fully committing to our conversation.

"Maybe you could get in touch with them now," I say in earnest. "A baby often changes things."

She shakes her head. "It's too late. They're on the other side of the world now. They have their lives and I have mine. I'm Sasha, by the way," she shouts as she waves. "I like your bracelet."

"Tori," I say loudly, waving to her as I look down at my gold link bracelet with the dangling star charm. "My Armenian grandmother gave it to me when I turned sixteen. Her mother gave it to her when she married my grandfather."

"I can tell it's not from here. It's quite unique."

We spend the next twenty minutes chatting about a million different things. Feeling my throat growing sore from all the shouting back and forth, I suggest we move closer to each other. She nods and I pull my towel over next to hers and we talk about her employment options.

"There are loads of hospitality jobs out here in the summer," I say. "The Hamptons are full of tourists with lots of money. You should be able to find something."

She grins. "Lots of money? Maybe I'll find a rich father for Liam, and a sugar daddy for me."

I wonder if she *is* kidding as I reply. "I'm sure being a single mother isn't easy."

"You don't know the half of it. Right after I had my son, which ironically was on Valentine's Day, I got so depressed. I was completely alone and for a while, it was awful."

"Are you still feeling sad?"

"It wasn't sad so much as feeling nothing. I had this beautiful baby, but I was totally empty inside. The first few weeks after he was born were terrible. I'm much better now. I try to do more self-care, get enough sleep, eat well and have regular massages. That helps a lot."

I nod. I love massages too, so I get it.

"Yesterday," she says, becoming more animated, "I had the most amazing massage in town with this woman name Chloe. Do you know about her? She's got a storefront in that strip mall next to the farmers' market. I have two words for her — magic fingers. When I left her place, I was a totally new woman. You have to go."

I make a mental note about 'Chloe with the magic fingers' by the farmers' market, because I'm always on the lookout for a good massage. We sit without talking for a few moments looking out at the sea. Then, I break the silence.

"So, tomorrow you begin your job hunt?"

"First, I have to buy a used car. Then, I start looking for a job. You can't work out here without a car. Public transportation is very spotty."

"How did you get out here today?"

"We took the bus from the center of town."

"With all your baby stuff?"

Her son begins to sputter. Sasha takes a bottle out of her bag and lifts him from his carrier. Cradling him in her arms, she slips the nipple into his eager mouth. For the first time, I can see all of him and he's absolutely delicious.

"He's perfect," I say.

"He's an easy baby. Sleeps through the night and everything. Would you like to hold him?"

Thrilled, I take the little boy into my arms and feed him the remainder of his bottle. By the time Liam finishes, he's drifting off to sleep. I return him to his mother, who puts him over her shoulder, burps him and places him back into his makeshift beach crib.

It's midday now, the sun is high and it's getting hotter. The shady tree no longer provides as much protection and there's only a small patch of shade left between us.

"Can I ask you a huge favor?" says Sasha, wiping her brow as she looks at me over the top of her glasses.

"Sure."

"I'm absolutely roasting. Since Liam's asleep, would you mind watching him for a few minutes so I can go for a quick dip in the water to cool off? Would that be all right? I'll do a couple of laps and come right back."

I find her request a little surprising considering she hardly knows me. What kind of mother leaves her baby on a beach with a total stranger? Of course, we had been talking intimately with each other for nearly two hours so technically, I'm not a stranger. And, the truth is, our conversation was so intimate that I know more about Sasha than some people I've known for years.

"No problem," I say, pleased she trusts me that much. "Take your time. I love babies."

CHAPTER TWO

Sasha stands, pulls off her hat and glasses and tosses them onto her towel. She takes a pink hair elastic off of her wrist, whips her long hair into a ponytail. Then, she retrieves a hot-pink bathing cap from her bag. Artfully, she tucks all of her hair into the pink cap, puts a pair of goggles on her head and adjusts the straps of her suit.

Before she moves, she looks up at the sky and makes a face. "Shit. I forgot my sunscreen."

"I have some," I say, handing her a blue bottle of SPF 70 from my bag. She slathers some on her face, the back of her neck and her arms and the tops of her hands and tosses it back to me.

"Thanks, Tori. You're a lifesaver. I'll be back in ten minutes," she says as she walks towards the water.

I'm sitting over to the side near the dunes where it's slightly elevated. From there, I have a good view of the water and the entire beach. My eyes follow Sasha in the distance as she steps into the water. Then, I look down at the still-sleeping Liam and smile.

When I look up, Sasha is wading in up to her knees and going deeper into the water. When she's up to her waist, she dives into a ripple of a wave and begins to swim. The ocean is a little rough, which is why the yellow flags are out. I watch her move beyond the point where the waves break so she can swim parallel to the shore without being disrupted. As her pink cap bobs rhythmically across the water, I notice she's got good form and a nice strong even stroke. She swims all the way to the left side of the beach, flips over and swims back to the right. I watch her go back and forth for several minutes until I hear Liam making noise. He's awake. I look in Sasha's bag for the pacifier she told me to give him. Carefully, I pick up the baby and cradle him in my arms. He opens his mouth and accepts the plastic nipple and instantly quiets down.

I'm examining his facial features thinking how perfect he is when there's a long, loud whistle sound followed by four short ones. Far in the distance, I see the lifeguards jump off their tall white chair waving their arms. I look out at the water. A number of people swimming come out of the water, but I can't see the pink cap. Cupping my hand over my eyes to block the glare, I look around the water a second time, no pink cap. While one lifeguard signals for people to get out of the way, the others grab flotation devices and run into the surf. People from all over the beach get up and move towards the water. They form a line along the shoreline blocking most of my view. I can't see the pink cap. I can't see Liam's mother.

Desperate to know what's going on, I pick up the baby and, holding him tight, carry him down closer to the water's edge. As I walk, I call out to others, gleaning bits of information as I go. When I get closer, the scene in the water is pure chaos. The lifeguards are frantically searching for someone. A man next to me is on his phone and I interrupt him.

"Did someone drown?" I say, clutching the baby close.

"Looks like it," he says as he goes back to his call.

A wave of nausea passes over me as I watch the growing commotion in the water. Now, everyone on the beach is down by the water and several bystanders wade in to help with the search. Frozen, I clutch the baby tighter.

"See that rocky jetty over there?" says an older woman standing next to me pointing at the formidable rock structure, "when the currents are real strong, the undertow at this beach can hurl a person right into those rocks. I'll bet that's what happened to her."

Happened to who? To Sasha? Where the hell is Liam's mother?

As the minutes pass and Sasha doesn't appear, I start to panic. It's been at least fifteen minutes since I last saw her pink cap moving across the water. The baby is squirming now in my arms. His soft skin feels so good next to mine as he nuzzles into my neck. If Sasha *is* okay, she'd be looking for me and her baby by now. But I don't see her and I start to think the worst.

A young woman in the water who had been trying to help the lifeguards walks out of the surf and runs up the beach in my direction.

"What's going on?" I shout as she passes.

"It not good. All I know is that some woman in a pink cap went under. The current is really bad today, it almost pulled me down. That's why I got out. She must have drowned."

My legs start to buckle underneath me and my arms suddenly feel weak holding the weight of the baby. I need to put him down or I'm going to fall over and possibly drop him. A million crazy notions run through my mind. I force myself to walk to my towel while trying to collect my thoughts.

My eyes fill with tears as I slip the sweet baby into his carrier. There's a visor on the top of the portable car seat. I open it to protect him from the sun. He looks up at me with innocent, trusting eyes. He has no idea he just lost his mother.

Taking a deep breath, I scan the water one last time still looking for that bobbing pink head. *Where are you, Sasha? You trusted me to watch your son. What am I supposed to do now?*

My trance is broken when the baby starts crying. I lean over and pick him up. Clutching Sasha's child to me, I continue watching what appears to be futile lifesaving maneuvers going on in the water. That's when the terrible reality becomes clear — Sasha's probably dead, which means the baby I'm holding is an orphan.

While my brain grapples with the horrendous series of events, my body goes on auto pilot. Without realizing it, I've already stuffed Sasha's and my towels into the beach bags as I break camp. A voice inside my head asks, "What are you doing?" as I put on her floppy hat and sunglasses. *What am I doing?* It's like someone else is directing my actions and I'm simply following orders. At the same time, my supposedly weak sickly heart is beating like a fucking jackhammer. Sweat pours off of me as I continue packing up. *Do I have any choice? Sasha's got to be dead. I can't leave the baby here. She trusted him to me.*

I stop for a split second to review my life. For three years, Daniel and I have tried to get pregnant. When the doctors finally told me another IVF was out of the question because of my medical situation, we were devastated. The only choice left was to put our name on a wait list for an adoption. We did, but the agency told us it could take years.

I gather everything up from the sand and look up at the distant parking lot behind me. *Am I really doing this? What if Sasha isn't dead? Maybe she's one of the people down by the water trying to help find a different missing person? Maybe she's alive?*

I turn my head and look at the water one last time half hoping to see her pink cap bobbing again. I don't. I'm about to start moving towards my car when a young couple passes me, deep in conversation.

"She's dead for sure," the young man says loudly to his girlfriend. "No way she's still alive. Been too long."

I reflect before I move.

I promised Sasha I'd take care of her son. I have to honor that, don't I? This baby has no family. If I turn him over to the authorities, he'll go straight into foster care. I can't let that happen.

Clipping Sasha's diaper bag to the handle of the baby carrier, I look down. Liam smiles at me as I lift him.

"I won't let them take you," I say softly as I start my trek to the car. Seconds later, the police race onto the beach and I almost lose it. I take a deep breath. Every nerve in my body is activated, but I keep going and walk past them to my car.

Once on the road, I'm in full panic mode and already have second thoughts. *I could still call child services now. No crime will have been committed. I'll have rescued an abandoned baby on a beach and be a hero, a Good Samaritan.*

I continue driving on the highway, torn by competing emotions. *This beautiful child has nobody. His father and grandparents don't know he exists. Suffolk County will definitely put him into foster care, which means a lifetime of misery. I can't allow that to happen to this sweet little boy.*

A car passes me and honks. I'm going well below the speed limit so I push down on the gas pedal. I don't want to draw any attention to myself.

It's my moral obligation to take him home with me. I've heard the stories of what happens to orphans in this country. If this sweet child goes into the system, he'll be shuffled from one awful place to the next. He'll be neglected or possibly worse. What kind of monster would that make me for turning him over?

Cooing noises come from the back seat and I look into my rearview mirror. When I see his little face, my heart literally melts. Pulling over to the side of the road several blocks from my parents' house, I stop the car and turn off the engine. Daniel and I've been through so much — all the IVF procedures followed by the bitter disappointment when they didn't take. After all those tests, and all that poking around in my body, the doctors told me the drugs involved were too risky with my heart problem. Fuck my stupid heart.

A tear trickles out of my right eye and onto my cheek. I brush it away as I take out my phone and punch in my husband's number. It rings four times before he answers.

"Daniel, you're not going to believe what happened. I have the most wonderful news," I say. "The adoption agency called. They have a four-month-old baby for us. I'm on my way to pick him up right now. Daniel, can you hear me? You're going to be a father."

CHAPTER THREE

I pull up to the stop sign at the intersection of my parents' street and make a hard left. Their charming old rambling cottage is ahead, up on a hill. You can see the ocean from their backyard. It's my happy place.

About to turn into their driveway, I hit the brakes when I see an empty, blue, two-door Toyota parked on the right side of the garage. My parents are out of town and they don't have a car like that. Alarm bells sound in my head.

Someone's looking for the baby. They know.

I pull into the left side of the driveway and turn off the engine. Unsure of what I'm going to find, I call out through my open car window. "Hello?" I say several times, but no one answers.

I get out of the car and reach into the back seat to remove my special cargo. Carefully, I carry the baby up the front walk.

The front door is ajar and I feel my shitty heart start to pound. There's a noise, the sound of a motor running coming from inside. Since I have no idea who's in my parents' house, I should turn around, get back in my car and call the police. But I can't call the cops, not now, not ever. Not after what I just did. I push the door so it swings open.

"Hello?" I say as I walk through the front foyer, following the whirring noise. When I get to the archway of the living room, I see a middle-aged blonde woman vacuuming the rug. She obviously can't hear me over the sound of the motor. I shout, "Hello," again and wave at her to get her attention.

When she sees me she jumps back and shuts off the machine.

"Who are you?" I say.

"I'm Eva. I'm the cleaning woman. Who are you?" she says, peering at me as she takes another step backwards, creating more distance between us.

I point to an old family photo on the mantle. It's a thirty-eight-year-old picture of me when I was five taken with my parents when they were in their thirties. Mom, as always, is totally put together like the model she once was — dirty-blonde hair and a perfect bone structure. My father just looks intense. He's not a handsome man but makes up for it by being a force of nature that women always find appealing. He's shorter than my statuesque mother and has a dark Mediterranean complexion, hooded eyes and an abundance of flesh on his face.

"I'm Tori Petrosian, Tori Fowler now. The Petrosians are my parents."

Eva picks up the picture and examines it, keeping one eye on me. Relief finally flashes across her face. I presume she's decided I'm not in the house to murder her.

"I see the resemblance now. You look like your father," she says, studying me.

Eva nails it. I look exactly like my father, having not inherited any physical attributes from my German/Italian beauty of a mother. I'm one hundred percent Petrosian. People tell me I'm attractive and have great hair. That's not the same as being pretty. After years of therapy, I finally realized that I have other talents my mother doesn't have. It's not easy being average-looking when your mother's a knockout. I'm okay with it now, but it took a while.

"My parents didn't tell me anyone would be here," I say, still not entirely sure about her.

"I clean every other Wednesday, rain or shine."

"But they're gone for the whole summer?"

"I water plants, make sure nothing's leaking and I dust. Things get very dusty here. Your mamma always likes things to be perfect."

Having someone clean an empty house seems rather extravagant to me. But these days, my parents have more money than they know what to do with. If it makes them happy to have a clean house when they're not here, go for it.

"I didn't know Mr. and Mrs. Petrosian had grandchildren."

I smile. *She's assumed the baby's mine and my parents are his grandparents. This is going to work.*

"Can you keep a secret? The truth is, Eva, my parents don't even know yet. I just picked him up from the adoption agency. It came out of nowhere. My husband didn't know either. He's in California on business. I just called him and told him he's a father."

She smiles and walks over to admire my son. "Is it a boy or a girl?"

"A boy."

"He's very beautiful. Congratulations. What's his name?"

I smile again. "I don't know, it all happened so quickly. Of course, I'll have to discuss his name with my husband, but I'm thinking of calling him Jonah. What do you think of that? Jonah Fowler. That's sounds pretty good, don't you think?"

"That's a nice solid name from the Bible."

After a few more minutes of polite conversation, Eva gets back to her cleaning and I bring the baby into the kitchen. The first thing I do is dig through Sasha's diaper bag to see what kind of supplies she's left for me. There are three clean diapers, which is good because my nose tells me Jonah needs a diaper change pronto. In some of the bag's side pockets I find a jar of baby food, a spoon, a package of wipes, a couple of empty bottles and a few assorted rattles and toys.

I take out the beach towel, fold it in half, lay it on the kitchen table and place my son gently down on it. Unsnapping his pants, I remove the soiled diaper, clean him, put on a fresh one and snap him up. He looks up at me and smiles. *He knows I'm his mother already.* I put him on my shoulder. His soft, tiny body feels so wonderful.

"I'll always watch over and protect you, sweet Jonah. No matter what," I whisper into his ear.

Bouncing him lightly, I make a list in my head of all the things I need to get for a baby. I don't have a crib, food or anything. I google 'baby furniture rental' and within ten minutes arrange for a crib, changing table, high chair and swing to be delivered later that afternoon.

I'm pretty pleased with myself for being so resourceful until Jonah starts fussing. I don't have any additional food for him other than the half-full bottle of formula and a jar of mashed peaches. I can't take him out in public. What if someone recognized him? The motor from the vacuum starts again in another part of the house, reminding me the cleaning woman is still here.

With Jonah nestled on my shoulder, I find Eva under the dining room table and wave for her to turn off the machine.

"Eva, I have a little job for you, if you don't mind. As you know, the adoption happened very suddenly. With my parents and husband gone, I need to go into town to buy some basics like diapers and formula. It should only take me about an hour. Could I ask you to watch Jonah for me? I'll pay you a hundred dollars for your time."

Her eyes light up and she stretches out her arms. "Give him to me and do whatever you need to do. I'm in no rush."

For a second I hesitate. I'm handing my baby over to a virtual stranger, but I really have no choice. He needs food and diapers, so I'll have to take a chance. I kiss Jonah on the top of his head and place him in her arms. When she hugs him, my fears subside . . . a little.

"I'll be as quick as I can," I say grabbing my wallet and car keys as I hand her a half-empty bottle of formula, the last of his food.

"Don't worry. We'll be fine," she says, settling into an armchair in the living room with Jonah on her lap. I give her the two rattles from the diaper bag and head for the front door. "I left my phone number on the kitchen table. If you have any problem, call me and I'll come straight back."

I drive to our local pharmacy/general store, making a random list in my head of all the things one needs for a baby. Pulling into the parking spot, I marvel at how my entire life has changed within a few hours. This morning, I had planned to spend the day lounging with a juicy book on the beach. Instead, I met Sasha. I liked her right away and thought we might have become friends. I really do feel very bad about her drowning. She was so young. I did what I had to do. I couldn't let Jonah go into foster care.

Being a mother changes everything. With Jonah, our family is complete. Now, Daniel and I will live happily ever after with our new son.

CHAPTER FOUR

The cashier at the pharmacy rings me up. I've spent nearly seven hundred dollars on baby stuff. Who would have guessed formula and diapers were so expensive? Fortunately, I found a coupon for a certain type of formula in Sasha's diaper bag and know exactly what kind he gets.

I buy so much stuff in CVS that the clerk offers to help me carry the bags to my car. I've got rattles, bottles, wipes and sippy cups. I don't even know if Jonah knows how to use a cup, but I've got one anyway.

Driving back to my parents' house, I check the time. It's nearly five o'clock and the furniture delivery is coming at six. Dying to tell my parents the amazing news, I calculate the time difference between New York and Paris. It's nearly eleven there.

I pull into the driveway and call my father while unloading the car.

"What's wrong, Tori?" he says when he picks up. "Why are you calling so late?"

"Nothing's wrong, Dad. In fact, everything is incredibly right."

"You're getting a divorce?"

I roll my eyes. "No, Dad, Daniel and I are fine. I've got really big news. Put me on speaker so Mom can hear, too."

My father does as I ask and I begin. "What's the one thing you two want more than anything in the world?"

"For the stock market to turn around," says my father. "I've had a terrible month."

"Sam, let Tori speak," says my mother. "Go ahead, sweetheart."

"Mom, Dad, you are both now officially grandparents."

"What?" they both say in unison.

"It happened this morning. I was doing some work out at the beach house and I got a call from the adoption agency. There was a baby who was supposed to go to another family. Something happened and they couldn't take him. Somehow we got moved up on the list. I didn't ask why. I'm just so happy we were next on the list."

"Did you say 'him'?" my mother says, practically squealing. "I have a grandson?"

"His name is Jonah. And Mom, he's gorgeous. When they said I could pick him up today, I got right into my car and drove straight there. I picked him up this afternoon. It's like a miracle."

"Do you know anything about the baby's real parents?" says my father.

"I am his *real* parent," I snap.

"Honey, of course you are," says Mom, starting to sniffle. "We're so happy for you. We're so happy for us. This is what you've wanted for so many years. Your father and I will catch the next flight home to New York."

"You don't need to do that. Besides, Daniel won't be here until tomorrow night."

I convince my parents to finish their trip.

"Daniel and I need some quiet time with our new baby first. Jonah will be here when you get back."

After more tears of joy from my mother along with a long list of everything she's planning to buy for her grandson, I hang up and go into the house.

Eva is still sitting in the same chair. Jonah is asleep in her arms. "I fed him the rest of his bottle, burped him and then he went out like a light," she says smiling. "You've got a beautiful little boy here. So perfect."

I ask her if she would stay a little longer until the furniture is delivered. She agrees to watch him so I can unpack all the things I bought. At a little after six, the doorbell rings. Two men enter and set up the crib and changing table in my bedroom. A high chair and swing go in the kitchen.

After they leave, I give Eva a hundred and fifty bucks and ask her if she has any time to help me out this coming week.

"Sure," she says as I walk her to the front door, Jonah draped over my shoulder. "Call me anytime."

I'm about to close the door when she stops me. "I almost forgot," she says as she reaches into her pocket. "While you were at the store, I was looking for another toy for Jonah. I looked through the diaper bag and found your phone in a zippered pocket. I thought maybe you forgot it." I look down at her hand. She's holding an android phone that I've never seen before. "I guess you forgot to take it with you when you went to the store. Good thing I didn't need to reach you while you were gone because . . ."

As she speaks, her eyes drift down to the iPhone in my right hand.

"But you already have your phone. Then, whose phone is this?" she says, holding up Sasha's phone and examining it more closely.

I try to remain calm. My answer has to sound credible so she doesn't ask any more questions. Sasha left her phone in the bag.

"I-I . . . actually have two phones," I say, grabbing Sasha's phone from the cleaning woman's hand and jamming it into my pocket. "One for work and the other for personal use. Keeps things cleaner."

"Oh," she says, the confused look still on her face. "What kind of work do you do?"

"I manage an art gallery in the city. The Pierce-Woolsey Gallery, have you heard of it?"

She shakes her head as she shuffles towards the door, saying she looks forward to seeing me and my baby again. I force a smile as I turn the lock knowing I won't ever have her back here. She asks too many questions and I can't take any chances.

Now, the house is silent. For the first time, I'm completely alone with my son. My body is tingling on the inside. I'm having a normal moment — a mother holding her child, gently rocking his little body as I move around the house. After a while, it occurs to me that I probably should feed him.

I open a can of formula, pour it into a bottle and warm it up in the microwave, checking to make sure it's not too hot. Then, I settle into a chair with my new baby in my arms. Within a few minutes, he's consumed the entire thing and I'm oddly so proud.

I take him over to the changing table to undress him. Luckily, Sasha kept an extra outfit for him in her diaper bag. I'll have to remember to do that. You never know when a baby might spit up.

After Daniel arrives, I'll drive down to a local store and buy Jonah some new clothes. In another day or two, my mother will be spending a small fortune on baby clothes and other kiddie paraphernalia at Bloomingdales and Saks. But for now, Target will have to do.

I put a fresh diaper on my son and gently clean his face, neck and ears with a baby wipe. Already, I feel my love for this child radiating out from my heart. This is what it feels like to be a mother. I was born to do this. When the diaper change is complete, I lean over, sniffing his sweet scent and kiss him on his nose, which makes him laugh. He gurgles and that sound melts my heart again.

It's time for bed, so I place him in the rented crib. He cries for a moment when I put him down, so I stand over him gently rubbing his tummy. When he's finally quiet, I creep out of the room. It's nearly nine thirty by the time I enter the kitchen. I haven't had anything to eat or drink since this morning. There's pizza in the fridge from the night before, so I warm it up and pour myself a celebratory glass of red wine. As I sit down at the kitchen table I think about the amazing day I've had. Tomorrow will be even better. That's when Jonah meets his father for the first time.

CHAPTER FIVE

That first night, my little angel wakes only once at three a.m. I warm up a bottle and bring him into bed with me. By three thirty, he's asleep again and I place him back into his crib. I should be exhausted given what's transpired over the past twenty-four hours, but for some reason, I'm wide awake and feeling exhilarated.

Lying in bed, my mind flits from one topic to another. When I think about Sasha, my heart races. As awful as her death is, they say every cloud has a silver lining. I'm going to make sure Sasha's son has an amazing life with me. Life is so unpredictable. Less than a day ago, Sasha and I were two women gossiping and laughing on a beach. Now one of us is dead, and the other, a new mother.

Wondering if the police have found her body, I reach for my iPhone on the nightstand. I put in my earphones so I don't wake Jonah and google 'woman drowned today Hamptons NY'. A slew of news headlines pops up and I click on one after another. All the information seems to be the same: *A woman wearing a pink bathing cap was seen swimming by several people on the beach as well as one of the lifeguards before she went under.*

I click on the local cable News12 covering Suffolk County. There's a video segment of the police chief giving a press conference.

> *"Two eyewitnesses confirmed that they saw a woman in a pink bathing cap doing laps in the water yesterday. The lifeguard on duty said the swimmer was out beyond where the waves break. Because she was out so far, he kept an eye on her. At one point, he saw her head go under. That's when he blew his whistle and ran into the water.*
>
> *Two other lifeguards and several onlookers attempted to find the missing woman, but the current was extremely strong yesterday. The coastguard has been called in, but so far the divers have been unsuccessful in finding her. Because of the surf conditions, it's possible she has been pulled out to sea. At this time, we have been unable to ID the victim. Law enforcement officers canvassed the beach and no one identified her. None of her belongings were found, and no vehicle was left in the parking lot. Clearly, she didn't walk to the beach with nothing but her bathing suit, so we're asking for the public's help. Perhaps someone remembers giving her a lift to the beach? Or maybe accompanied her to the beach but later left with the missing woman's things. If you have any information about the identity of this person, please call..."*

I put my phone down after learning all I need to know. The police have no clues about Sasha's identity, which means they don't know she's a mother and aren't looking for a missing baby. If she was pulled out to sea, they may never find her or learn who the woman in the pink cap was. I may be the only person on the planet who knows the real story, and that's how it's going to stay. Revealing the truth now won't bring her back.

I snuggle into my crisp cotton sheets comforted by the knowledge that my secret, at least for now, appears to be safe. With that resolved, I say a little prayer that my usual loud snoring doesn't wake up my baby. Gradually, I fall off to sleep.

Three hours later, my son's cries wake me. I'm exhausted emotionally and physically, and the thought of getting up now seems impossible. As a rule, I don't sleep well. I haven't had a good night's sleep since I was a kid. Daniel and my parents have taken me to different doctors who specialize in sleep problems. One physician wanted me to take all kinds of drugs and another insisted I wear one of those awful nighttime breathing machines. Naturally, I politely declined and instead power through my tired mornings with extra coffee. However, after yesterday and everything that's happened, I'm much more out of it than usual.

Jonah continues to cry, and I rouse myself with some stern self-talk. *You're a mother now. Jonah comes first. You sleep when he sleeps.* Forcing myself out of bed, I drag my exhausted body across the room and lift Jonah from his crib. The minute I pick him up, he stops crying. He already knows I'm his mother.

During my first full day alone with my new son, I get to know his routine. He sleeps a lot, which gives me a break every few hours. I use that time to tidy up the house. I want everything to be perfect for when Daniel arrives and meets his son for the first time.

It's early evening and Jonah's sleeping again. I must have dozed off because I'm awakened by the doorbell. I look at my watch. It has to be Daniel. I fly to the front door and open it. My husband is standing in the doorway holding a huge bouquet of summer flowers. He has a gigantic grin on his face as I leap into his arms. Then, he kisses me long and hard.

"Hello, Mama-cita," he says as he comically kisses my neck a dozen times. "Every minute I was on the plane felt like an hour."

"Hello, Daddy-O," I say with an equally big smile.

We're both laughing, crying and talking over each other as we go into the house. When I close the door, he drops his bags on the floor. "Where is my son?"

I take his hand and lead him into our bedroom. We hear Jonah lightly snoring as we quietly tiptoe over to the crib. I stand back to give Daniel the time and space to take it all in.

He bends over the crib and kisses our little boy for the first time. My heart is so full, I'm sure it's going to burst. As Daniel gently rubs our baby's head, I can feel his love for Jonah. It's palpable. I reach for my husband's hand and he squeezes mine. I've never felt more connected to Daniel than in this moment.

"I love you," he says as we sit down at the kitchen table and share a glass of Merlot. I say the same to him and we toast.

He can never learn the truth. He must never find out.

We finish our wine and go into our room to gaze down at our sleeping son. Jonah's making adorable soft breathing sounds that warm my heart with each subsequent exhale. Daniel puts his arm around my waist and we stand there silently in awe of our sleeping child.

"We're finally parents," I whisper. "We're a family now."

He squeezes my waist, yawns and tips his head towards the bed. I'm tired, too. It's been a whirlwind few days. What had started out as a rather ordinary beach day turned horrible and just as quickly ended up being the luckiest day of my life.

We climb into bed and kiss each other goodnight and both fall asleep. An hour later, Daniel wakes me.

"You're snoring again," he says. "You're going to wake the baby." Barely conscious, I flip over as I do almost every night when I wake up my husband with my loud breathing.

At three forty-five in the morning, I hear Jonah crying. Not fully awake, I get out of bed, scoop up my son from his crib and take him into the kitchen. I place him in his portable carrier sitting on the kitchen table and heat up a quarter bottle of formula hoping a little snack will help him go back to sleep. He eagerly takes the bottle and before it's finished, he's out for the count. I let out a happy sigh and we both go back to bed.

Come seven a.m., my little boy is chattering happily in his crib. With my eyes still closed, I turn my head towards my husband and mumble, "Your turn."

On his side with his back to me, Daniel groans and puts his pillow over his ear. "He's happy. He'll play for another five minutes."

Despite my groggy state, it strikes me that Daniel's comment about Jonah playing for another five minutes is a weak ploy to get out of his shift. I laugh, roll over and look at him. "Nice try, Daddy. Your son needs a diaper change and there are bottles ready to be heated in the fridge."

Daniel groans again but gets up, pulls on a T-shirt and picks up the baby. From the bed, I watch them and can already see a bond growing between them. My husband is smitten just the way I am. Through my half-closed eyes, I watch him make faces at Jonah. The baby giggles and coos to his father's every move.

They leave the room and I lay my head back down on the pillow, thinking about all the things I now need to do. I hear Daniel talking to Jonah in the kitchen. Not wanting to miss anything from these first few days, I drag myself out of bed and head to the kitchen to have breakfast with my two favorite boys.

"I thought you were going to sleep in," says Daniel as he takes the heated bottle out of the microwave.

I'm about to tell him to sprinkle some of the formula on his forearm to be sure it's not too hot, when he does it without prompting from me.

"How did you know to do that? I say, impressed by my husband's innate baby knowledge.

"My mom always did that when my little sister was a baby."

Daniel settles into a chair to feed Jonah, and I gaze lovingly at my son. "Isn't he beautiful? Don't we have the most gorgeous baby? Look at his eyes. They're blue right now. Do you think they'll turn brown? He even looks a bit like you, don't you think?"

Daniel looks up at me and smirks. "That might be wishful thinking on your part. It doesn't matter if he looks like us. I'm just happy he's here."

"You're right, who cares? All that matters is that he's ours."

CHAPTER SIX

This is a day of firsts for the three of us as a family. Most couples have nine months to plan and read up on all things baby. Daniel and I had been so focused on getting pregnant that we spent no time learning what to do after the baby is born.

That's why I bought everything they had for babies at the pharmacy. I even bought a nasal suctioning syringe thing. I have no idea what it's for, but I have one just in case I need it. Becoming parents so suddenly means Daniel and I need to get organized — fast.

While he feeds Jonah his breakfast, I place a spiral notebook on the kitchen table and begin to write.

"We need to get Jonah on a regular schedule for feeding and naps," I say as I scrawl in bold print. "I googled it and a four-month-old should get about five to six ounces of formula four times a day."

"Okay," says my husband as Jonah finishes his first bottle. "Let's take him to the beach tomorrow. We can dip his feet into the water and give him his first taste of the ocean."

"No," I say loudly, pressing the pencil down so hard on the paper that the point breaks off and flies across the room. When I look up, Daniel is staring at me. "He's too young. I don't want to risk him getting too much sun."

"Who knows when we'll be out here again? It might not be until next summer. It's nice out today. We can go to your favorite little beach, the one with the shady tree."

"I don't want to." Abruptly, I get up and walk over to the sink to get a glass of water. Even with my back to him, I can feel the tenor of the room is thick. My husband must be bewildered by my reaction to his seemingly innocuous suggestion. I turn around with a big smile on my face which confuses him even more.

"I'm sorry," I say. "I didn't mean to bite your head off. The beach is a wonderful idea, just not this week. Everything is so new. I need time to adjust. We'll come back out to visit my parents in a few weeks and can take Jonah then."

"Okay," he says, continuing to examine my face. "I meant to ask you, when's Jonah's birthday?"

I freeze. *Shit. Of course, I should know his birthday. I could make it up, but I remember Sasha said something about it. It was on a holiday, it was . . . Valentine's Day.*

"February fourteenth," I say. "Isn't that amazing? Our son was born on Valentine's Day. It's poetic because he's bringing so much love into our lives."

My husband smiles. "It will be easy to remember. Did the agency tell you anything about his parents?"

Shit, another detail I should know.

"They didn't tell me much," I say, trying to buy myself time to come up with a decent story. "They said the mother wanted to remain anonymous but that she was a single teenager."

"Did they give you any historical medical information? We should have a family history for him."

I should have planned for this line of questioning. That was stupid on my part. These are all good questions, ones that I would ask if our roles were reversed. Of course, my parents would want to know that too, especially my father.

"I didn't get a family history because," I say dragging out my words to give me time to invent a plausible answer, "everything happened so quickly. The agency barely had time to get the basic paperwork ready. I'll go back to see them next week and pick up the remaining documents."

"We should get that. It's important. We also need to find a pediatrician for him."

I hadn't thought about needing *legitimate* documentation. I can probably find a bogus birth certificate online but medical insurance fraud, that's a whole other thing.

"I'm thinking of taking him to Dr. Kalajian, our family's doctor. He's been taking care of me since I was a little girl. His son is taking over the practice. They're expensive and they don't take insurance, but they're the best pediatricians in the city. It will be worth the extra money."

Daniel nods. "Whatever you want. Did you find out why we got moved up on the list and why it was so last-minute? From what you told me, they gave you only a few hours' notice."

I walk over to the refrigerator and open the door so he can't see my face as I make up another lie. "Yes, they told me what happened. It's a terrible story. Apparently, another couple in New Jersey was supposed to get Jonah. The day before they were to pick him up, the wife got some devastating medical news and they couldn't move forward."

"Cancer?"

"I don't know, but it was bad," I say. "The agency didn't elaborate and I didn't want to pry."

"Oh, my God. That's awful," Daniel says.

"Let's not dwell on that," I say, attempting to redirect him away from my lie. "Let's stay in the moment and enjoy our new baby."

"But we weren't next on the list. The last time we checked, they told us there were more than a dozen couples ahead of us."

Why does he keep asking me so many questions? "Honey," I say, "forget the list. All that matters is that he's ours now, right?"

My husband nods, laughs at his own paranoia as he gets up, crosses the room and plants a kiss on my cheek. "You're right. That *is* all that matters."

Thank God.

"Somebody needs a diaper change," he says sniffing the air. "We'd better do this together. I don't have a lot of experience with diapers."

"Me neither," I reply as we both laugh, pick up our baby and head to the bedroom. Before we do anything, given the pathetic job I did earlier with Jonah's diaper, I suggest we watch a video on YouTube to see exactly how to do it. When it's over, Daniel takes the lead. He deftly removes Jonah's dirty diaper, cleans him and in several smooth moves has the new one on securely. I'm impressed.

How did he learn to do that so fast? My husband is full of surprises, but then again, so am I.

CHAPTER SEVEN

The rest of our time in the Hamptons is spent getting to know our new son and each other as parents. We have a few hiccups but figure them out. Now that there are three of us, it feels like Daniel and I have fallen even more in love than we already were. After a magical week at the beach, it's time to return to our real life back in Brooklyn.

Our three-story townhouse is in the Cobble Hill section of Brooklyn. It wasn't a fancy neighborhood when my parents bought the place in 1979. My father, Sam Petrosian, also known as the "Carpet King", had just opened his second store. By the time I finished high school, he had had twenty-two locations in the New York Metro area. While I was in college, my parents moved out of Cobble Hill to a much larger five-bedroom apartment on Park Avenue in Manhattan. Unwilling to part with their beloved Brooklyn townhouse where they raised me, they kept it and rented it out over the years.

When Daniel and I got engaged, my father took me out to lunch.

"I don't think there's a man living who's good enough for you," he said reaching across the table and patting my hand. "Daniel's better than some you've brought home, but worse than others."

I remember my body temperature rising. I didn't want to have that conversation with my father. It felt so disloyal to Daniel.

"It concerns me," my father continues, "that Daniel doesn't have a steady job or an inclination to get one."

"That's not true. Daniel works extremely hard. He's an actor, Dad. Most actors don't have steady jobs unless they're big stars. He's trying to build his career. Besides, he makes money doing all sorts of other things like trade shows and modeling."

My father snorts. "Conveniently, he's marrying a girl who will one day inherit a not-so-small fortune."

I roll my eyes. "It would be the same for anyone who marries me."

My father laughs. "True. Indulge your old man, will ya? I only want to protect you. You currently receive a monthly allowance that lets you live very comfortably. However, the money I have earmarked for your future inheritance will be going into a trust that can't be touched by a spouse in the event of a divorce."

"Why does everything always have to be about money?"

My father shushes me. "There's more. Let me finish. I'm only sixty-six and hopefully, your full inheritance is a long way off. In the interim, your mother and I would like to give you the Cobble Hill house as a pre-wedding present."

The truth is, my father is a shrewd man who never does anything by accident. I look at his smiling face across the table, trying to work out exactly what his scheme is. Then, it hits me.

"I get it," I say. "This is a 'pre-wedding gift' because in the state of New York any money or property acquired during the marriage would be equally split between the two parties if there was a dissolution of the marriage. But, if I inherit the house now, before I marry Daniel, he'll have no claim on it."

"That's my girl. I always said you should have gone to law school."

"You don't understand Daniel at all. He doesn't care about money. He's not into material things. He only cares about me and acting and that's it."

My father smiles. "Then he won't mind this arrangement and I'll sleep better at night."

So much has happened since that lunch. Flash forward and we're in Brooklyn with our new baby beginning life in the city as a family. When we get back to our house, Daniel takes the baby upstairs. Once he's gone, I take out Sasha's diaper bag still filled with all of her stuff. I look inside and see her phone is still in the bag. I'm not sure why, but I take it out and stick it in the back of a kitchen cabinet so it's out of sight.

"Daniel," I shout up the stairs, "we've got nothing to eat. I'm going to run to the market. Be back in forty-five minutes. You okay to be alone with the baby?"

He makes a snarky comment about him being a "baby whisperer" and tells me to take my time.

Once outside, I walk down two blocks and over three where I grab a taxi to Dumbo, another neighborhood in Brooklyn near the bridge. I get out of the cab on a commercial street. Walking for a few blocks, I find what I'm looking for — a large dumpster in an alley next to a fruit-and-vegetable store. As I lift the heavy green metal lid on the garbage container, the summer stench from inside is overpowering. The large bin is three quarters full of rotting organic garbage. I figure with that repugnant smell, no one will be rummaging around inside of the bin. I slip the diaper bag filled with Sasha's things into the dumpster. There can be no connection between Sasha and me. As I walk away from the metal container, I'm confident Sasha's belongings will soon be in a landfill and no longer a danger to me or my son.

I hail a cab and head back to Cobble Hill. No matter how I try, I can't get Sasha out of my mind. I don't feel guilt. It's not like I killed her. I didn't suggest she go for a swim that day. I didn't tell her to put on that pink cap and dive into the surf when there was a strong current warning. It was all her choice. I was very nice to her. I told her all about the Hamptons and good places to eat. I gave her a piece of gum and then I watched her baby. And, I'm still doing that, just like I promised. She had no family. There's no father to take the baby. Jonah would have ended up with people who didn't love him. That's no way for a child to grow up. With Daniel and me as his parents, Jonah will have a life filled with love, laughter and many trips to Disney World and Legoland.

When I get home from the market, Daniel and Jonah are asleep together on our bed. Standing in the doorway of my bedroom, drinking in the heartwarming scene, I know I did the right thing that day on the beach.

CHAPTER EIGHT

As we work out the kinks and logistics of our new roles, Daniel and I acknowledge that we'll both have to make a lot of changes to our schedules now that Jonah is part of our life.

It's early days and though my primary focus is on being a good mother, I keep my eyes on the investigation in the Hamptons regarding Sasha's death. Several times a day I search online to study the latest information about the Rocky Point Beach drowning.

Initially, there were a lot of articles online and on local TV about the missing woman in the pink cap. But in the weeks that follow, there's almost nothing — which surprises me.

"Sadly, it happens," says an East End police captain being interviewed on News12. "The ocean currents out here can be very powerful, even for a strong swimmer. People often forget that when they go in the water. As of today, no one has reported anyone missing and we've been unable to identify her. Whoever she is, the missing woman left no belongings on the beach to help us. As of now, this investigation is still open."

For the first two weeks that's all I find. No one has reported anyone missing and the police don't have a body,

ID, or car. Three weeks after that fateful day, the cops release a different theory.

> *News12 Video*
> *"We had been treating this investigation as an accidental drowning. We're now looking at the possibility of a deliberate action. Due to the fact that there was no trace of the woman, police now think it's possible that the swimmer in the pink cap intentionally went under. We're treating this now as a possible suicide."*

I play the video three times before the reporter's words sink in. *Suicide? That makes no sense.* I can't get my head around that theory. The girl I met had been through a lot but seemed like she had it together. Besides, why would she move all the way from Chicago to New York to kill herself? That doesn't ring true. Of course, she did tell me she had postpartum depression but said she was over it. I watched her interacting with the baby. She was very loving and gentle with him. She talked about the future and all the things she was planning to do. I don't buy the suicide theory.

Dumbfounded, I sit at my computer for a long time contemplating the possibilities. Suddenly, Daniel walks into the room. I quickly close my browser and sit back.

"Ready to go to the park?" he says. "I've got everything loaded into the stroller."

I mumble something about needing to return a call to one of the gallery's biggest clients and ask if he can give me ten more minutes. I need time to think.

If Sasha drowned intentionally, then when she asked me to watch her baby, she knew she was never coming back. That means she wanted me to be his mother. I told her how I wanted children. She chose me.

I'm trying to work out this incredible revelation when Daniel impatiently calls to me from downstairs. "It's going to rain in a few hours, Tori. Let's go."

"Be right down," I say as I close my computer and put on my sneakers. As I tie the laces, I wonder, did Sasha set me up?

I replay every word that was said that day on the beach but in my mind, it still doesn't add up to a suicide. Also, she borrowed my sunscreen. Why would a woman planning to kill herself put on sunscreen? Seems to me you wouldn't care about UV rays or sun damage if you were about to kiss this life goodbye.

"Tori, come on," shouts Daniel again from the floor below. "Jonah's getting antsy."

I walk to the top of the stairs and something else occurs to me. Sasha couldn't have set me up to take the baby. I was the one who sat near her, not the other way around. I wanted to sit in the shade and barged in on her space. I also started our conversation, she didn't.

"Tori?" says Daniel, looking up at me from the bottom of the stairs. I take a deep breath and bounce down the steps, planning to give it more thought later. Now is family time and I need to focus on that.

We step out into the beautiful warm day and take Jonah down to the waterfront in Brooklyn Heights for a walk along the promenade. The walkway is buzzing with New Yorkers enjoying the sunshine. We look out at the single World Trade Center tower across the water, while passing playgrounds filled with hordes of children, open-air exercise classes, and an endless parade of baby carriages. For years I envied all those lucky people pushing strollers. Now, through some twisted miracle, I'm one of them.

Daniel looks over at me. "What are you smiling about?" he says.

"All this," I say looking up at him and waving my hand. "Being here with you and Jonah. This is all I've ever wanted."

Over the next few weeks, Daniel, Jonah and I settle into a routine. I've taken maternity leave from the gallery for three months. Luckily, Daniel doesn't have a lot of auditions or jobs lined up right now, so we've been doing almost everything together.

"We should talk about the future," I say one evening in the kitchen after Jonah is asleep. "I'm eventually going back to the gallery. What are we going to do about the baby?"

Daniel doesn't work every day. Sometimes he doesn't have work for weeks or even months. I'm hoping he'll agree to take over the childcare when I'm at work.

"What if I have an audition or get a part?" he says as he loads dishes into the dishwasher. "I have to be available to go meet people like my agent or a casting director. Sometimes the turnaround on meetings can be a matter of hours."

"Maybe we should consider getting a nanny?"

"You want to leave our son with a stranger?" says my husband, his brows knitting together.

"They wouldn't be a stranger once we got to know them. We'd carefully vet this person and get a ton of references."

"It's not what I'd envisioned," he says as he dries a plate. "We went through so much to get him and now we're going to hire someone else to raise our son?"

I look at Daniel and there's a part of me that agrees. But I really love my career. Realistically, we're going to need some help. I walk over to him at the sink and touch his back. "Millions of people have nannies, Daniel. I think it's something we should consider."

We table the discussion for another day to give each of us time to process having a babysitter in our house taking care of our child.

The next morning, I'm in the kitchen feeding Jonah some baby cereal when the doorbell rings. I shout to Daniel upstairs, asking him to get the door. He doesn't answer so I figure he must be in the shower. Slipping the tray of the highchair out slightly, I lift up my cereal-covered son, plant him on my hip and head to the front door. Looking out through the side glass panels, I see two uniformed police officers.

Shit.

"May I help you?" I say opening the door slowly.

The cops explain they're investigating a missing person's case in the Hamptons. Apparently, they tell me, some video camera picked up my car's license plate near Rocky Point Beach on the day a woman drowned. They want to speak with me and my husband. I let them in and walk over to the staircase.

"Daniel," I shout up to the second floor, "can you come down here, please?"

A minute later, Daniel, Jonah and I are seated in our living room with the officers.

"I'm not sure how we can help you," I say before the cops ask any questions, hoping I didn't seem too defensive.

Shut up Tori, let them speak.

"As I said, Mrs. Fowler, we're investigating a missing person, a possible drowning or suicide that may have taken place on June twenty-second of this year. We've got camera footage from the highway that leads to the beach. Your car — Audi license plate *VKP 184* was tagged heading towards the beach the same day that the woman disappeared."

I'm about to tell them I don't know anything but decide this time to wait and hear them out.

Breathe.

"Were either of you in the Hamptons in June, specifically on June twenty-second?"

There's a long moment of silence before I speak. "I was staying out at my parents' beach house that week. Daniel joined me on the twenty-third or twenty-fourth. I don't remember the exact date."

"It was the twenty-third," Daniel says jumping right in. "I remember because I flew in from California to New York on the evening of the twenty-third."

"I see," said the older police officer, making a note and then looking directly at me. "The cameras also clocked your car leaving the beach around the same time the local police arrived on the scene. Can you tell us anything about what happened that day?"

All eyes are on me. Shit. I've got to say something.

"I'm pretty sure I went to Rocky Point Beach once or twice that week," I say slowly, considering every word. "I couldn't tell you the exact days I was there. Although, now that you mention it, one day there was some commotion down by the water. I'd received a very important and time-sensitive call and had to leave the beach immediately.

I didn't pay much attention to what was going on. I do remember that as I was getting into my vehicle to leave, a few police cars pulled into the parking lot. I was in such a rush so I didn't wait around to find out what was going on."

The older of the two cops makes a few more notations on an official looking writing tablet and looks into my eyes. "Ms. Fowler, do you remember seeing a woman in a pink bathing cap walking on the beach or swimming in the water?"

Shit.

"I'm afraid I don't. I always bring a trashy book with me when I go to the beach. I'm sure I had my nose in it the entire time. Also, I usually sit way back from the water, so I wouldn't have had a very good view of the ocean."

After a few more simple questions, the officers seem satisfied, stand and thank us for our time. When I open the front door to let them out, the older cop turns and looks at me. A bead of sweat trickles slowly down my spine.

"One more question, Ms. Fowler. You said you got an important phone call and had to leave. Where did you have to go?"

"I can answer that one, officers," says my husband smiling, holding Jonah on his shoulder. "Tori and I had been on a waiting list for an adoption for a long time. That was the day Tori got a call from the agency. They had a baby for us."

Both officers' eyes light up and they smile. "I'd say that qualifies as an important call," says the older cop, stepping outside. "Congratulations, he's a very cute little guy. We'll be in touch if we have any other questions."

I watch them walk down my front steps as a river of sweat pours down the center of my back.

"What's wrong with you?" Daniel says, staring at me. "You have a weird look on your face."

Shaken from my trance, I look up at my husband. "The story about the woman in the pink cap who died, it's so sad."

CHAPTER NINE

The same day the Suffolk County cops came knocking on my door, my parents finally return from Europe. My mother calls me the second they get into their apartment.

"We're back!" she says a little too loudly. "The food in Italy was incredible, which is why I'm starting my diet tomorrow. Your father and I can't wait to meet our new grandson. I'm going shopping in the morning and we'll be over in the afternoon. The pictures you sent of Jonah are simply darling. Buying things for him will be so much fun. When I get finished at Saks, there won't be a single outfit left in the baby section."

I hang up the phone and rub my temples. I adore my parents, but they can be . . . a lot. Mom always says everything is 'marvelous,' 'fabulous' and 'amazing' and laughs all the time. My father is more serious, a man who doesn't suffer fools. He's not a big laugher, but when he does, it makes me smile because it's so rare.

True to my mother's word, the two of them need our help carrying in the ridiculous number of gifts they've bought for Jonah. After unwrapping everything, I'm convinced my son's technology, toy and clothing needs have been satisfied for the next ten to fifteen years. I won't have to buy him anything until he goes off to college.

"This is a handsome boy," says my father, holding Jonah on his lap and bouncing him. "He looks a bit like me, don't you think? You're going to teach him to swim, right? Swimming's very important, Tori."

I must be looking at my father like he's bat shit crazy because I see my husband across the room stifle a laugh.

"Swimming? He's not even six months old, Dad," I say.

"You don't want him drowning in a swimming pool. Jonah's gotta have lessons. We put you in the water when you were three, didn't we, Marion?"

"Sam," says my mother, "Jonah's just a baby. He's not going swimming now. Although it's never too early to sign him up for the right schools. The waiting lists for the good private schools are horrendous. I know someone on the board at the Wilson-Hewitt School who could help us. You leave it to me."

I know my parents are excited and want only the best for their grandson, but he's only a few months old and this conversation seems ridiculous. We have an early dinner that night, take-out from a local Chinese place. As I expected, my parents pepper me with questions about the adoption and how it all happened.

"The call came out of the blue?" says my father, rocking the crib of the now-sleeping Jonah.

"It took me completely by surprise," I say. "Daniel was out of town at a trade show when I heard from them."

"Did you get a job?" says my father, looking away from me and directly at my husband.

"It was a five-day modeling gig at this technology show," Daniel mutters. "I've got a lot of other irons in the fire, though. Big things are happening."

My phone rings and I look down at the caller ID. It's Neville Pierce, the general manager of the Pierce-Woolsey Gallery that I work for. This is his second call to me in less than thirty minutes. I figure it's something important so I excuse myself.

Sitting alone at the kitchen table, I call him back.

"Tori, dearest," he says as he answers, "how is motherhood treating you?" Before I have a chance to reply, he starts talking. "Things have been so horribly chaotic at the gallery without your steady hand on the tiller."

I've heard this kind of talk from him before. He's buttering me up for something he wants. "Neville, you have a remarkable tendency to exaggerate things, especially when it's something negative."

"Not this time," he says in a mournful tone. "Nothing's going right. We had a sculpture show last week and it was an absolute disaster. Anton called it a travesty and I agree with him. No one who's anyone in New York came. We hardly sold a thing. Frankly, it was devastating for all concerned."

Neville Pierce and his business partner and husband, Anton Woolsey, in their mid-sixties, have been together for as long as anyone could remember. But when the two of them are left to their own devices there is always plenty of drama. Big or small problems are given the same amount of attention and gravitas. If the gallery is out of coffee or milk or if one of them can't get an Uber in under five minutes, it is classified as a disaster.

I've worked with both of them for more than ten years. When they take something minor and turn it into a catastrophe, I've learned not to get worked up over it. I know how to bring their temperatures down and the sanity back. That's my special gift. And the truth is, I absolutely adore them and they me.

"I'm sure the opening wasn't that bad, Neville. You did sell something, right?"

"Of course we sold something, petunia. I didn't just fall off a turnip truck. But we didn't sell everything. If you had been here, it would have been so much better and . . ."

"The baby is wonderful, thanks for asking," I say.

Neville pauses but only for a second. "I was just about to ask you about little Joseph."

"Jonah."

"Of course . . . Jonah. I knew that. I was testing you."

I laugh to myself because I'm impressed Neville even remembered I had a baby and that it was a boy. That in itself is astounding and a clear sign of his affection for me. Babies are not on his or Anton's radar. For them, it's all about the art world and the gossip that goes along with it.

"What do you want, Neville? I'm still on my maternity leave."

"There's just this one tiny thing. You know you're the only person at the gallery that Mr. Ornish will work with. I promised Rodrigo Balaz we'd sell his horse sculpture by the end of the summer and I thought if you . . ."

After I let Neville grovel for a while, I promise to call Ornish, one of Pierce-Woolsey's wealthiest clients. Mr. Ornish had taken a liking to me right after I started with the gallery. Since then, he's refused to deal with anyone but me. I know him fairly well and am pretty sure I can get him interested in adding the Balaz horse to his already robust sculpture collection. I tell the ever-fretting Neville that I will call Ornish in the morning.

Back in the living room, my father, with Jonah now on his lap, is grilling Daniel about his job prospects. My husband is pale as he and my father volley back and forth. From the look on Daniel's face, he's losing the match. The minute I walk into the room, Daniel's eyes implore me to rescue him. I don't have to do much because I'm the apple of my father's eye. The moment I sit down, my father shifts his attention to me.

"Sweetheart, you were telling us about the day you got Jonah," says my father, now all smiles.

Daniel's body relaxes as I pick up the conversation. "It was a totally surreal day. I was sitting in my favorite spot at Rocky Point Beach when I got a call from the adoption agency we registered with. They said they had a baby for us and I could get him that same day. I literally grabbed my towel, ran off the beach and drove for two hours to their facility in Garden City. I walked into the building alone, terrified and excited at the same time. Three hours later, after a ton of paperwork and instructions on baby care, I walked out with Jonah in my arms."

"Why did you go back out to the Hamptons? Why didn't you go home to Brooklyn with Jonah?" my mother asks.

That's a really good question, Mom. I stall to give myself time to come up with a credible answer. "Well, there were a lot of reasons."

"I meant to ask you that, too," Daniel says, leaning forward. "Why didn't you take him home to Brooklyn?"

Three pairs of eyes are now focused on me. "Because . . . I drove directly to the agency in my bathing suit with just a little wrap skirt on. I didn't have any of my things with me. I had to go back to the Hamptons house to get my stuff. Besides, I thought it would be really nice to spend our first week as a family out at the beach."

Based on the nods of all three heads, it's clear my answer is sufficient. My mother takes Jonah in her arms as he's about to fade out. We all chit-chat softly for another half hour until my parents finally leave. Jonah wakes up right after they walk out the door and Daniel volunteers to feed him.

Tired from the long day, I give my husband a grateful kiss as he gets a bottle of formula and goes into the TV room to feed the baby. Once alone in the kitchen, I reach into the back of one of the cabinets and retrieve Sasha's phone. Jamming it into my pocket, I go upstairs to my bedroom and close the door.

I found an old charger that fit Sasha's phone and charged it up earlier this morning while Daniel was working out with his personal trainer. One thing my husband is religious about is his thrice-weekly training sessions. Never misses one of those.

"My body is an instrument. It's all I've got to sell. That's why I take good care of it," he says whenever I tease him about all his dietary requirements, supplements and rigorous training schedule.

"You're so regimented," I say. "You could cheat now and then."

"You see this," he often says, pointing to himself. "If I don't stay in top condition, I've got nothing to sell. I am the product."

I stretch out on my king-sized bed and turn on Sasha's fully charged phone. When I try to open it, it tells me I need a passcode. *Shit.* I had hoped maybe that wouldn't be the case. Disappointed, I turn it off and put it under a box of silk scarves in my nightstand drawer. I'm convinced the keys to Sasha's secrets are on that phone and intend to find out what they are. I need to know what's on that device and have to find a way to break in. It's the only way I can protect my son.

CHAPTER TEN

Shortly after Jonah enters our lives, my sleeping and breathing issues deteriorate. I've snored and had restless nights since I was a teenager. Growing up, it was totally normal for me to wake in the morning with a headache and then feel exhausted all day. I learned to live with it.

After I finished college, my sleep problems got worse and my parents took me to see an army of doctors. I saw a neurologist, a cardiologist, a lipidologist and a bunch of other doctor-ologists. They administered every available test in modern medicine including CT scans and MRIs. After I was poked and prodded for months, they diagnosed my problem.

The verdict: I have a rare congenital heart problem that can be life-threatening, if I don't take care of myself. The doctors put me on a special diet and gave me a list of do's and don'ts. Then, I was evaluated by a sleep specialist who diagnosed me with mild obstructive sleep apnea. Though it wasn't too severe, given my heart issues, the doctors were adamant that I pay full attention to my overall health. I wasn't prescribed anything back then. They told me to lose five pounds, avoid alcohol and call if the sleeping problems got any worse.

I was twenty-two and not ready to become a hermit. I wanted to go out and party and have fun like everyone else my age. In retrospect, I probably should have been a little more medically compliant.

By my thirties, shortly before I met Daniel, my sleep issues escalated. In addition to the morning headaches, I was often irritable and, if I'm being honest, a little depressed. At the urging of my parents, I went back to see another sleep specialist. This time like the first time, they had me wear a sleep monitor at home for a week so they could see exactly what was going on. Several weeks of tests concluded that now I had high blood pressure and *moderate* obstructive sleep apnea. Great. Things were going from bad to worse.

After examining my airways, the doctor also recommended I have a "simple surgery" to open up some of my breathing pathways. In my mind, the words "simple" and "surgery" don't ever go together, but I also didn't want to choke to death in my sleep, so I agreed.

The surgery went well and after I healed, my doctors did a new week-long sleep test on me. Unfortunately, there had been no discernible improvement in my condition. That's when it was recommended I wear a CPAP mask every night.

I'd seen what those things looked like when I was doing my research on sleep apnea. I wasn't going to wear one of those devices. As a single woman in my thirties, wearing one of those would ensure I'd never have sex again, so I refused. Instead, I lost five pounds and limited my alcohol — most of the time.

Naturally, my parents weighed in.

"Tori, this is your life we're talking about," said my mother on the brink of tears. "What if you stop breathing in your sleep?"

"Just try it, honey," said my father, "and see how it goes. You might start feeling a lot better."

My father was right. I did feel chronically shitty, so I agreed to try it for a few weeks. The first night I put it on should have been caught on video. After a few failed attempts,

I finally got the damn thing on right and stood in front of the mirror in my bathroom and cried. I looked like some kind of undersea robot. All I could think was, what guy will want to be with me when I'm wearing this fucking thing?

I had promised my parents I'd give it a shot, so I took one last look in the mirror and went to bed. Much to my surprise, I slept through the entire night. That almost never happened. When the alarm went off in the morning, I sat up and removed the mask. Swinging my legs out of the bed, I prepared myself for the morning pain in my head I always felt as soon as I moved. That day, there was no pain. I remember smiling. It felt great to wake up without a knife stuck in my skull.

Later that day, I was working at the gallery. Midway through the afternoon, one of my co-workers looked at me suspiciously. "Why are you so happy?" they asked.

"What are you talking about?"

"You've been smiling all day, Tori. You're way more cheerful than usual. New boyfriend?"

She was right and wrong. No new boyfriend, but I *was* happy that day and not tired like I normally was. The wheels in my head started turning. Maybe that hideous CPAP works?

Since I wasn't seeing anyone at the time, I didn't have to worry about romantic interludes, so I started wearing it every night. The change was amazing. For years I had been tired, depressed and cranky. But now, I was good, really good. Until then, I don't think I'd had a good night's sleep in twenty years.

Later, when I met Daniel and things started heating up, I thought it was important to tell him about my "mask" in advance. Wouldn't want to spring that on a guy last minute.

"You don't have to wear it while you're having sex, do you?" he said, a somewhat alarmed expression in his eyes.

I laughed. "No, only when I sleep, unless you want me to."

Daniel was really great about it. His reaction might have been one of the things that made me fall in love with him.

He never made me feel funny about wearing it. In fact, he'd often remind me to put it on when I was feeling lazy or simply forgot. I wore it about seventy percent of the time.

About six months after Daniel and I started seeing each other, I told him about my heart problem.

"Why didn't you tell me this before?" he said, stroking my hair. "It sounds serious."

"It's no big deal," I remember saying. "I just wanted you to know. I'm fine. Really."

Not long after that, my snoring increased and got louder. Soon, even with the CPAP, the headaches and irritability returned. At first, I was in denial until I started waking up several times a night unable to take a breath. Sometimes, I'd dream I couldn't breathe and then I'd wake up choking. It was the weirdest thing, and a little scary. After a while, both Daniel and my parents convinced me to go back to the sleep doctor.

This time, I checked into an in-house sleep center so they could watch me and collect data while I slept. After the testing period was over, my mother and I met with the medical team.

"Tori, your condition has become more concerning and severe since the last time we monitored you," said the doctor. "It's unusual given your age. I'd like you to meet with a surgeon in my practice. He may recommend removing your adenoids and tonsils to help clear your airways."

"More surgery?" I said, looking over at my mother.

"It's nothing major and it might help," said the doctor. "Also, I'm going to move you up to a more comprehensive CPAP device. I can't stress more strongly that you must wear this every time you sleep, including naps, and particularly if you're alone."

The look on the doctor's face frightened me a little. It was clear he wasn't joking.

"What if I fall asleep by accident and don't have it on?" I said.

"I don't want to alarm you, but it could be serious," said the doctor. "Your condition is rare, but I've seen it before. You should be fine, if you religiously use the device."

"And, if I don't?" I asked.

The doctor glanced at my mother before giving me a long, intense look. "It's a remote possibility, but with your blood pressure being high and your heart issue, there's a chance you could have heart failure or a stroke."

After that sobering meeting, my CPAP device went on *every* night after I brushed my teeth. I became a model sleep apnea patient, a totally compliant lamb. I had too much of life ahead of me to risk having a massive cardiovascular event.

After my tonsils and adenoids were removed, I went back to the sleep center for observation. The results — my sleep apnea was worse. And, the surgery didn't help at all.

CHAPTER ELEVEN

I don't know if it's the stress of having a new baby and all the stuff that goes with it, but lately, my sleep issues have started to escalate. I often wake up gasping, unable to take in a breath. Whenever it happens, Daniel holds me and tries to calm me down. It's really scary.

"You need to go see the doctor again," my husband says emphatically after another episode. "You've taken on too much. You've got the baby, you're still working for the gallery from home and a million other things."

"Okay, I'll go see someone," I say trying to end the conversation.

"Promise?"

I nod, knowing I probably won't go to another doctor, at least not right now. I'm sick of doctors. Next month, after I go back to the gallery, I'm sure things will calm down.

Daniel looks at me. He knows me better than I think and doesn't believe me. "Clearly, I can't control you, but I do have a say in how this household runs. If you're going back to work," he says, "we're going to get some help."

I shake my head. "I thought you didn't want anyone else to take care of our child."

"I don't. But your health concerns me and what if I'm in a play, or have to travel somewhere for a shoot? You know my hours can be crazy. Sometimes auditions are last minute and missing one could kill my career."

I thought he was being a little dramatic. I love my husband and he's a great actor who just needs a break. When he played Stanley Kowalski in an Off-Off-Broadway showcase of *Streetcar*, there wasn't a dry eye in the house. I was so proud that night. But the truth is, his career isn't exactly booming. When we met at a charity event, he'd already been at the acting game for a good seven or eight years. Now it's been eleven.

Since I've known him, he's had an assortment of small acting roles but nothing of significance. Most of the money he makes comes from the occasional modeling job. That money is usually poured right back into his personal maintenance and acting classes. Of course, he's got to do it. Without his handsome face and fit body, he's got nothing to sell, as he often reminds me.

"It's like taking care of a house," he said one night after plunking down a ridiculous amount of money for a series of facials. "If you don't fix the roof, eventually your ceilings are going to cave in and then you've got nothing to sell."

Still, no matter how hard he's tried, his acting has never taken off. It breaks my heart because all the rejections chip away at his self-esteem. The truth is, we don't need the money he earns. I've got a trust fund that can more than cover our expenses. I want him to be happy and not feel like a failure.

Having Jonah has been a huge positive distraction for Daniel. With a new baby, he can take a little break from all the theatrical disappointments. He adores our son and that makes me so happy. It means everything I did was worth it. Sometimes, I have doubts when I feel the burden of the secrets I've kept. But, when I see Daniel with Jonah together, and the look of pure joy and love on their faces, I know I did the right thing. No regrets.

Daniel and I resume the conversation about getting a babysitter and we make a list of requirements on a piece of paper.

"I'd want her to live in," I say, looking at my first line item. "That way we always have someone here."

"Except," says Daniel, "it means we *always* have someone here. We'd have no privacy."

"We have a huge three-story house with a basement. She can stay on the third floor. We'll hardly ever see her."

After a few minutes of cajoling, my husband agrees to a live-in nanny. "She should be young because babies take a lot of energy," I say. "And, she has to speak English well. We have Jonah's speech development to consider. And, no smoking."

Daniel adds washing the baby's clothes and bedding and outlines a daily walking schedule. I approve. As on most things, we're in sync. I'll start my quest for the perfect nanny the following day. We've got four weeks until I'm due back at work.

I put my feelers out in the universe for babysitter recommendations. I call a bunch of friends, some old sorority sisters from college and several clients from the gallery who have kids. My mother and father, the ultimate doting grandparents, do the same. We place an ad on a local website and Daniel asks around in his acting circles for any leads. I'm confident we'll find someone amazing.

Over the next few days, Daniel's got a four-day modeling job at the Javits Center. I'm at home with Jonah, happy as a clam. He's crawling now and has immense curiosity about everything. No words yet, but he makes all sorts of sounds as if he's trying to communicate with me. He's so darn cute.

It's afternoon when I put him down for a nap. He resists and cries for a good ten minutes. My heart breaks when I hear him in distress. But according to all the baby books, I'm supposed to let him cry and put himself to sleep. It kills me every time.

Finally, he's quiet and I pick up several of his toys scattered around the TV room. Jonah's barely been in our lives for two months, but I honestly can't remember life without him. Knowing I have at least an hour before he wakes, I go to my computer to catch up on some gallery business.

After I respond to a couple of emails, I start thinking about Sasha — again. I momentarily get teary. She was a nice girl who had really bad luck. I try to picture her but I can't see her face anymore, only her long dark hair and perfect eyebrows. The rest of her is gone now.

I want to know more about her and what kind of gene pool my son comes from. Was there depression in her family? What about cancer or autoimmune diseases? I need to know these things to make the best choices for Jonah. I type the word "Sasha" and "Chicago" and "Ohio" into the search bar and get nothing.

Then, a little information nugget pops into my head. I remember something she said to me that day at the beach. "I had the most amazing massage yesterday with this incredible woman named Chloe. She's got a little place in a strip mall next to the farmer's market."

I type *Chloe + masseuse + Hamptons NY* into the search bar and I get a hit. Body Therapy by Chloe is located in a strip mall on Montauk Highway in East Hampton. The next time I go out there, which will now be sooner than I planned, I'm going to get a massage with Chloe. I need to find out everything I can about Sasha — to protect my son.

CHAPTER TWELVE

Two days later, a plain, middle-aged woman wearing a red sweater and a knee-length gray skirt waits in the entrance foyer of our home. She's the fourth of thirteen nanny applicants we will interview this weekend. Daniel took an active interest in the process and pre-screened all of them on the telephone. Only the women he liked will we meet in person. The first three were okay, but none of them set my world on fire. Daniel didn't like them either. I get it. Our nanny has to be special. Nothing short of Mary Poppins will do.

We lead "Number Four" into the living room. Daniel and I sit on the couch while she plants herself in the adjacent armchair. Jonah is in his swing rocking back and forth next to me. He watches everything.

The first thing I look for in a potential nanny is how quickly they engage with my child. Number Four scores a few points when she goes directly over to Jonah the moment she walks into the room. Daniel and I exchange a positive look. Number Four passes the first hurdle.

Over the next twenty minutes we learn that Number Four has had two long-term babysitting jobs, one for a set of nine-year-old twins and the other for a boy, age five.

"You haven't had any experience with babies then?" I say, hoping I'm wrong because everything else about her seems pretty good.

"I haven't. But I'm willing to learn," she says.

Nope, I say to myself. *I can't have you possibly making mistakes with my child.*

Before giving Daniel a chance to weigh in, I make an executive decision and abruptly end the interview. Within sixty seconds, Number Four is on the outside of our front door and I lock the latch.

I walk back into the living room, letting out a disappointed sigh as I sit down.

"Close but not close enough," I say.

My husband stares at me, and not in a good way.

"What the hell was that?" he says.

"What was what?" I say, a little defensively.

"What just happened here?"

"She wasn't right for us. She never took care of a baby before. I thought you and I were on the same page."

"C'mon, she was good. She was mature, calm and had great references. And Jonah responded very well to her."

"I didn't love her," I say as the doorbell chimes. Daniel shakes his head as he gets up to answer the door, muttering something about how "it's going to be a long day."

He returns with Number Five, a twenty-eight-year-old grad student in anthropology. Five goes to school part-time taking one or two classes a semester at Columbia. She's cute and bubbly and, if she's going to Columbia, she must be smart. She also goes directly over to Jonah and engages with him.

"Tell us a little about your experience," Daniel says with a smile.

Five nods. "I was a nanny for the Grangers for about a year. They have an adorable two-year-old little girl. When Mr. Granger's company transferred him to London, they asked me to go with them. Oh, my God, I would love to live in London, but I'm in school and that's gotta be my priority."

I feel myself fidgeting in my seat and tap my pen on my folder. This girl isn't right for us and I wonder why Daniel is still conversing with her. She said it quite plainly. School is her priority and that is a deal-breaker for me. Our nanny must consider childcare to be her priority. I cross Number Five off of my list while Daniel continues to ask her more questions. I don't want to cut him off again like I did with the previous candidate, so I remain silent.

I watch them converse. They're laughing and joking like old friends. That's when I add another absolute requirement to our future nanny's profile. She can't be super cute, young and bubbly like this one. I know my husband loves me, but you'd have to be an idiot to hire someone who looks like this girl. That would only be inviting trouble. She's looking at my husband now with stars in her eyes after he shares that he's an actor. Daniel's lapping up her admiration. I don't blame her for being dazzled by him. My husband is very handsome. Still, I can't have that banter going on all day, every day.

"Tori, do you have any other questions for her?" my husband says interrupting my inner conversation.

"Nope. I think she's answered everything we need to know. I'm good."

Naturally, Daniel offers to walk her out. I hear them continue to chit-chat in the foyer for what in my opinion is an unnecessarily long time. *Let the woman out, Daniel.*

The front door opens and closes. In the meantime, Jonah has fallen asleep in his rocker. I pick him up as my husband comes back into the living room.

"She was great, don't ya think?" he says all smiles. "I think we've found our nanny."

"She was all right," I say guarding my words, trying not to sound too negative.

"You didn't like her? I thought she was awesome. I'm starting to get the sense you won't like anyone."

I do a quick calculation in my head. If I submarine this last woman because she said school was her priority, Daniel will think I'm being petty and he'll get annoyed. I have only one play left: appeal to what he understands — his inherent effect on women.

"I know I'm being silly," I say, laying it on thick, "but the truth is, I don't want someone that attractive in my house every day."

He laughs. "Is that what's going on in your head? You're jealous?" he says as he comes over and puts his arms around me and our sleeping baby. "You know I love you. Nothing is more important to me than you and our son."

I stand there in his arms, feeling all my anxiety slip away. The warmth of his body next to mine makes me feel safe and wanted. I look up into his eyes and smile gratefully for his loving reassurances.

"Can you try to be a little more open-minded while we interview the rest of the nannies?" he says, kissing me on the forehead. I nod as the bell rings again.

Number Six has no sense of humor whatsoever and thankfully Daniel doesn't like her either. Number Seven is a no-show and Number Eight smells like cigarettes, which is out of the question. After spending the better part of a Saturday interviewing nannies, we are no closer.

The next morning we try to remain optimistic as we prepare to interview the remaining five women. Number Nine seems great. She's had one other babysitting job for two years with a family in Manhattan. She's bilingual in English and Spanish, something Daniel and I think is a huge plus. She's thirty-two, single. She's pleasant looking but not too pretty, which takes her up a notch in my book. She says all the right things, but I notice she barely looks at Jonah. The entire thirty minutes she remains focused only on Daniel and me.

Jonah's chattering and happily playing with his rattle in his playpen.

"Would you like to pick him up?" I say to Number Nine, hoping her lack of interest in my son is just nerves.

She shakes her head. "That's okay. I don't want to disturb him. He seems happy right now. I don't believe in picking up babies too much. They need to learn to entertain themselves. It helps them build coping skills."

Daniel and I give each other a sideways glance. Thankfully, he doesn't like her answer either and we soon send her packing. Number Ten is too old. Number Eleven chewed gum the entire time. Number Twelve is from South America. After twenty minutes, she reveals that she is illegally in this country. She's hoping whoever she works for will sponsor her.

I understand her plight, really I do, but I don't want to get involved in that kind of a commitment with a total stranger. What if we start sponsoring her and decide we don't like her? Or what if immigration officers show up one day and take her away? We could get into big trouble.

We're wrapping up with Number Twelve when our house phone rings in the kitchen. We let the machine pick it up. Daniel walks the young woman to the front door and I hear it close with a heavy thud. When he comes back into the living room, he's got an exasperated look on his face.

"I didn't think finding a nanny was going to be this hard," he says, scratching his head. "With the exception of the pretty girl you vetoed, none of them were truly great. When I spoke to them on the phone they all seemed fine."

"We still have one more coming," I say, looking at the time on my phone.

"Given how it's been going so far, I'm not hopeful about number thirteen, are you?" he says walking out of the room to get a glass of water before the next candidate arrives.

"Check the machine and see who called," I shout as I flip through the texts on my phone. I'm reading a confusing series of messages from one of our gallery's biggest artists when Daniel returns. His forehead is wrinkled and his eyes are narrowed.

"What's wrong?" I say.

"There was the strangest message on the machine."

"What do you mean?"

"It was the adoption agency where we got Jonah," he says. "They wanted to let us know they expect to have a baby for us sooner than they expected."

CHAPTER THIRTEEN

The minute the words come out of Daniel's mouth, my heart starts pounding. Every part of my body is on high alert. I can't catch my breath. I wonder if today is the day I'm going to have that heart attack they've been warning me about.

"Tori?" says my husband, looking me straight in the eye. "Why did the adoption agency say they were going to have a baby for us?"

I need to say something logical, something that makes sense. The best I come up with is: "I don't know." *Ugh.*

"Something's not right," he says. "I'm going to call them back to see what's going on. Why would they leave a message like that?"

Desperately trying to come up with a plausible answer, I'm literally saved by the bell when our doorbell rings. I pop out of my seat like a jack-in-the-box and run to the door. Number Thirteen's early arrival has gotten me off the hot seat, which makes me like her before I even see her.

I lead her into the living room, assessing her appearance and gait. She walks like a truck driver. She's not the least bit ladylike and her accent has a slight Southern lilt to it. I'm thinking Kentucky or West Virginia. At first, she calls me ma'am, which I put a stop to immediately.

"Daniel, meet Eden," I say to my husband as I walk the young woman into the living room. Daniel seems preoccupied. I can tell he's still focused on the message from the adoption agency. To get him to switch gears, I jump right into the interview, asking Eden about her previous babysitting experience.

She looks young. She's got light, slightly curly, strawberry-blonde hair half-pulled into a ponytail, the remaining strands are loose, but not in a casual chic way, in a messy way. My guess is she's no more than twenty-five. She rattles off information about her previous employer, while I hyperfocus on her pale skin that has an almost blueish cast to it. Her features are washed out. Her pale-blue eyes practically fade into her face. She could use some make-up. But it almost doesn't matter because she's wearing glasses with a thick dark frame that overwhelm her face. I can't tell if she's fat or thin because she's got on baggy pants with an oversized sweatshirt. There are sneakers on her feet and a large cross-body bag, its strap resting diagonally over her chest. Physically, she's a bit of a hot mess. But I kind of like her.

"And this is Jonah," Daniel says as he picks up our son. I look over at my husband holding our boy and notice Jonah's strawberry birthmark has finally disappeared. His pediatrician said it would fade and now it has.

Eden lumbers over to the baby, gingerly taking him from Daniel's arms. I watch the whole encounter carefully to see if there's a connection between Eden and my child. She's tentative at first, but then she wraps her arms around him and starts to sing. I don't know the tune, but it's pretty and Jonah smiles at her. Eden smiles back and the two lock eyes.

"You like music, don't you?" she says as she walks around the room, gently bouncing him on her shoulder. Jonah makes happy sounds and she responds perfectly. It appears that Eden checks all of my boxes. She's dumpy and frumpy which means she's a zero threat to my marriage. Not that I have any doubts about Daniel, but who wants a hottie walking around the house in bike shorts and a cut-off T-shirt?

It's obvious Eden loves babies and handles them with ease. Jonah took to her instantly. It was pretty amazing to watch.

She hands us a fantastic written reference from her last employer. Naturally, I'll call them to double check that it's legit. Don't want to take any chances. I have to admit, though, I do like her. She's a little rough around the edges, but we're not hiring a fashion model. We're hiring a person to take care of our baby.

I look over at Daniel. He's not smiling and I wonder why. She seems perfect to me.

"Do you have any more questions for Eden?" I ask my husband.

"No," he says looking at his phone like he has something more important to do.

For some reason, he's not a fan of this young woman and I really like her. I've got to save this.

"Do you have any questions for us?" I say to Eden. She asks about the hours and if she could see the room she'd be staying in. I take her up to the third floor to show her the bedroom and bath that would be hers. Daniel remains downstairs in the living room while I show Eden around the house.

"Can I see the baby's room?" she asks, her Southern drawl creeping in.

My heart is full. She wants to see his room. This young woman is already clearly invested in Jonah. I take her into the nursery and she flits from one shelf to the next looking at his toys and the books in the bookcase.

"I love this series," she says picking up one. "I read them to the last baby I took care of. I love to sing and play and read my kids stories. This is a beautiful room, by the way."

Compared to all the others we've met, this woman is hands down the best. I'm completely sold. Eden is our nanny. I have to get Daniel on board.

As we walk down the stairs, it occurs to me that she may not want the job and my anxiety creeps in. Daniel is waiting for us in the living room.

"You have a wonderful home," says Eden to my husband.

"Thank you," he says, not looking her in the eye.

"You have a very impressive reference," I say. "As a matter of fact, I think you'd be perfect for—"

"For many families," interrupts my husband. "Thank you for coming. Tori and I've met quite a few people this weekend. We need to talk things over. We'll get back to you tomorrow."

"Of course. This is a big decision for any family," says Eden as she walks over to Jonah and picks him up again. He melts into her arms. "In order for this to work, it's got to be a good fit for all of us, but most importantly for Jonah."

I smile and nod to Daniel and then show Eden to the door. Before she leaves, I shake her hand and tell her she'll be hearing from us soon. Back in the living room, I'm brimming with excitement and optimism, and ready to change Daniel's mind.

"Wasn't she great?" I say, a big, encouraging smile on my face.

"She was all right," he says, playing with his phone again. "She dresses like a slob."

"We're not hiring her to walk the runway. We're hiring her to love, nurture and take care of our child. Who cares what she looks like?"

Daniel paces around the room. "That's not the song you were singing when you thought one of the nannies was too attractive. I don't know about this one. She was pretty rough around the edges."

"But she was great with the baby. You saw the way Jonah responded to her. He doesn't act that way with everyone."

"I'll admit, she was good with him. But when was the last time she combed her hair?"

"Oh, my God, Daniel. She takes care of babies. We're talking spit-up, dirty diapers, baby food disasters. She spends her days on the floor, picking up toys and pushing a stroller. She's not working at a law firm or an ad agency. She's a nanny."

Daniel sighs. He knows when he's beat. "You really like her?"

"I do."

"Okay, but let me call her reference first before we offer her the job. I want to talk to them. Fair?"

"Absolutely," I say, breathing a sigh of relief. Daniel puts his phone on speaker and punches in the number Eden provided of her previous employer. He gets their voicemail and leaves a detailed message.

"What if they don't call us back?" I say, already panicking.

"They'll call back," he says, walking towards the kitchen. "If they really value her, like she said, they'll want to help her get a new job, right?" He reaches the archway to the hall and spins around. "I'm still puzzled about that message on the answering machine from the adoption agency. The woman was very specific and she knew our personal details. How could she not know they just placed a baby with us? Don't you think that's weird?"

During Eden's interview, I came up with a reason for the odd agency phone call in case he brought it up again.

"I should have told you, but on the day I picked up Jonah, the administrator at the agency asked if we'd ever be interested in a second baby to round out our family. I told her yes."

"Wait a minute. We never discussed getting a second baby. How could you do that without consulting me first?"

"I know, I'm sorry. It was a knee-jerk reaction. I was so surprised and overcome with emotion and joy that day. When the woman asked me, I wasn't thinking clearly. I'll call them tomorrow and tell them we're not interested in another baby at this time. Jonah is more than enough for me."

CHAPTER FOURTEEN

On Monday morning, Daniel has an early audition for a car insurance commercial. He promises me he'll try Eden's reference again while he waits for his audition time slot. On pins and needles, I busy myself with Jonah's laundry and tidy up his room to help me to stop obsessing over losing my perfect nanny.

At eleven a.m., Eden calls asking if we've made any decision yet.

"It's great to hear from you," I say in the syrupiest voice I can conjure. "We're very close. Just waiting to hear back from your reference. You still want the job, don't you?"

There's a long pause, too long and I feel my stomach churn.

"Yes, of course I do. But another family has offered me a position. They're insisting on an answer today. The family is very nice, but they have three older kids. I'd much rather take care of Jonah, but I need a job."

"Eden, we both loved you and I know we're a perfect match. But my husband needs to check your reference first, that's how he's wired. I promise you, we'll get back to you within a few hours. Maybe you can give your old employer a call and ask them to get in touch with us?"

Eden agrees to reach out to her previous employer. "I think we're the perfect match too," she says. "I love babies and Jonah is the cutest one I've ever seen. I would love taking care of him."

Over the next few hours, I call Daniel seven times only to get his voicemail. I text him nine times, but they remain unread. Where the hell is he? The clock is ticking and I'm about to lose our nanny and my mind. At one thirty p.m., I'm pacing around my living room like a caged lion with Jonah on my shoulder. The front door opens and I race to the hallway as Daniel comes in.

"Where have you been?" I say. "I've been calling and texting you for hours."

"I was at an audition. And yes, it went well, they're calling me back. Thanks for asking," he says as he tosses his house keys into a large silver bowl by our front door.

"Why didn't you answer me?"

"You know I always turn my phone off when I'm at an audition," he says as he walks down the hall towards the kitchen, me following behind.

"I guess I forgot," I say, talking a little too fast. "I'm so wound up about the nanny situation. Did you listen to my messages? She's got another offer. We have to make a decision now. Did you talk to her reference? Please tell me you've talked to them."

"Slow down. Yes, I talked to them," he says, opening the refrigerator and rummaging around. "I called them back as soon as I got out of my audition."

"And?"

"Make Eden the offer."

"What? The reference was good? I knew it would be. What did they say?"

He pops a piece of rye bread into the toaster and faces me. "They said she's phenomenal. They couldn't stop gushing about her. Talked about how they begged her to come with them when they move but she wants to stay in New York. The woman told me how her daughter loves Eden and how much they love her. The father told me his wife cried when Eden told them she couldn't go with them."

An enormous smile spreads across my face. "You're totally on board with her?"

"She's a little different than what I'd envisioned. But, after that glowing reference and the fact that you like her so much, let's do it. If she doesn't work out, we'll get rid of her."

I race back to the living room, grab my phone and call Eden. She answers and within five minutes, I close the deal. She'll finish up with the other family and start with us in two weeks. When I hang up, my whole body relaxes. Getting the right childcare is so important. The wrong choice could be a disaster. I can't make any mistakes with Jonah. He's my one and only.

I call my parents to tell them we've hired a nanny. My father says something to the effect of 'maybe I should meet her first.' I politely decline his offer.

"Daniel and I have already made our decision," I say.

My mother volunteers to help me redecorate the room that Eden will be staying in. It's a small room on the third floor with its own bath. When I was growing up in this house, it had been a guest room. It hasn't been updated in twenty years. I agree with my mother, it's time for a refresh. I'm hopeless when it comes to interior decorating. My mother, on the other hand, has a good eye and a passion for it. It didn't take much convincing for me to turn the decorating reins over to her.

"I'm thinking sleek, modern and unfussy. What do you think of a Scandinavian motif?" she says, already off to the races. "It's so much easier to keep clean and in my opinion, it's a timeless look."

I agree with everything my mother says because I don't really care. I just want the room to look good and feel homey when Eden arrives. The better our nanny feels, the better care she'll take of our son. Someone once told me 'people don't run from good.' I think that's true for lots of things — relationships, jobs, the arts and nannies.

I've found a gem and I don't want someone else stealing her away from me. I've heard about parents who look for a new babysitter in playgrounds. They go there and observe how other nannies interact with their kids. When they spot one that appears super engaged, gentle and loving, they make their approach. It starts with a casual conversation. The parent might compliment the nanny on her childcare skills. Soon, an offer for employment is made. I don't want that to happen to me, so I'm going to make sure Eden loves living here. I give my mother the green light to redo Eden's room, and off she goes.

Ten days later, the bedroom on the third floor has been transformed. The walls have been painted white and icy blue. My mother selects a blond bedroom set from a Swedish furniture company and has the order expedited so it arrives within a week. A new luxury mattress arrives the following day. Crisp white cotton sheets along with a fluffy white comforter that has navy ticking go on the queen-sized bed. White-and-navy towels are placed in the white tile bathroom.

"It looks amazing, Mom," I say to my mother as she places the last navy-and-white throw pillow on the bed. "Thank you for doing this."

"There are still a few prints I want to hang on the walls," she says. "Your father's coming over later with his hammer."

"Daniel or I can do that."

"Tori," says my mother with an incredulous look, "I've seen your interior decorating handiwork before and Daniel is all thumbs. Let your father do it. Besides, it's an excuse for him to come over and see you and Jonah."

An hour later while my parents argue over the height of a framed print on the bedroom wall, my phone rings. The caller ID says Abercrombie Adoptions of New York. *Shit*. I run down to the second floor, duck into another guest room and shut the door.

"This is Tori," I say softly.

"Hello, it's Jennifer Hazelton from the Abercrombie Adoption Agency. I didn't hear back from you and wanted to make sure everything was okay. We need some additional paperwork for the adoption. We estimate the timing to be in about five months. What I need from you now is . . ."

This can't be happening.

"Ms. Hazelton, let me stop you. Due to some other unforeseen family issues, we won't be able to adopt a baby at this time."

Dead silence.

"I'm sorry to hear that," she finally says. "I'm a little surprised. You called so often to check in. You and your husband were so anxious to move things along. Is this a postponement or a . . . ?"

I've got to put an end to this now.

"We're getting divorced."

CHAPTER FIFTEEN

I sip my morning coffee reading the news on my phone, my body relaxed. Everything is finally coming together. My little white lie about getting divorced means that the Abercrombie Adoption Agency is no longer a nagging problem. I can finally stop looking over my shoulder.

I still check the police reports and newspapers every day for anything new on the drowning. So far, there's been no connection between Jonah, Sasha and me. They still don't know the identity of the woman who drowned, and they've never recovered a body. Nobody reported seeing Sasha with a baby at the beach that day. I'm starting to believe we're in the clear.

Several theories have been posted on online bulletin boards and in the local Hamptons newspapers. The general consensus: the missing pink-capped woman swam out too far, got caught in a current and went under. Some have suggested there was no woman in a pink cap at all. One poster believes the pink-capped swimmer was a hysterical collective figment of people's imagination. Their contention — after the lifeguard *thought* he saw something and reported it, everyone else piled on. Personally, I think that's a stretch. Besides, I was there. I talked to her. Sasha was real.

The third theory circulating is that the woman in the pink cap *intended* to harm herself. They say she swam way out and simply let herself go under. A possible theory, I suppose, but not true. I was the last person to speak to her. I'll admit she'd had a tough life, but she was still very positive and appeared resilient. She talked about finding a job, buying a car and getting herself settled. She even joked about finding herself a rich Hamptons husband. And she put on sunscreen. I can't get that thought out of my mind.

She didn't sound like someone on the brink of killing herself. Also, Sasha was a mother. Maternal instinct is strong. I know how I feel about Jonah. There's literally nothing I wouldn't do for him. A mother wouldn't deliberately leave her baby alone on a beach with a total stranger. No, Sasha drowned because she got caught in a riptide, case closed.

I make myself another cup of coffee even though I've already had one and a second will make my heart race, but I don't care. I need some extra energy today. Eden is moving in this morning and I'm so excited.

When the bell rings I race to the front door and yank it open, a gigantic welcoming smile on my face.

"Eden," I say with possibly too much enthusiasm, "we're so glad you're here."

She's wearing a bulky gray hooded sweatshirt over thick gray sweatpants and sneakers. Her frizzy golden ringlets are pulled back into an unkempt ponytail again and a pair of large tortoiseshell eyeglasses sits on the bridge of her nose. Once again, I detect no trace of make-up. Appearance isn't her forte, which suits me just fine. Daniel won't be distracted and she can devote all of her energy to my son.

I help her bring in several duffel bags and what looks like a large art portfolio.

"Are you an artist?" I say, getting nosey already.

Her pale white skin goes a little pink. "I sketch with pencils and paper. I'm not very good, but I enjoy it. Where's Jonah?" she says, looking around the minute she steps inside the foyer.

I call up the stairs for my husband, who comes down with the baby in his arms. Daniel's barely on the bottom step before Eden races over to him, her arms outstretched.

"There's my baby," she says as Daniel gently passes our son to his new caregiver. "Jonah, I've missed you so much. You and I are gonna have a good time together. I'm gonna take you to the park and we'll go for long walks and read lots of stories."

My son seems delighted by his new nanny and smiles and squeals, fully engaging the dimples on his cheeks. Eden blows air into his face. At first, he's surprised, but then he laughs. He reaches out for her curly hair with his tiny hands, grasps and then pulls it. She doesn't seem to mind and only laughs as she sits down in a nearby chair with him in her arms. Soon she's singing *Edelweiss* to him in a beautiful soprano voice.

I watch Jonah. His eyes follow Eden's every move. He smiles, gurgles and giggles as she finishes her song and kisses him on his head.

"You really have a way with babies," I say, a little jealous at how easy she makes it all look.

"Practice, I guess. I was the oldest of five kids. My parents both worked. I often had to take care of my younger siblings."

"When I see the way Jonah responds to you, it melts my heart. I can't tell you how important that is to me. We're both so glad you're here, aren't we, Daniel?"

As soon as those words come out of my mouth, I look at my husband. He hasn't said a single word since Eden arrived. I look at him waiting for a response.

"Yes, very glad," he says as he walks out of the room headed towards the kitchen.

I don't think Eden notices Daniel's aloofness, but I know him and something's definitely wrong. Once I get her settled in her room, I bring her down to the nursery on the second floor to play with the baby. Only then do I go looking for my husband.

"Daniel," I shout from the second-floor landing. "Where are you?"

"Down here," he yells from the kitchen.

I find him seated at our large pine table. He's got an espresso in front of him while he plays on his phone.

"What was that all about?" I say.

"What do you mean?"

"You were short and abrupt with our new nanny. That wasn't very welcoming."

"I carried all of her stuff upstairs. I shook her hand when she arrived and I smiled several times."

"That's not how it looked to me. You looked distant and detached. Do we have a problem?"

Daniel gets up from the table, puts his demitasse cup in the dishwasher and faces me. "Did you see her outfit? She looks like she just rolled out of bed. There hasn't been a comb in her hair in months."

"Shhh," I say, gesturing for him to lower his voice. Sometimes my husband can be so superficial. "She's not auditioning for a beauty pageant, Daniel."

He lets out a snort. "That's for damn sure."

"You need to get over this," I say, lowering my voice even more. "She's great with the baby and that's all I care about. That's all you should care about, too."

He mutters, "Fine," as he leaves the kitchen and heads down to the basement to our home gym for his daily two-hour workout. "Gotta maintain my six pack if I'm going to get any jobs," he says whenever I complain about the amount of time he spends down there.

I still hear him going down the old creaky stairs when my mother calls. She's up in the Berkshires in Massachusetts for the month and wants me to go out to the beach house next weekend to let a repairman in.

I knew I'd go back there one day but not this week. The mere mention of going back to the scene of my crime sends a shiver down my spine. The hairs on the back of my neck stand up. I become instantly nauseated and start making excuses.

"But I already have other commitments this week and—"

"I'd really appreciate you being there to let him in and check on the house, too," says my mother, talking over me. "Your father and I haven't been out east in a while. With all the rain they've had out there, I'm worried about leaks."

"But Mom, our nanny just started and . . ."

"Plus, it's so beautiful out on the East End in September. You can put Jonah's feet in the water," she says, trying to convince me to change my weekend plans. "That's about the same age you were when we first took you to the beach. Take a picture of Jonah in the water when you go and send it to me."

After a lengthy back and forth, I reluctantly agree to go. The truth is, I have to go sometime. I can't boycott the beach for the rest of my life. But I didn't think it would be this soon.

I'm pacing around the kitchen when it dawns on me that going back to the Hamptons isn't a totally bad thing. I need to find the masseuse that Sasha went to, Chloe, the only person Sasha had physical contact with after arriving in New York. I have to know if Chloe remembers Sasha or the baby. More importantly, I've got to find out if Chloe's followed the news and made any connection between Sasha and the missing woman who drowned. Not knowing who knows what has made me feel vulnerable and it's been driving me crazy.

I go back upstairs to check on our new nanny. Eden and my seven-month-old son are in his playroom. He's sitting up on the gray-and-blue oval braided rug holding a rubber panda. Eden's on the floor next to him. There are a dozen small stuffed animals piled on her stomach. She takes each one and flies them like an airplane around Jonah's head. I stand silently in the doorway smiling as Jonah grabs for the soaring bears and lambs, laughing with delight.

"Looks like you two are getting along just fine," I say.

"He's wonderful," she says as she sits up. "He's so alert and bright. Jonah notices everything."

I beam with pride and nod because I couldn't agree more. My son *is* incredibly intelligent and I'm so lucky to be his mother. Just thinking that a child like him could have been thrown into foster care makes me sick.

I did the right thing, I know I did. Sasha would have wanted me to keep him. I promised her I'd take care of him.

"This week we'll get you settled here in Brooklyn. But next weekend I have a little surprise for you," I say. "My parents have a four-bedroom beach house out in the Hamptons. They've asked me to go out to check on something at the house. We'll make a weekend of it. How does that sound?"

"I've never been out there."

"You'll love it. And, you'll be there for Jonah's first time at the beach."

Since we're all going out to my parents' house in a few days, I call and make an appointment for a massage with Chloe and her magic fingers. She may be the only connection left to Sasha.

CHAPTER SIXTEEN

Eden's first week goes beautifully. She's polite, attentive and totally focused on Jonah's needs, which is exactly what I hoped. With me going back to work and Daniel out at auditions or occasionally working, I need to know Jonah is in good, loving, capable hands.

It's Friday morning and Eden and I pack up all the baby things we'll need for our three-day weekend in the Hamptons. We've amassed a large pile in the foyer by the front door.

"That's a lot of stuff," she says, wearing a dubious expression.

"I know. I don't think it's all going to fit in the car," I say with a defeated groan. "I've never traveled with a baby before."

As we're debating what to leave behind, Daniel comes down the stairs carrying a small leather weekend bag and looks at the pile in front of him.

"What the hell is all this?" he says, standing in front of the mountain of strollers and stuffed animals.

I take a moment before answering knowing I overdid it. "The baby's things."

"You've got enough toys here for a nursery school. What's that?" he says, pointing to a large white metal pail.

"It's a UV light diaper pail," I say. "I just got it."

My husband tilts his head to one side and looks at me. "I thought we were only bringing essential items."

"We are," I say. "UV light eliminates bacteria and germs that cause odors and viruses."

"Tori, we're only going to be at the beach for three days," he says. "There's only room in the car for a quarter of this stuff. Can't you improvise a little?"

"I'm not sacrificing our son's health because of car space. We'll have to take two cars."

From the corner of my eye I see Eden backing slowly out of the foyer. Who could blame her? She doesn't want to witness her married employers have an argument. In an effort to maintain family harmony, I let Daniel win this one and remove the diaper pail from the mix.

"You'll need to get rid of more than that pail," he says as he picks up a large plastic baby bathtub and moves it to the side. "I'm going to make a cup of coffee. When you've got that pile small enough to get into one car, call me and I'll load it up."

When I go back to my room to grab my diaper bag, I hear Eden calling to me from the foot of the stairs.

"Did you bring Jonah's ear drops?" she shouts.

Shit. What kind of a horrible mother am I? I forgot all about his drops. I took Jonah to the pediatrician yesterday because one of his ears was red and he was a little cranky. The doctor said he needs the drops twice a day for a week.

"I've got them," I say as I walk down the stairs, not wanting her to know that I'd forgotten.

Forty-five minutes later, with less than half of what I'm sure we'll need to survive the weekend, we're on the Southern State Parkway heading east. It's a picture-perfect September day, warm like August, but with much less humidity. The windows are cracked and the air feels good on my skin. Daniel's unusually quiet, so I chatter about our weekend plans to fill the silence.

In the back seat, Eden, armed with rattles and toys squeezes and shakes them to keep my son amused. He responds to her every attempt with a smile and a squeal. They've really connected.

We pull into the driveway of my parents' house. It's got a second story but only in one part of the house. Most of the living space is on the first floor, including two of the bedrooms. To make our lives easier, we'll use the two bedrooms downstairs. As Daniel assembles Jonah's crib in Eden's room, I carry my son on my shoulder while I give her a tour of the house.

Opening the sliding glass doors in the back, we walk out onto the pool deck adjacent to the house. We gaze out at the distant ocean sparkling in the sun.

"This is beautiful," says Eden, taking it all in.

I smile. Growing up, all my summers were spent at this house. It's not huge, only 2,400 square feet, but my mother has it beautifully decorated and the ocean view property is magnificent.

"This was my happy place when I was a kid. My parents were still renting a small apartment in the city when they bought it. It was all they could afford back then. That was over forty years ago. I think they paid less than a hundred thousand for it. Now it's worth a fortune."

"Wow."

"When Jonah takes his nap, you can go for a dip in the pool if you like. You must be hot in those sweats," I say, puzzling over Eden's lack of clothing diversity.

She gives me a peculiar look. "I didn't bring a bathing suit."

"We could probably get one for you in town."

"That's okay, I'm just happy to be here. I'll be fine."

I wonder how a person could forget to bring a bathing suit to a beach house. Then it occurs to me that maybe she doesn't own one. I make a mental note to buy her one as a little surprise. Next summer, we're going to spend a lot of time out at the beach and she'll need a suit.

We walk back into the living room from the deck and I close the doors and lock them. I explain to Eden the importance of making sure the doors are always closed and locked at all times.

"Jonah's crawling and with the pool being right out back, the doors have to remain closed. Are we clear on that?"

"Absolutely, I couldn't agree more. I thought pools had to be fenced?"

"They usually are, but my parents bought this place so long ago the no-fence thing was grandfathered. I'm planning to talk to my mother about putting in a fence. I can't bring Jonah out here worrying all the time about him drowning."

Daniel brings in the last of our things from the car and lets out a sigh. It's warm out and he's sweating.

"I'm going to jump in the pool," he says as he heads into our room to put on his bathing suit. It's after one and Jonah needs to eat and take his nap. While Eden puts him into his baby seat, I warm up his food. Minutes later, Daniel reappears in his trunks carrying a beach towel. As usual, he looks like he stepped out of *GQ*.

"If anyone needs me, you know where to find me," he says as he pulls open the slider.

I get Eden all squared away feeding Jonah and go into my room to change. A swim sounds pretty good to me, too. I pull on my new Eres black one-piece swimsuit, grab my straw bucket hat, sunglasses and a book and head into the kitchen. Jonah has finished eating and Eden is cleaning him up. I notice his eyes are closing.

"He's tired. It's past his nap time," I say as I give him a kiss on the top of his head and walk over to the sliding doors. "Put him down for his nap. I'll be outside if you need me. We'll go to the beach when he wakes up."

I close the door behind me and watch Eden through the glass as she lifts my sleepy son out of his chair and cradles him on her shoulder. She's so gentle with him, caressing as she holds him. He responds by nuzzling into her and I smile because he's in such good hands.

I've heard horror stories about nannies. One woman told me her au pair left her infant home alone for three hours to go see her boyfriend. Three hours? What if there had been a fire? I say a little prayer and thank the universe. Eden is one in a million.

CHAPTER SEVENTEEN

Dozing on a chaise lounge by the pool, I wake an hour later from the faint sound of my son crying inside the house. They say a mother can hear her baby crying in a thunderstorm. I believe that. I'm about to get up to go to him, when the crying suddenly stops. Eden must have picked him up. I reach over and give my snoozing husband a nudge.

"Hey, wake up. I told Eden we'd take Jonah down to the beach after his nap," I say as I throw on my cover-up and walk towards the house.

At five p.m., Daniel, Eden and I push Jonah in his carriage down to the beach. This beach is within walking distance to my parents' house. It's a different beach from the one where I met Sasha.

Early evening is the perfect time of day to take Jonah because the sun isn't too strong. I make a mental note to order Jonah a full-body sun protection suit for next summer. It's never too early to start protecting a baby's skin. Eden must subscribe to that philosophy because she's wearing a long-sleeved cotton shirt, gray sweatpants, a baseball hat and sneakers.

"Won't you be hot in that?" I say.

"I'll be fine. I'm always cold."

Daniel snorts. "It's eighty-something degrees out."

"I'll be fine," she says as she looks down at Jonah.

"Do you have sunglasses?" I say to her squinting as I lift mine up. "It's really bright out. With your light-blue eyes, you must be sensitive to the sun."

"I'm okay."

Daniel lets out a sigh. "She says she's fine, Tori. Can we move on?"

As we walk, I point out various streets and houses, giving Eden a little backstory on the neighborhood.

"Here is our secret pathway onto the beach," I announce proudly as we walk through what appears to be someone's private property. It is. It's the McKenna's yard.

"The people who live here are old friends of my parents," I say as I lead her through their gate. "I've known the McKennas since I was a kid. Our families had cut-through rights for the past thirty-five years. It's a well-kept secret. The family is hardly ever out here anymore. The house is usually empty."

Eden nods as the four of us walk across the manicured lawns. The McKennas may not be there, but they're loaded and their yard is always pristine. We leave Jonah's carriage in their backyard while Daniel carries him down onto the beach. We walk close to the water, kick off our flip-flops and throw our towels down on the sand.

"Why don't you take your shoes off," I say to Eden. She nods and unties her laces. Daniel sits on his towel, balancing Jonah on his knees, making surprise faces to entertain him. Each time my husband makes a new one, Jonah laughs, making Eden and me do the same.

"Can I bring him down to the water?" Eden says, standing over Daniel. My husband hands her the baby and she gently lifts him onto her shoulder.

"You ready for your first dip in the ocean, little man?" she says, giving him a squeeze. He babbles something unintelligible as Eden walks towards the water. Daniel gets up to follow her but stops and turns back to me.

"Would you look at what she's got on. Who dresses like that for the beach?" he says as he walks away towards the water. I follow them, bringing my camera to record Jonah's first moment feeling the ocean on his toes. The sea is calm. Eden has rolled up her pants and has waded into the water. Daniel stands next to her, watching. Carefully, she holds Jonah under his arms and lowers him down, allowing his tiny feet to skim the top of the cool water.

From behind, I'm recording the whole thing. Daniel and Eden take turns dipping Jonah's feet in the surf as I snap shots and videos for my mother. Eventually, Daniel takes Jonah alone for a walk down the beach and Eden and I go back and sit on our towels.

"How did you and Daniel meet?" she says.

I smile. "At a charity event, a Junior League fundraiser."

"What were they raising money for?"

I laugh. "I honestly can't remember. I used to go to a million of those things. Then one night, I was seated next to this incredibly handsome man. From the minute he sat down, I talked to no one else."

"Was it love at first sight?"

I laugh again. "Pretty close. I know I was mesmerized. Daniel was so charming and when he flashed that smile, I could barely get a word out. Then, I learned he was a struggling actor, which made him even more interesting. I never met actors. I mainly dated Wall Street types or publishing people. But Daniel was different and so handsome. He asked me to marry him five months after we met."

"Fast."

"When you know, you know," I say as my husband approaches with Jonah in his arms. "Ready to head home?"

Daniel nods as he hands Jonah to Eden. "I think someone's got a dirty diaper."

Eden stands and takes Jonah from his father and places him back down on her towel.

"How did you like your first visit to the beach?" she coos to my son as she cleans him and puts on a fresh diaper.

"He likes the water," I say, remembering that it's not Jonah's first visit to the beach.

Later that night, Daniel and I are out on the pool deck enjoying a glass of wine while Eden gets Jonah ready for bed. When he's in his pajamas, she brings him downstairs to say goodnight.

"There's my baby," I say, taking him from her arms and smothering him with kisses. "Mommy loves you so much."

As I hand him to Daniel, who does more of the same, Eden walks over to me. "Can you give me Jonah's ear drops? He's got to have them before bed."

"Right," I say as I get up and go to my diaper bag sitting on the kitchen counter. I dig into the zippered pocket where I had put the drops, but it's not there. I distinctly remember placing the drops in that pocket for safekeeping. We were so rushed leaving the house, and Daniel was on me about packing too much. *Maybe I didn't put it in there? Did I?*

I rummage through my bag, searching through what feels like a hundred pockets. Why do they put so many pockets in these bags, to confuse people? Unable to find his medicine, I pull everything out of the bag, dumping the contents on the kitchen table. I hear Daniel and Eden in the other room entertaining Jonah as I frantically turn everything upside-down.

I'm shaking my bag out when Eden and Daniel come into the kitchen with the baby.

"What are you doing?" says my husband, one of his eyebrows slightly arched.

"I'm looking for Jonah's ear drops."

"Are you sure you brought them?" he says in a slightly accusatory tone. "What are we supposed to do now? Is Jonah going to be okay without them?"

"I know I put them in the inside pocket," I say. "I'm sure of it."

"Don't worry," says Eden. "It was a twin pack, remember? I packed the unopened one, just in case. I've got it in my bag."

Wow. Eden's only been with us for a few days and already I don't know what I'd do without her. "Oh, my God,

Eden. You're so smart to have brought it with you. Thank you."

"No problem," she says as she takes Jonah from Daniel. "I'm a little neurotic. I've got doubles of almost everything Jonah needs. I'll put his ear drops in now. Say goodnight, Jonah." Daniel and I wave to our son as he leaves the room and I let out a sigh before looking guiltily at my husband.

"It was a chaotic morning," he says supportively. "So, you forgot the drops. It doesn't make you the worst mother in the world."

"But I know I put them in . . ."

"Forget it. Let's crack open a bottle of wine and go back outside."

I smile gratefully and we go out to look at the moon and reminisce about our first day at the beach with our son.

Two hours later, I'm feeling a little drunk as I get ready for bed. Daniel's already under the sheets as I pull the cotton blanket back to get in.

"Where's your scuba gear?" he says with one eye open. That's what my husband calls my CPAP breathing device.

"I don't feel like wearing it tonight," I say, climbing into bed and pulling the sheets up to my neck.

"Tori, we've talked about this more times than I can count. You're supposed to wear it. You know what the doctor said. Scuba gear is not optional."

I roll my eyes, get up and drag myself back to the bathroom to put on my "sleep equipment." I hate that goddamn thing.

CHAPTER EIGHTEEN

The next morning, I wake up and the sun is shining. Daniel, already out of bed, is singing show tunes in the hall shower. I personally like to belt out a little Motown or some country when I'm washing my hair. Daniel, the actor, is serenading me with a few tunes from *Les Misérables* and *Hamilton*. He's got a great voice, but I still tease him.

"Keep it down in there," I say as I walk past the bathroom door and bang on it. "How about a little something from *West Side Story*?" As usual, he ignores me and sings louder. I laugh and head off to find Eden and Jonah in their bedrooms, but they're gone. I go down to the kitchen and find Jonah seated in his chair as Eden attempts to feed him breakfast. My son is covered in baby oatmeal. From the grin on his face, it's clear he's having a wonderful time.

I wet a paper towel and begin to wipe his face. "Jonah," I scold lovingly as I clean him up, "look at you. You're a big fat mess." Happy chattering sounds come out of his toothless smiling mouth and I look over at Eden. "Looks like there's more oatmeal on him, than in him."

"Don't worry, he's had plenty to eat," says Eden as she puts his dishes in the dishwasher. "That's his second bowl. He already ate the first one."

Once my son is clean, I put him on my lap at the kitchen table while I drink my coffee. The warmth of his tiny body against my skin feels so good.

"What are your plans today?" Eden says as she sponges down Jonah's highchair.

I know exactly what I'm going to do today, but I won't share that with Eden. I'm going to find Chloe, the masseuse.

"I was thinking of going for a massage," I say, casually twisting my neck and shoulders for effect. "My neck is so tight and I've got a nagging pain in the center of my back. I really need a good massage."

"I've never had one," says Eden, washing out some of the baby's cups.

"What? Never? They're incredible. I always feel like a new person after I go," I say, pretending to google around on my phone for a local massage place. Within a few seconds, I find the number for Body Therapy by Chloe and call. A woman answers.

"I'd like to book a massage with Chloe. Someone I met recommended her to me."

I make the appointment for a deep tissue massage at two. "It will be with Chloe, right?"

"That's me. I'm the only one here," says the woman on the phone. "See you later."

Daniel has taken a bicycle from my parents' garage to ride into town to get a haircut. Since I'm leaving Eden alone with Jonah, I stop by her room to say goodbye before I leave. Jonah's asleep in his crib and I lean down and kiss his cheek.

"I'm going into town for my massage now," I whisper as Eden and I close the bedroom door and walk to the front of the house.

"I hope your neck feels better," she says as she opens the front door for me. I remember then that she told me she never had a massage and I spin around.

"Eden, I know what we'll do. If this massage is good, I'll treat you to one the next time we come out here. How's that?"

She smiles, gives me a thumbs up and nods enthusiastically. "That would be so nice. Thank you."

Walking to my car, I make a mental note to regularly do nice things for Eden. I don't want to lose her. 'People don't run from good.'

I drive into town and park next to the farmers' market. I'm ten minutes early, but that's exactly how I planned it. Hopefully, it will give me some extra time to case the joint. The waiting area is extremely small with room for only three brown plastic chairs and a small side table with a lamp on it. A few out-of-date magazines are spread across a radiator cover on the far wall. There's a small counter that has glass display shelves underneath showcasing various spiritual items for sale like crystals and essential oils.

A sign on the counter tells me to: *Please take a seat*, but I don't. Another sign says: *Chloe is in session and will be back shortly*. I use the waiting time to examine every item in the reception area to get a better handle on who exactly Chloe is. Is she a curious person who might pull a thread and follow it? Or is she a Simple Simon who has no interest in anything outside of her own bailiwick?

I scrutinize a framed, slightly yellowed newspaper clipping hanging on the wall. It's about a local fundraiser for an animal rescue shelter. The picture in the article is of Chloe and several other local entrepreneurs who had participated in the event. What have I learned? Chloe's civic-minded and likes animals. Neither of those bits of info is helpful to me.

A door opens in the back and I jump on the nearest plastic chair. I dive into my phone as two women walk in through the hallway door. I recognize Chloe immediately from the picture on the wall. She's forty-ish, thin and willowy with long red hair neatly braided down her back. After she charges her customer's credit card she gives her a little namaste prayer gesture, and then turns her attention to me.

There's a part of me that's dying to give her a little namaste bow, but I restrain myself.

"Tori?" she says in a quiet and calm voice. "Please, come on in."

I do as she commands and follow her down the hallway. My mission today has a dual purpose. I need to find out what she knows about Sasha. But also, my back truly is killing me and I desperately *need* a massage. Magic fingers are hard to find.

Chloe brings me into a semi-darkened room. Somewhere the sound of wind chimes and harps play an ethereal melody. The moment I enter, the relaxing smell of eucalyptus envelops me and I feel myself start to let go. She hands me a pale-green robe and tells me she'll be back in a few minutes.

When she returns I'm lying on my stomach waiting for the magic to commence. And oh, does it ever. This woman is so good. No, I take that back, she's incredible. With each move of her hand my muscles loosen and my anxieties slip away from my body. After nearly thirty minutes of the one-hour massage, I'm so caught up in the physical experience while she kneads my aching lower back that I almost forget the real reason I'm here.

"Flip over," she says and I obey her command. She starts on my feet, which is heaven. I start to drift off when a little voice in my head shakes me into reality. *Talk to her. You don't have much more time.* I snap myself out of my massage coma and strike up a conversation.

"This feels wonderful," I say.

"I'm glad. You're very tight, especially in the shoulders. That's where you hold all of your tension. I can feel it."

Is it me or do massage therapists always act like they're a little psychic? "You're right," I say. "Whenever something bad happens, my shoulders freeze up immediately."

"I can tell," she says as she moves up my calf. It feels great. She does have magic fingers, just like Sasha said.

"I met this woman at the park in town. She's the one who told me about you. She said you were amazing, the best massage she'd ever had. I had to see for myself."

"And?"

"I think she was right." I open my eyes and look up at Chloe. She's smiling. I'm about to ask some pointed questions when she beats me to the punch.

"Who was the person who referred you to me?"

"I only got her first name, Sasha. I met her in late June when I was out here for a few days. She and I started talking by the duck pond in town. She noticed I was stretching my neck out and mentioned that she had just been to a fantastic massage therapist near the farmers' market. I got your name from her."

Chloe continues working on my calf. "What did she look like?" she says.

I describe her as a dark beauty with long black hair and brown eyes, extremely fit with a beauty mark by her right eye.

"I think I know who it is. She only came in once. I remember her because she was so complimentary and made another appointment but never showed up. To be honest, I was little annoyed at the time. Why don't people call and cancel? I could have booked someone else."

Chloe begins working on my other leg. I drift back into a blissful state after deciding to wait a few minutes before asking another question. I don't want her to think I'm weird or draw too much attention to myself. When she finishes the massage, she leaves me alone to dress. I meet her out front and hand over my Visa card.

"That was wonderful. Sasha was right," I say, reintroducing the Sasha topic.

"I looked her up on my calendar while you were dressing. There was a Sasha who came in on June twenty-first."

Chloe leans over the counter and shows me her iPhone calendar. It shows Sasha at eleven a.m. on June 21 and another appointment at four p.m. on June 25. She never made it to her second appointment. I met her at the beach on the 22nd, the day she drowned — the same day I became a mother. A wave of sadness passes over me, but I carry on. I need to work quickly because Chloe's next appointment could arrive at any moment. "Do you remember anything else about her?"

Chloe shrugs. "I think she told me she was single, just moved into town and was looking for a job. I told her the Lobster Den Cafe was hiring."

Chloe's next appointment arrives and I make one last attempt at picking her brain. "Sasha gave me her phone number but I lost it. You wouldn't still have it, would you?" I say trying to sound casual as I look at the crystals in the display case.

The masseuse looks back at her calendar. "Here it is." She scribbles Sasha's number on a piece of paper and hands it to me. I have no idea what I'm going to do with the number. I already have her phone and she's dead, but I take it anyway.

She tells her next appointment to go in the back and change while we wrap up.

"Now, I remember, Sasha told me that she had a new baby," says Chloe. "She said it was the first time she'd been out alone without him. Guess she got a sitter. Every mother needs a little pampering now and then."

I nod, smile weakly, and tell her I'll be back. "It was really great," I say as I open the front door.

"If you talk to Sasha, please tell her to come back. I understand what it's like to be a new mother," says Chloe as she turns and heads to the back room.

I walk out into the warm autumn sunshine thinking only one thing: I'm screwed.

There are two people out here who met Sasha and knew she had a baby. Chloe is one, and now this mysterious babysitter is the other. Chloe never saw the baby, so she's less of a threat. But the babysitter interacted with Sasha and spent time taking care of my son. I've got to find who that person is and fast.

CHAPTER NINETEEN

I wake the next morning with one agenda — find out which Airbnb Sasha stayed in. If I know that, I might be able to identify who the babysitter was and how much he or she knows. My gut tells me it's probably a neighbor because Sasha had only just arrived here and didn't have a car. But you never know.

Sasha told me she paid for her three-month rental fee in advance. That means technically it's still hers. Even now, it's possible no one yet knows she's not there. I can use that time to my advantage.

I download the Airbnb app and search for rentals within a five-mile radius of the town center. Sasha said she took the bus from town to the beach. With a baby and all her stuff, she couldn't have been that far from the center. I set the rental parameters for a two-bedroom or smaller. Once the results appear, I check the reservation calendar for each listing making a note of those that had been fully rented for the summer. When I finish ticking them off, there are only seven possible places that could have been hers.

I send messages to each owner/manager asking generic house questions. I explain that I'm looking for a four-month rental and happen to be in the Hamptons this week visiting friends. I say I'm hoping to drive by their property just to see the location while I'm here.

Throughout the morning and early afternoon, responses trickle in. Eventually, all of them send me the exact address of their apartment/house so I can do an unescorted drive by. I plan to do much more than that.

I've got a lot of ground to cover and only a day and a half before we go back to Brooklyn. Daniel's out in the backyard on the far side of the pool reading a new play he wants to audition for. Standing by the back sliding doors, I call out to my husband to tell him I have some errands to run in town. He nods and I walk over to the pool. Eden, wearing loose gym shorts and a baggy T-shirt, is knee deep in the shallow end holding Jonah. She's singing nursery songs to him while dipping his feet in and out of the water. Each time his toes hit the water, he giggles. My heart is so full just watching them.

For a second I consider chucking my plans and putting on my bathing suit. But I can't. There are too many loose ends I need to take care of.

I walk towards my husband, who's sitting on a lounge chair with his back to me.

"Daniel," I say loudly to get his attention

He turns his head. He's on the phone. I mouth "sorry" and wait patiently until he finishes his call. I'm not close enough to hear what he's saying but from his tone, it sounds important. Then, he gets up and starts to pace. Moments later, the call ends, he puts his phone in his pocket and flashes a big smile at me. His eyes are literally sparkling.

"What's going on?" I say.

"I got another call back for that Off-Broadway play. I told you about it," he says as he puts his arms around me. "That was my agent. I'm up for the lead. It's between me and two other guys. They want me to come in again and read."

I smile and start to giggle with joy. Daniel's worked so hard for so long, but he hasn't been able to break through. Maybe this is it? He really needs validation. I can tell his tank is nearly empty. Lately, he's been so emotionally erratic that

I wonder if he's going to give up on acting entirely. Being in the theatre is a hard life, often accompanied by rejections and disappointments. You have to have a really thick skin. I couldn't do it.

"What's the play? What's the part?" I say, giddy with excitement for him.

"I can't tell you that. Even talking about it might jinx it," he says as he twirls around on the grass and lets out a low primal scream.

"I'm not gonna lie," he whispers loudly, "I'm really excited about this play."

The truth is, my husband is always excited when he gets a call back. That's nothing new. Still, all you need is one, right? I turn towards my son in the water and shout, "Jonah, your daddy's up for a big Off-Broadway part. He's going to be a huge star."

"Congratulations," says Eden, all smiles.

A worried look crosses my husband's face. "We're not going to say another word about this, or it will bring bad luck. Okay?"

I nod and turn to Eden. "Daniel never likes to discuss any parts he's up for," I tell my confused nanny. "He thinks talking about it brings him bad karma."

"No point in taking any chances," he says as he walks me into the house. "Sorry to do this, but I need to catch the train back to the city this afternoon."

"What? Why?"

"The director wants to have breakfast with me tomorrow morning. I want to get home tonight, get a good night's sleep, and look fresh when I see him. I hate to leave you and Jonah but . . ."

"Don't worry about us. Eden's here. We'll be fine. I'll miss you."

Truthfully, while I'm disappointed he's leaving, it gives me more free time to do my reconnaissance on the mystery babysitter.

Twenty minutes later, Daniel's showered, packed and waiting by the front door.

"Come on, Tori, we've got to go or I'll miss the train," he shouts.

I look at my watch as I pass him in the hall. It's only one o'clock. His train isn't until much later and the station is less than ten minutes away.

"We've got plenty of time," I say as I walk to the kitchen. Jonah's in his highchair and Eden is giving him a snack. As I plant a kiss on Jonah's head, Daniel follows me into the room.

"Tori, we've got to go now," he says. "My train is at one thirty."

"You told me you were taking the four thirty train," I say.

"I said the one thirty."

Daniel gives me a wary look, and I wrack my brain trying to find an instant replay of our earlier conversation but am unable to retrieve it.

As Eden lifts Jonah from his highchair into her arms kissing him on his nose, I remember she overheard our conversation.

"Eden was there," I say. "Eden, what train did Daniel tell us he was going to take back to the city?"

My husband stares at our nanny. "Yes, Eden. Please tell Tori exactly what I said."

With Jonah sitting on her right hip, she looks down at the floor. "I don't really remember," she says.

"It's not a big deal," I say. "Just tell us what you heard."

After a moment, she lifts her head. "I think . . . Daniel said . . . he was catching the train at one thirty."

"Vindicated," my husband bellows as he walks towards the front door. "Let's go."

"I'm sorry," says Eden softly to me.

I assure her it's no big deal and look around for my bag and car keys. "I'm going to drive Daniel to the station now and then do a few errands. There's hamburger meat in the fridge. How about we throw some burgers on the grill for dinner when I get home?"

She nods enthusiastically and I go meet my husband out front. As we drive to the station, Daniel's busy on his phone while I sing along to a few classic rock songs playing on the car radio. When I pull up in front of the station, Daniel gets out and grabs his bag from the back seat.

"Do I get a kiss?" I shout through the open passenger window as he starts to walk away.

He turns, smiles, and walks around to my side of the car. Slowly, he leans down and kisses me on the cheek. "See you in two days, honey," he says. "Wish me luck."

Before I have a chance to say something encouraging, he's gone.

Wasting no time, I pull around the corner and take out the map. I've already marked it up pinpointing the addresses of the Airbnbs Sasha may have rented. Not wanting to leave Jonah for too long, I estimate I can get through the entire list in under ninety minutes.

The first house is a small two-bedroom cottage. I walk up the driveway, take a look around and knock on the door. After several minutes with no answer, I go over to the house next door and ring their bell. A middle-aged woman answers.

"Can I help you?" she says peering at me suspiciously through her screen door. "You're not selling something, are ya? Cause I don't need anything."

I shake my head. "I'm trying to find a friend who just moved out here. She gave me her address and phone number, but I lost it. She told me she was renting a two-bedroom Airbnb for the summer. So, I looked up all the Airbnbs in this area. The house next door is on the list. I knocked on the door over there but no one answered. By any chance, do you know the renter who's staying there?"

"I might," she says, still dubious.

"If I describe her to you, maybe you could let me know if I found the right place."

"Don't need any descriptions. I can tell you right now you got the wrong place."

"But, I haven't told you . . ."

"Cause the people renting that apartment for the summer are two brothers in their twenties. Can't be your girlfriend then, can it?"

I thank her and head to my car crossing off the address on my map. For the next three stops, I actually meet the tenants. Two of the Airbnbs are rented by couples and the third is a single male. I cross them all off the map and focus on the remaining three. If it's not one of those, then I don't know what to do next.

CHAPTER TWENTY

I drive down Heather Lane and stop my car in front of a gray two-story clapboard beach house with white trim. According to the Airbnb listing, the apartment rental is located in the free-standing garage on the side of the house. I walk up the driveway and rap on the side door of the garage. There's a sound of a lock turning and the door swings open.

A diminutive woman in her sixties appears, waiting for me to speak. I spit out the same bullshit story I gave to all the others about losing a friend's phone number. At this point, I don't care if she buys my tall tale or not. It's obvious she's not Sasha. My question was answered when she opened the door. Just to be sure, though, I ask her how long she's been staying at this Airbnb.

"Here?" she says. "About three months, but I'm leaving next week. Place has cockroaches. Hope you find your friend."

I've got two more places to check out before I head back to my parents' house. I hate missing the afternoon in the pool with Jonah, but I have no choice. Finding out who knows about Sasha and the baby is critical to my family's existence. As I drive to the next location, I call Eden to see how everything is going.

"We've had a great afternoon," she says. "Jonah saw some yellow butterflies in the backyard. He couldn't take his eyes off of them."

I feel another pang of jealousy having missed another of Jonah's first moments. I tamp down my envious feelings and remind myself that I'm on a mission to protect and keep Jonah safe. Sacrificing one afternoon is well worth the price to keep him with me always.

I park in front of the sixth house. It's another small two-bedroom ranch, and the farthest one from town. I almost didn't include this rental in the mix because of its distance but added it at the last minute.

I survey the neighborhood from my car and get out slowly noticing there's no car in the driveway. I ring the bell four times, but there's no answer.

Walking around to the back, I stand on my toes and look in through the kitchen window. If I see baby things scattered anywhere then this may be the house Sasha rented. Everything would have been left as it was on the day she died. I look around the room but see nothing out of the ordinary and no baby paraphernalia. Moving to the side of the house, I peek through another window into what appears to be the living room. It's an ordinary room: couch, coffee table, TV, end tables flanking the couch and a big easy chair. But no sign of a baby.

I'm about to return to my car when out of the corner of my eye I spot a stuffed teddy bear on the floor next to the couch. My heart starts to pound and I feel my body flush. My damn heart is racing so fast that I need to hold onto the outside windowsill to steady myself.

Somehow, I know this is the right place. This is or was Sasha's house. It has to be. I look in the window again to determine if there is three months' worth of undisturbed dust on the furniture. From where I'm standing, it's hard to tell.

My only recourse now is to knock on a few of the neighboring homes to see if anyone knew Sasha or interacted with her. The most important question, does anyone know anything about Jonah? I look up and down the street and wonder if it was a neighbor who took care of my son while Sasha got her massage. What kind of mother leaves her baby with strangers to go for a massage, or a swim for that matter? Maybe Sasha wasn't a very good mother after all.

I'm standing out front trying to decide which neighbor's house to approach first when a car pulls into a driveway directly across the street. I cross over and walk up behind a blonde woman in her forties unloading groceries from her trunk.

"Excuse me," I say, a big friendly Hamptons smile on my face. Startled, the woman spins around. "I'm wondering if you can help me. I'm looking for a friend and I've lost their address and phone number. I think they may have rented that house across the street."

A relieved look flashes across her face, probably because I'm not asking for a donation or a signature on a petition.

"I'm happy to help. Can you give me a minute?" she says, holding up a finger. "I've got ice cream in the bags that I need to get into the freezer. Wait on the front porch and I'll be right out."

I sit down on a wooden rocking chair and gaze out at what might be Sasha's house.

A minute later, the blonde introduces herself and for the tenth time that day, I tell the same bullshit story.

"I think that may be her address," I say pointing at the house across the street, "but I'm not a hundred percent sure."

"What's the name of the person you're looking for?" she says, her eyebrows raised.

Not wanting to give her Sasha's real name, I look around as if I'm worried someone is following me. I take my voice down to a loud whisper and lean in.

"The truth is, my friend was in a horrible relationship. She's been in hiding from her physically abusive boyfriend. He threatened to kill her several times. I doubt she's using her real name."

"Oh, my God, that's awful. They should lock people like that up."

"I totally agree. In the meantime, could you describe your neighbor to me?"

"Megan didn't tell me anything about a boyfriend," says the woman. "She said she was an artist out here to paint for the summer. She's been taking art classes. Is this awful boyfriend her baby's father?"

Holy moly, shut the front door! This Megan person who lives across the street has a baby. I didn't say anything about a baby. Megan has to be Sasha. If that's the case, then the blonde woman I'm talking to could be the babysitter I'm looking for.

I've got to play this right. "Yes, he's the baby's father and he's mean and violent. My friend got a restraining order against him, but he harassed and stalked her anyway. It's a mess."

"That's terrible," the blonde says, shaking her head. "Where are my manners? Would you like something cold to drink?"

Thirty seconds later I'm sitting in her kitchen with a cold glass of iced tea in my hand. While we chat, I make stuff up about "Megan" to keep her interested. Since I'm winging it, I don't want to paint myself into a felonious corner by giving her too much information. The woman blathers on about the state of the world and domestic violence. After a while, I interrupt her to ask the critical question.

"Did you ever watch Megan's baby? He's cute, isn't he?"

"He's a cutie, all right," she says as we walk back into her living room. "I only watched him once a few months ago, right after she moved in. I think she had a doctor's appointment or something like that."

From everything she says, I'm more and more convinced that we're both talking about Sasha. The blonde has also acknowledged that the baby was a boy. I go in for the kill and ask the final question.

"When was the last time you saw my friend?" I say, holding my breath.

She takes a moment before she speaks. "It's been a while, at least a couple of months," she says, looking out the front window while biting the inside of her cheek.

"You haven't seen her recently?"

"The first week she moved in, she was coming and going all the time. We had quite a few nice conversations."

As the words leave the woman's mouth, a small black SUV drives down the street and pulls into the driveway of the house we've been talking about.

"Would you look at that?" says the blonde woman. "There's Megan's car parking in the driveway right now."

CHAPTER TWENTY-ONE

I lean in closer to the window and peer out as the taillights on the car across the street turn off. A surge of adrenaline courses through my veins as I try to make sense out of this development. Could Sasha still be alive and living across the street? None of this makes any sense. If she's alive, then why isn't she looking for her baby? I've been following the news like a hawk. There have been no missing baby reports.

Standing behind the blonde woman, I crane my neck to get a better glimpse as the driver gets out of the vehicle. The car door opens and a woman with dark hair gets out. Her back is to me. She's wearing aviator sunglasses, nothing like the oversized fashion glasses Sasha wore that day at the beach. She's also wearing a baseball cap with a long dark ponytail sticking out the back. Her hair is similar to how I remember Sasha's. I examine her body. She's small and sinewy, like Sasha. She's pretty far away, but I believe it could be her. I won't be sure until I get a look at her face. I need to see those dark-brown eyes with perfect brows and that beauty mark next to her right eye.

I'm about to go outside and get a closer look when something stops me and I freeze.

Sasha can't see me. If she does, she'll take Jonah away from me. She'll call the police. I'll lose my son and Daniel and go to jail for kidnapping.

As I slink behind the blonde woman to shield myself, my eyes are glued to the woman across the street removing groceries from her car. She carries several bags into the house and returns for more.

"You all right? You look like you've seen a ghost. Is that your friend?" says the blonde woman staring at me, a puzzled look on her face. I'm so lost in my own thoughts that I forget I'm not alone and in someone's house.

"I'm not sure if it's her," I say trying to remain calm as my entire body pulsates. "She's too far away."

"Why don't you go outside and say hello? That should settle it."

Good question, Blondie. Why don't I go outside and say hello? Well, there's kidnapping, for starters. I rack my brain for an appropriate answer to her question but none come.

"I-I-I don't want to startle her," I say, my eyes still fixed on the activity across the street. "I just need another minute."

"Suit yourself," says my host, plopping into a chair. "I ain't got nowhere else to go."

The woman across the street comes out of the house again for the remaining bags in her trunk. Despite what the blonde woman told me, the woman I'm watching doesn't have a baby with her. Maybe she is Sasha. She wouldn't have a baby. I have her baby.

"Would you look at the time, it's after five," says my host, getting up. "I'm going to make myself a little gin and tonic. You want to join me?"

"What?" I say, still consumed by the action outside as the woman across the street disappears into her house again. The driver's side door of her car is still open so I know she'll be back.

"I said, do you want a gin and tonic?" says the blonde woman a little louder as if I have a hearing problem. "I hate drinking alone, but I will if I have to. You want one?"

On some level, I'm aware my host is speaking English, but I'm so engrossed in what's happening outside I'm not comprehending anything.

"A drink?" I say. "No . . . thank you."

"Suit yourself," she says as she saunters off to the kitchen. As I hear ice being tossed into a glass, the woman across the street emerges from her house again. I scrutinize her face, but it's still hard to tell with that hat and glasses and the distance between us. *Is it Sasha? If she didn't drown, why didn't she go to the police and report her baby missing? Why isn't everyone in Suffolk County looking for a missing child? There hasn't been a thing on the news about it. Are the cops hiding something? None of this makes any sense.*

"You should go over and talk to her," says my host, strolling back into the room with a large ice-filled goblet presumably containing gin. As she settles into an armchair and takes a big gulp, the woman across the street bolts out of her house. She runs to the open driver's side back door of her car and leans in. A second later she lifts out a sleeping child.

My heartbeat slows ever so slightly and the intense pulsing in my hands and feet diminishes. I start to come down from my heightened state, but only a little.

That woman has a baby. That woman isn't Sasha.

CHAPTER TWENTY-TWO

With two more Airbnb's to hit, I head towards the second to last destination on my list. It is a one-bedroom apartment on the second floor of a house on Raymond Lane. Given that Sasha had a baby with all sorts of baby junk, it's unlikely she'd rent a second-floor unit. But, not willing to take any chances, I park my car in front of number twenty-four.

I walk up to the front door. There are two sets of bells. One has a name written underneath, Pinella. The other is nameless. I assume the nameless one is the Airbnb and ring it three times. While I wait, I look around the yard. When no one answers, I ring the other bell. I figure, what the hell, I'm already here. Soon the sound of shuffling footsteps come towards me from the other side of the door. It opens, revealing a very tall young man with long brown hair. He's obviously been woken up by me.

"Can I help you?" he says, yawning.

"I'm not sure. I hope so," I say with as much perkiness as I can muster. "I'm trying to locate a friend and . . ."

I tell my familiar phony story, embellishing the evil boyfriend and restraining order bit, and it works like a charm. The fake story gives me the cover I need to continue my inquiry without raising suspicions.

"What the hell is wrong with people today?" he says loudly, shaking his head. "I'll never understand how any man can do that."

"I know, it's awful," I mutter. "Have you lived here long?"

"About a year."

"I thought my friend might be living in the upstairs apartment. I rang the bell but no one answered."

"Nope. Sorry, but your friend doesn't live here. The place upstairs is rented for the summer by a bunch of young party girls from the city. They're only out here on weekends and none of them have kids."

Before I drive away, I cross off the listing and call Eden. It's nearly seven o'clock and she's probably wondering where the hell I am. If she is worried, I can't tell when I speak to her. She tells me everything is quiet and she's reading Jonah a book. I smile. My son is being well taken care of while his lunatic of a mother is out canvassing half of the Hamptons looking for a dead woman.

"I'll be home in half an hour," I tell her as I drive to the last location. If this isn't the right one, I'm at a loss as to where to go or what to do next. As long as there's someone out there who's spent time with Jonah and knows who his real mother is, my family remains at risk.

Ten minutes later, I turn onto Goose Head Road looking for number thirty-nine. I don't feel well now. I haven't eaten in a while. I'm not supposed to do that. My doctors have said that letting my blood sugar drop is dangerous. I usually carry a granola bar in my bag, but I forgot to pack one. I tell myself I'll be fine even though I'm having a little trouble breathing.

Number thirty-nine is a small brown colonial house with white trim. It looks old and the yard hasn't been taken care of, which is unusual for a Hamptons property. Sweat is beading up on the back of my neck. I take a few deep breaths to calm my body down before getting out of the car. All I know is that I've got to keep going for Jonah's sake.

Though it's a few minutes past seven p.m., it's still light out as I walk to the front door and ring the bell. This is my last chance, there are no more rentals on my list. If Sasha opens this door, I'm not sure what I'll say to her — remember me, I'm the woman who ran off with your baby while you were drowning? When you look at it like that, it sounds really bad. I shrug it off and ring the bell a second time and then a third and a fourth.

Somewhere in the house, a light goes on. Seconds later, a middle-aged couple stands in the open doorway. They're not what I was expecting.

I launch into my surefire story about my missing friend and the restraining order. I get the appropriate amount of concern from the two people but soon find out they've been staying there since early May, over a month before I met Sasha. They have no knowledge of anyone answering the description of the woman I'm looking for.

I drag my sorry ass back to my car. An entire afternoon wasted and I'm no closer to the truth. And, I missed time with my son that I'll never get back. Feeling defeated, I stop at the town market and pick up a tub of locally made coffee and chocolate chip ice cream to help soothe my soul.

By the time I get back to my parents' house, it's nearly eight. Eden has already fed and bathed Jonah and put him to bed. She's also cooked the burgers and made a salad and wrapped a plate up for me. I thank her. She's so competent. After she tells me about every one of their afternoon activities — what Jonah ate and all the cute things he did, she excuses herself to go to her room and read. I'm so emotionally spent from a day lying to everyone I met that I'm glad to have some alone time. While I munch on my burger, I check my phone. It was on silent all afternoon. Scrolling through, I see Daniel called twice but didn't leave a message.

"Hey," I say when I call him back.

"Hey," he says with his usual cool casual demeanor, the same persona that sucked me in when I first met him. "I just got home."

"Just now? You left here five hours ago."

"Went to the gym. Can't slack off, Tori. Got to stay in shape, the competition in my age group is intense."

"I don't know what you're talking about. You look amazing."

"What did you do with your day after I left?" he says, changing the subject.

For some reason I get a vibe he's baiting me. "Not much," I say carefully. "Played with the baby, got some sun. Nothing special."

He pauses before he speaks. "That's funny. I called you this afternoon around five and again at six thirty. When I didn't hear back, I got worried and called Eden."

"Did you? She didn't mention it."

"I told her it wasn't important and that I'd call you later."

"Okay. So, why did you call?"

"Do I need a reason? Can't I call my wife to tell her I love her?" He's teasing me, so I start to let down my guard.

"Absolutely. You can tell me that every day."

There's another long-ish pause before Daniel speaks. "I'm having a little disconnect. When I spoke to Eden, she said you'd been out all afternoon. But you just told me you were home all day with the baby."

The pit of my stomach churns. I've been caught red-handed in a stupid lie, an unnecessary one at that. I could have easily said I went shopping and that would have been the end of it. *Think, Tori, think. Keep it simple.*

"You got me. I went shopping and was too embarrassed to tell you. Forgive me?"

There's another pause. "You don't have to lie to me, Tori. I thought we didn't keep secrets from each other. It's all your money anyway. If you want to spend it, that's your prerogative. It's just that you always say how you want to spend more time with Jonah before you go back to work. I'm surprised you left him for the whole day to go shopping, that's all."

Fuck. He's left me no choice now. I have to pull out my trump card — my shitty heart. I go for it. What choice do I have?

I let out a sigh. "The truth is, Daniel, I wasn't feeling well this afternoon. After I dropped you off at the train station, I started feeling lightheaded and nauseated. My heart was racing."

"You should have called me," he says, a mixture of irritation and concern in his voice.

"You were already on the train to the city. What were you going to do for me? I drove myself to the Urgent Care to get checked out. They agreed my heart was beating much faster than normal but didn't find anything else out of the ordinary. They had me stay in one of their rooms for a couple of hours to monitor me. After a while, I felt better and they let me go after promising I'd call my cardiologist."

"And, did you?"

"Of course, I did. Dr. Baum wants to see me when I get back to the city."

I apologize for lying to him three or four times. Eventually, our phone call ends on a happy note. I've got enough going on with the whole Sasha debacle. The last thing I need is a problem between Daniel and me. Nothing is more important than my family.

I wander around the kitchen looking for something else to eat when I remember the coffee ice cream. I pull it out of the freezer and am filling my bowl when Eden appears in the kitchen doorway in her pajamas.

"You want some?" I ask, hoping she says yes. Dr. Baum made me promise to lose ten pounds during my last check-up, which I've not done. Eating ice cream *with* Eden will make me feel less guilty.

We sit down at the kitchen table and she tells me more about Jonah's accomplishments that day. I glow with pride at each little story.

"Do you want to have children of your own one day?" I say. "You're so good with them. You'd be a wonderful mother."

She smiles and nods. "I hope so. But that's a long way off."

"Don't wait too long. I didn't start trying until I was in my late thirties and then I couldn't."

"Why did you wait so long?"

I smile ruefully. "I had three serious boyfriends before Daniel. Naturally, my father hated all of them. He's convinced every man who looks at me only sees dollar signs. I almost married one, but in the end, none of them were right for me. They all looked good on paper but they were so serious and dry. There was no spark for me."

"Until you met Daniel?"

I nod. "He was different. Daniel was creative and he made me laugh. And, unlike the others, he didn't recoil the first time he saw me in my CPAP mask. He didn't make me feel ugly."

I notice Eden is staring at me, her mouth slightly open. I wonder if I've shared too much personal information. "Anyway, the moral of the story is that some women can have babies well into their forties. I wasn't one of them. That's why we adopted Jonah."

Eden nods again as she takes another spoonful.

"When I first met you and Daniel, I didn't know Jonah was adopted. I figured it out later and I was surprised."

"Why?"

"Because he looks so much like you."

CHAPTER TWENTY-THREE

The next morning I'm up early to make the most of our last day at the beach. I feed Jonah his breakfast and take him to the carpeted living room floor to play. My son delights in every little game I dream up. I fly a teddy bear over his head and he thinks it's hysterical.

As we play, Eden's strange comment from the night before reverberates. She thinks Jonah looks like me. The truth is, as Jonah gets older, I also thought he looked a little bit like me. I brushed it off as wishful thinking.

One day soon after we first got Jonah, I had him out in a stroller on the Brooklyn Heights Promenade when an elderly woman stopped to admire him.

"How old is he?" she said as she leaned down and made silly faces at my son, which he loved.

"Five months," I replied like a peacock with my feathers fully spread. "His name is Jonah."

"He's beautiful and looks exactly like his mama," she said with a wink before walking off. I remember thinking how lucky it was that Jonah and I had the same coloring. We both have dark hair, eyes and complexions, although my hair is highlighted blonde. Still, our facial resemblance is close enough that strangers always assume he's my biological son.

Daniel, on the other hand, looks nothing like Jonah. My husband has dark hair, but his blue eyes, fair skin and facial structure are completely different. Even Eden thought I was Jonah's birth mother. That makes me so happy.

I'm singing "Under the Sea" from *The Little Mermaid* while simultaneously making two stuffed frogs dance for my son when Eden appears in the room.

"Do you want me to take him?" she says, wearing the same oversized shirt, sweatpants and sneakers that she wears every day. Her large black framed glasses don't do her any favors. A little lipstick wouldn't hurt either. Her strawberry-blonde hair hangs loosely around her shoulders but doesn't appear to be recently combed.

She's so devoted to Jonah, but honestly, if she ever plans on getting married and having a family, she'll have to try a little harder. It's one thing to go au natural but another to look like you're a panhandler. Personally, I don't care, as long as she takes good care of my son. It's Daniel who has a bug up his ass about her appearance, not me.

"How she looks reflects back on us," he said one time after Eden took Jonah out for a walk looking like 'something a cat dragged in' according to him. "What happens when Jonah goes to nursery school? What will the other parents think when they see Eden wearing stained clothes with holes in them?"

I defended her but made a mental note to buy her some new clothes so they'd be stain- and hole-free. "Maybe I'll offer to treat her to a haircut?" I said.

"It's going to take more than a haircut to fix that wreck," he had said all snarky.

"Tori? Do you want me to take Jonah?" Eden says a second time as she walks towards me, her arms outstretched. I pick up my son from the rug, nuzzle his neck and give him a kiss before handing him over.

"I have a few errands to run this morning," I say as I get up off of the floor. "I'm going to take a quick shower and get everything done early so we can take Jonah to the beach this afternoon. Since we're leaving tomorrow, this will probably be our last time to do it until next summer."

Forty minutes later, I'm in the car on my way to Target to buy an untraceable burner phone. If I'm going to track down Sasha and make sure no one's aware of or looking for my son, I need a phone that can't be tracked or traced. I've watched enough episodes of *Law & Order* to know about these things.

I find a young male clerk in the electronics department who's totally into phones, computers and gaming. I let him talk. Eventually, he hands me a cheap flip phone with prepaid minutes. When I'm done with it, I'll simply toss it in the garbage.

I go back to my car and search the *Hampton Gazette*'s website for the story about the woman who drowned months earlier at Rocky Point Beach. A dozen or so articles pop up, each getting shorter as time went on and no new leads being reported. I review all the articles so they're fresh in my mind. There are conflicting theories on what happened to the woman. A horrible accident? A suicide? Or did she even exist at all?

I look for the name of the reporter. They're all written by the same person — Kevin Jordan. His profile says he covers the crime beat.

Using my new burner phone, I dial his number and he answers.

I clear my throat. "Hello, Mr. Jordan, my name is Ann Livingston. I read your series of articles about the woman who disappeared and drowned at Rocky Point Beach a few months back. I'm an author and I'm writing a book about unusual deaths and disappearances in popular vacation areas. I was wondering if I could pick your brain for a minute or two?"

I hold my breath waiting to see if he buys my story or suspects I'm not who I say I am.

"Sure, how can I help you?" he says.

I'm in. I walk him through what I know and ask him to confirm or deny my assumptions as I go.

"What's your personal opinion on this case?" I say. "Do you think the woman was a figment of the imagination?"

"No, I don't," he says. "Too many people recall seeing her. She was real."

"I agree. What do you think happened to her?"

I hear him let out a breath before he speaks. "At first the local police thought she was pulled out by a current. It's happened before. Five years ago a twenty-one-year-old college senior was pulled out and drowned. The day the woman in the pink cap disappeared, there was a strong undertow but not that strong. Someone said they saw her doing laps, so she must have been a decent swimmer. The currents that day were only at a medium level."

"I see. So, what's your theory?"

"From day one, I always thought it was a suicide. The cops have to do their due diligence, but I think they've come around to that theory as well. My buddy over at the police station said they're not pursuing the case anymore. No family or friends have come forward demanding answers and the police have nothing else to go on."

"Hmm. So, it's pretty much a closed case?"

"I didn't say closed. As long as we don't have a definitive answer the case will remain open for a time. Bottom line — there's no body, no car in the parking lot, no chair or towel or bag on the beach, no family, no witnesses who are absolutely sure of what they saw. The most logical explanation is a suicide and her body was pulled out to sea by the current. I can tell you that the police department isn't putting any manpower on it anymore."

I thank him for his time and promise I'll give him a credit when the book gets published. Sitting in my car, I review everything he told me, thinking back to that day at the beach. It's something I've done a thousand times.

There's a set of nagging facts that still bother me. I don't think Sasha's disappearance was a suicide. I may be the only person who knows the different pieces of her story. But I can never tell, for obvious reasons.

What do I know for sure? Sasha was a mother with a baby. No mother would give her baby to a stranger if she wasn't coming back. She'd find a friend or someone she really trusted, not some woman she just met on a beach.

Another thing, she put on sunscreen while we were talking. Why would a woman about to kill herself care about UVA rays? That makes no sense. Also, she wore a bathing cap and goggles and did some laps. If she was going to drown herself, why would she do any of that? She also left all of her stuff behind including her phone, as if she'd be back in ten minutes. I was the one who removed everything from the beach, not her.

I come to my own conclusions. Sasha didn't commit suicide, she drowned. I also now have confirmed that the police aren't looking for her or are aware the missing woman had a baby with her.

I breathe a sigh of relief. My son and my secret are safe. Nobody is looking for Jonah and that's the way I want to keep it.

CHAPTER TWENTY-FOUR

Back in Brooklyn after our long weekend in the Hamptons, I try to get back into the swing of things. Even though I still have a little time left on my maternity leave, Neville's been calling more often about things going on at the gallery. Some of them are important but others, not so much. Daniel tells me I need to learn how to say "no" more often. He's right, but the truth is, I adore Neville and Anton and like to make them happy.

"Darling dearest Tori, I know you're still on leave," is how Neville's calls always start. "If you could tear yourself away from that adorable little boy for five teensy little minutes and look at the Peter Calaway contract, you'll be saving my life, literally."

It's a beautiful September day and I plan to take Jonah over to Prospect Park for some fresh air. It's still warm out, but soon it will be too chilly for the park.

"All right," I say to Neville, "but only five minutes. I have a date with my son today."

"Thank you, my darling, you're an angel. How old is little Jonah now?"

I think for a moment and do the math. Sasha said he was born on February 14th, Valentine's Day. "He'll be eight months in less than two weeks," I say triumphantly.

"Eight months, already? How time flies. You are planning a big extravaganza for his first birthday, aren't you? Promise me you'll let Uncle Neville and Uncle Anton be in charge of the birthday cake and flowers. I know the most divine bakery in Williamsburg and my florist in Soho is beyond fabulous."

And that's why I adore Neville. He lives to make the world a prettier place. Two minutes after hanging up the phone, several documents appear in my inbox from the gallery. I look them over. There's nothing in them that Neville couldn't have easily handled himself. Both he and Anton have grown dependent on me over the years. They prefer I make most of the big decisions. In some ways I kind of like it. Before Jonah came into my life, it was the gallery that gave me purpose. Now that I have a son, the goings-on at the gallery don't seem as important as they did before.

Jonah watches me from his swing in the kitchen while I review the contracts. It's ten o'clock by the time I send Neville my notes. It took more like thirty minutes to review them versus five. Regardless, I'm finished and free to spend the rest of the day being a mom.

I go into the kitchen to pack up everything we'll need for our outing. While I'm rummaging through the cabinets, Eden appears in the doorway. She has the day off, which is why I'm going to the park solo.

"I'm leaving in a few minutes," she says. "Do you need anything before I go?"

My nanny is in her usual gray ensemble, her stringy hair hanging limply on her shoulders.

"Going to do something fun today?" I say while placing various items into my diaper bag.

"I wouldn't say fun exactly. I have to go to the school library to work on a paper that's due in a few weeks."

I pour Cheerios into a small plastic container and snap on the lid. "Maybe you can do something fun afterwards. There's a great costume exhibit at the Met."

She walks over to the half-full coffee pot and pours herself a quarter cup. "I actually have a meeting with a . . . man later this afternoon."

"That's sounds mysterious," I say looking up at her. "A date?" She nods.

I'm not sure which is more surprising, that she *has* a date or that she's going to meet him dressed in her old sweaty grays. Maybe she's going to change?

"Are you coming home from the library before your date?"

"No, I'll be gone the whole day. I probably won't be back until about ten tonight. That's all right, isn't it?"

Eden is about seventeen years younger than me. I chalk up her wardrobe choices to our generational differences. Personally, I wouldn't be caught dead dressed like that, especially not for someone I might be romantically interested in.

I examine her face. She doesn't have terrible bones, but even someone with good bones needs to make a little effort. I squelch my impulse to be her mother and only nod and smile. I remember what it was like being on the receiving end of my own mother's disapproval of my appearance.

"You're going to wear that, Tori?" I can still hear my mother's voice. "That dress drains all the color from your face. You should never wear pastels. And, don't slouch, it makes you look dumpy. Good posture is so important."

It's not easy being the average-looking daughter of a great beauty. Growing up, I remember people meeting me for the first time and seeing the expression in their eyes. People always assumed that Marion Petrosian's daughter would have inherited her beauty.

As it happened, I look exactly like my Armenian father. He's not a handsome man, but he's loaded with confidence, charm, charisma and money . . . which makes him extremely attractive to women. To be clear, it hasn't been so easy for my beautiful mother. While my father adores her, he also has a persistent wandering eye. My mother has had to contend with that for their entire marriage. She threatened to leave him many times, but he always convinces her he'll never do it again . . . until the next time. I know he loves my mother. Honestly, I think he can't help himself.

Eden finishes her coffee and puts the cup into the dishwasher. "I guess I'll get going."

I hear Daniel bouncing down the stairs. The man never walks.

"Good morning," he says as he pours himself a half cup of coffee. "Big audition today, a men's hair color commercial. It's a national spot. You know what that means, huge residuals."

"Good luck, honey," I say as I lift my son from his swing.

Daniel picks up a banana from the large bowl on the counter and peels it. "Eden, I noticed all the lights are still on in your room and bathroom. You need to turn them off when you're not in your room. Electricity isn't free."

Eden appears flustered. "I'm going right back up. I just came down for a coffee and . . ."

"But you're not up there now, are you?" my husband says as he drops the banana peel into the trash can. "Try to remember in the future."

It's an awkward moment that I try to smooth over. "I'm sure Eden just forgot. We all forget to turn the lights out from time to time. I know I do."

"I don't," he says as he walks abruptly out of the kitchen towards the front door grabbing his portfolio off of the side table in the hallway. "Wish me luck."

"Good luck," I shout. "Don't forget my parents are coming for dinner tonight."

The front door opens and closes, leaving me wondering why my husband still has such an issue with Eden. I'll admit she's not the neatest-looking person, but she's amazing with our son.

Eden goes upstairs to get her things as I finish my preparations for our day in the park. I'm in the middle of changing Jonah's diaper when Eden comes back.

"I turned off all the lights," she says softly, looking at her feet.

"Please don't worry about that. Daniel always gets stressed out before an audition. He can be awful on those days. He bites my head off, too. Never saw that side of him when we first met."

Eden gives me a relieved smile and nods. "You mean at that charity dinner."

I smile at the chance to change the subject. "He was nothing like any of the men I'd dated before. Daniel was a breath of fresh air. Of course, he didn't have a pot to piss in, but I didn't care. He was creative, exciting and gorgeous. Now, we have Jonah and everything is so perfect."

"It's like a fairytale," says my nanny.

"This man you're meeting today, have you been out with him before?"

Eden's face goes a little red before she answers and she pushes those awful thick-framed glasses up the bridge of her nose. "Actually, we've been seeing each other for over two years."

Wow. I did not expect that answer. The last thing I anticipated when it came to Eden was a boyfriend. There are legions of attractive single women in this city who can't get a date. How did my nanny with the stringy hair, always dressed in a gray sweats uniform, find a boyfriend?

"Two years," I say trying not to look as surprised as I am, "that's a long time. Is it serious?"

She looks down at her feet and then into my eyes. "He's the love of my life. He's *my* Daniel."

CHAPTER TWENTY-FIVE

After Eden leaves, Jonah and I spend a glorious day in the park. The sun is shining, there's a gentle breeze and the humidity is low. It feels good being outside. I know I'm not supposed to, but I bring pieces of bread with me to feed the birds. I'm not supposed to do a lot of things.

Sitting on a bench beside the pond with seven-and-a-half-month-old Jonah on my lap, I'm so happy. Every time I throw some bread out to the birds, the flock flutters and delights my son. We wander around the park, Jonah nestled in his ridiculously expensive deluxe Bugaboo stroller that my mother insisted on buying for him.

"My grandson can't ride around in some pedestrian vehicle," she said after I protested it cost too much. "A bumpy ride might hurt his joints." I knew that statement was totally untrue, but I've learned to pick my battles with my mother. The price of a stroller didn't seem battle-worthy.

Towards the end of the day, I go back to the bench near the pond. Jonah's on my lap again and I'm quietly singing 1970s classic rock songs to him. An old man in his eighties with white hair and bright blue eyes sits down on the other end of the bench. He watches Jonah respond to my voice for a few minutes before he stands and faces me.

"You're a good mother," he says with a thick German accent. "He's a lucky boy."

As the old man walks away, I look into my son's dark-brown eyes and smile.

"Did you hear what he said, Jonah? He said you're a lucky boy." My son smiles back at me as if he understands and my heart melts.

On the way home, we wander in and out of cute boutiques and shops. It's after three and Jonah is asleep in his stroller when I arrive at the house. I push the carriage through the cast-iron gate out front and gently pick up my sleeping son, carrying him inside through the ground-floor entrance.

Moving slowly so not to wake him, I tiptoe through the house. Daniel is in the kitchen. I can tell he's about to say something in his usual booming TV announcer voice. I quickly shake my head and point at Jonah. He receives my signal and remains quiet. After I place Jonah in his crib and close the bedroom door halfway, I go back to the kitchen.

Daniel's at the kitchen table reading something on his phone.

"How was your audition?" I say, getting myself a glass of water and sitting down across from him.

"Total waste of my time," he says getting up and walking over to the counter to turn the kettle on. "The casting director met with me for less than five seconds."

"Maybe they're still thinking it over and—"

"I didn't get it, Tori. I can tell when they're not interested. Trust me, they weren't."

"But maybe if you—"

"Can we change the subject, please?" he says, placing a white ceramic mug down on the counter a little too loudly. Daniel's always grumpy after a bad audition. I get it. He's disappointed. Being an actor isn't an easy life unless you're a big star. I'd be in a fetal position if I got rejected day in and day out.

As he requests, I switch topics, telling him about my spectacular day with Jonah in the park. "He was so good and didn't cry once. I love him so much, don't you? I didn't think I could love anything the way I love our son."

"What about me?" Daniel says as he stirs his green tea.

"That's different," I say with a laugh. "You can't compare the two."

He takes a sip of his tea and looks out the window. "So, where's little Miss Muffet?"

"Don't call her that. I guess she's still out with her boyfriend."

"Boyfriend? The guy must be blind."

"What is it with you and Eden?" I say, standing up. "Why do you dislike her so much?" A wave of heat covers my whole body. I get up too fast and suddenly feel lightheaded, my legs tingling. I grab for the back of a kitchen chair to steady myself.

Daniel lunges for me. "Are you all right?" he says as he guides me to the couch in the adjacent family room and lays me down.

"I don't know what happened. Everything started spinning. I feel a little better now."

"Stay right here, I'm going to get a cool cloth and your inhaler."

"It's in my nightstand."

I lie on the couch, feeling a little better with each passing minute. The clock on the wall says it's after four thirty. I groan. My parents will be arriving for dinner in a little over an hour.

"Here you go," says my husband, walking into the room carrying a big glass of ice water and my inhaler. "Drink this. You're probably dehydrated again. Did you drink enough water today?"

I thought back on my water intake for the day. I had some coffee in the morning and a few sips of Jonah's apple juice while we were at the park, but nothing else. I don't tell Daniel because he gets annoyed and exasperated when I do stuff like this given my medical situation.

"You've got to be more careful," he says. "You don't take your health seriously."

"I do."

"You want to explain this?" he says as he pulls something out of his pocket and places my weekly pill box in my hand. "What's wrong with this picture?"

I look down at the container I'm holding and shrug. "I don't know. It's my pill box."

"Look at the days of the week, Tori. What's today?"

"Wednesday."

"Look at the compartments. Why are there still pills in Tuesday and Wednesday?"

"I don't know. I-I-I thought I took them."

"You haven't taken your medication for two whole days."

My brain starts firing. I remember taking my pills this morning, at least I think I did. I had so much going on and then Neville called. I was trying to get the baby ready to go out. Still, I could have sworn I took them. "I'm pretty sure I took my pills."

"I'm pretty sure you didn't. This is why you have a weekly pill case with the days on it so you'll know if you take them or not. This isn't a joke, Tori."

"I know," I say, looking down at the floor.

"I hear when you make jokes about your 'shitty heart.' Let me tell you something, joking about it doesn't make it go away. If you don't take your medicine, you could have a seizure or worse. Do you want that to happen? You're a mother now. What about Jonah? Don't you think he needs his mother?"

Daniel's right. I am a mother now. I can't be so cavalier about everything anymore. "You're right. I guess I haven't gotten my routine down yet. I'll be more careful, I promise."

Daniel sits down on the edge of the sofa and hands me my inhaler. I don't really need it now since I feel better. I use it anyway to show him I'm taking control of my health. I also promise to start following the doctor's orders about everything including wearing that damn CPAP device at bedtime.

I sit up. "My parents are going to be here soon."

"We'll order Chinese and make it easy," he says as he looks at his phone, studying something. "Holy shit. I can't believe it. My agent texted me. That casting director from today wants a few people to come back for a second look while they still have the studio space. I'm still in the running for the commercial."

"See, I told you. When do you have to go?"

"Now. They've got the space until seven thirty."

"But my parents are coming for dinner."

Daniel looks at me. I remind myself that his career has to take precedence over Chinese food with his in-laws and change course. "Go. You can join us for dessert."

He smiles, grabs his jacket and rushes out the door.

Three hours later, while my parents and I are finishing our Chinese take-out dinner, we hear the front door open and close. Eden waves to us from the hallway and starts to climb the stairs.

"Come in and say hello," I shout to her. She looks different when she steps into the kitchen. Her hair is pulled back, there's color in her normally pale skin and she's not wearing those hideous glasses. It's the first time I've seen her without them on. She even wore them in the pool when we were in the Hamptons.

She chats amiably with my parents for a couple of minutes and then offers to take Jonah, who's asleep on my mother's lap, up to his room. I notice she's flushed again and wonder if she got some action going with her boyfriend. Some people are full of surprises. I guess you could say the same about me.

After she leaves, my parents get ready to go.

"You're going back to work at the gallery soon. How is everything working out with your nanny?" says my mother.

"She's great. Jonah adores her. She's almost more doting than I am, if that's humanly possible."

My father puts on his jacket. "That's what you want when someone's taking care of your kid. Doting is a good thing. I was looking at her tonight without her glasses. She looks familiar."

Daniel gets home thirty minutes after my parents leave. He's humming and smiling when he walks through the door. I'm a little annoyed he's so late and ignore his jovial mood.

"I called you twice," I say. "I thought you'd be gone for an hour or two max." He rummages through the fridge, muttering that he's starving and pulls out all the white cardboard containers of leftover Chinese food. "What took you so long?"

"They kept calling me back in. I can't answer my phone in the middle of an audition."

"You could have texted me."

"Don't you want to know what happened?" he says, eating cold sesame noodles directly from the container using chop sticks.

"Okay."

"I got it. I got the part."

CHAPTER TWENTY-SIX

A week later, Daniel's already left for the gym and I'm in the kitchen in my robe having a cup of coffee. I'm going over a list of things to do before I return to the gallery. Jonah's nearby in his playpen dueling with a lamb plush toy. His one-way conversation with the lamb is extremely animated. I can't understand a word he says but from his tone, it's something very complicated.

Eden shuffles into the kitchen from the laundry room carrying a basket containing Jonah's clean clothes, sheets and blankets. I've been so stressed out about going back to work. Having her here makes it so much easier for me to leave him.

"Did I tell you Daniel got the part in the men's hair color commercial?"

Eden turns and smiles. "Some commercials pay big residuals if they run nationally, right?"

I'm surprised she knows what a residual is. "Yes, it can be very lucrative if it's a national campaign. How did you know that?"

"Daniel explained it to me this morning before he went to the gym."

Daniel actually had a normal conversation with Eden? Usually, he only talks to her if it has something to do with the baby. Maybe he's softening.

I chalk up his friendliness to his excitement about landing the commercial. "I'm very proud of him. He really needed a win."

She nods and turns to leave.

"Eden, I want to take Jonah with me to the gallery today. I've got a short meeting and everyone in the showroom wants to meet him. I'd like you to come with me. You can watch Jonah while I duck into the conference room. We'll leave in an hour."

I look at her outfit and cringe. I can't let her come into my workplace dressed like that.

"Since we're going into the gallery," I say, "do you have something else besides sweats you can wear?"

"I have a dress for special occasions."

"Wonderful. Wear that, please. We often have clients visiting and . . ."

"No problem," she says as she walks towards the stairs.

I want to ask if I could see the dress but decide it would be insulting and say nothing. I don't want to lose her. Whatever the dress looks like, it's got to be better than what she has on now.

Fifteen minutes later, I'm out of the shower standing in my bathroom combing leave-in conditioner into my thick blonde hair. My black roots are becoming noticeable and I make a mental note to set up an appointment with my colorist. My thick hair is one of the two positive physical characteristics I inherited from my father.

Putting on a little make-up, I use a pencil to outline my full lips before coating them with a rich burgundy lipstick. Squeezing my upper and lower lips together, I smile. My full lips are the other attribute I received from my father. Sadly, none of my mother's cover-girl looks attached to my DNA so I play up my lips and hair. You've got to work with what you've got.

I drop my make-up bag into the top drawer of the vanity and notice my weekly pill case sitting there. I look at the Thursday compartment, it's full. *Shit.* I thought I'd taken them earlier. *Get it together, Tori.* I open the latch, pour the pills into my hand and toss them down my throat.

Back downstairs, I collect Jonah and Eden for our outing. He's already buckled into his car seat looking adorable. Eden's dressed him in one of my favorite outfits for his debut at the gallery. She's so good.

The toilet flushes in the powder room off the kitchen and my nanny emerges. She's wearing a gray dress that looks like it's made of burlap. Honestly, if I'd seen it sitting on a table, I might have thought it was a large grocery sack. Her wavy hair is pulled loosely back in a low ponytail and she's wearing sneakers on her feet. Not exactly high fashion but better than the sweats.

She looks at me as if waiting for approval. I need to say something positive. "You look nice, Eden. Ready?"

A car waits out front to take us over to the Pierce-Woolsey Gallery in Manhattan. It's been weeks since I've been there. I'm looking forward to seeing everyone and for them to finally meet Jonah.

It's another beautiful warm late September morning. Our car sails over the iconic Brooklyn Bridge, giving us a spectacular view of lower Manhattan. Fifteen minutes later we pull up in front of the gallery located in the Meatpacking district. It's a super expensive area now. Several decades ago when Neville and Anton first opened, it was considered no man's land. They were smart and bought the building for next to nothing. Now, it's worth a fortune.

Holding my son in his car seat, we walk through the front doors of the cavernous gallery and are greeted by the staff. After a flurry of double kisses, an avalanche of compliments are directed at me and my son. What mother doesn't want to be told she has a beautiful baby?

I head over to my tiny office off the corner of the main room when Neville and Anton burst out from their large, shared office on the other side heading directly towards me.

"Darling dearest, you're finally back," yells Neville halfway across the main room with Anton following behind.

More kisses, hugs and praises of my son's handsome looks and 'obviously intelligent eyes.' I lap it all up. I am a proud mama, after all.

"Remember, I'm not back yet," I say firmly. "I still have another week and a half. I'm only in today because you wanted me to meet with Roberto so I'm here."

"You're the only one who can handle him," Anton half-whispers. "Neville is terrified of Roberto. The man is such a beast. If his paintings didn't fly out the door, we wouldn't work with him."

"He's not so bad," I say, lying through my teeth. The truth is, Roberto is awful. Everyone hates him including me. I often wonder how such a dreadful human being can create such magnificent art. I guess people are complicated. Even good people can do pretty terrible things if the situation is right.

A little later, I'm chatting with one of our employees when there's a loud commotion near the front of the house. I look up and see Roberto, trailed by two wafer-thin blonde women. The blondes are both wearing short skin-tight black dresses paired with high boots. Each carries a writing pad and pen. They appear to be copying down every word the artiste utters with him periodically asking, "Ya got that?" Behind the two blondes is a photographer snapping dozens of candid shots of Roberto for who knows what.

I throw my shoulders back and tell Eden to wait with the baby in my office. A knot in my stomach, I walk over to reluctantly greet one of Pierce-Woolsey's top-selling artists.

CHAPTER TWENTY-SEVEN

"Roberto," I say, a big phony smile plastered on my face, and my arms outstretched as I cross the gallery floor.

"Tori. Is it true? Am I now competing with a baby for your attention? You know I prefer working with you than with those other two," he says, tipping his head towards Anton and Neville's office. "Things go so much smoother when you're in charge."

I give him a hug and whisper into his ear, "Not to worry, Roberto, I'm back in the gallery in less than two weeks. I've already been doing work from home planning your next exhibition." He smiles.

After another staff member pulls Roberto away to look at some sketches for his next show, Neville grabs me. From the look on his face, though I'm sure he thought it was well hidden, he's going to ask me to do something I won't want to do.

"How did everything go with Roberto?" he says.

"All is well," I say, cocking my head and squinting at him slightly as I wait for the other shoe to drop. "What do you want now?"

"It will only take forty-five minutes, an hour at the most."

"What will only take forty-five minutes?"

"You have such a good eye and a way with creative types. I suppose that's why you married an actor because you—"

"Cut to the chase, Neville."

"There's an amazing new artist named Der Pflug. He's generating incredible buzz. Everyone in New York has been talking about him. They say he's the next Banksy, only he works on large canvas. We want his New York debut to be here at Pierce-Woolsey."

I nod, waiting for the part where I come in.

"I've heard through the grapevine," he continues, "that there are three other galleries trying to sign him right now. We've got to beat them to it. A friend called me this morning and told me Der Pflug is staying at the Clarkson Hotel in Chelsea. You and I need to run over there and see him today and—"

"Neville, I've got my baby with me. I'm not working today."

"Your nanny's here. It will only take a few minutes."

Neville widens his eyes like a lost puppy and I feel myself about to give in. "All right, but you owe me. One hour, not a minute more."

I walk away to find Eden. She's in my office with Jonah on her lap. She's reading him a book about farm animals. I watch from the doorway how gently she speaks while pointing to characters on the pages and moving his little finger to touch them. *I'm so lucky I found her.*

I explain to Eden what I have to do, which doesn't seem to faze her in the least. She'll take Jonah out for a walk in a nearby park while I'm gone. Five minutes later, Neville and I are in a cab headed uptown. I love being a mother, but I'm not going to lie, it feels good getting my hands back into the gallery. There's a part of me that thrives on Neville and Anton relying on me, as much as I hate to admit it.

Our cab pulls up in front of the boutique hotel and the car door is opened by a doorman. We walk through a large revolving door and go directly to the hotel's coffee lounge where we will meet Der Pflug. The table where we sit is partially hidden by a huge plant, but we can still see most of the lobby.

"Do you know what he looks like?" I say craning my neck to find an artsy-looking man.

"He's very minimalist," says Neville, now gazing out at the lobby. I'm looking over the coffee menu trying to decide on a latte or a cappuccino when Neville gasps.

I look up. "What's wrong?"

"Is that your father walking towards the elevators with a platinum blonde?"

I follow Neville's sightline and there's no mistaking it. My father has his arm around the waist of a much younger woman with short blonde hair. My heart starts to pound when I see him place his hand on the small of her back before whisking her into the waiting elevator. The overwhelming disappointment I feel is hard to describe. From where I'm sitting, I can't see the whole thing, but I could swear he leaned over and kissed her just as the elevator door closed.

I shake my head, hoping to erase the image before I look at Neville.

"I don't know what to say," he says. "I'm so sorry I pointed it out."

I sniff twice to hold back the tears accumulating in my eyes and wipe my face with my hands. "This isn't the first time. It's happened before but I thought it was in the past. So did my mother."

Neville reaches for my hand on the table and squeezes it. "Sorry. That's a terrible way to find out your dad's cheating."

I let out a sarcastic laugh. "Find out? He's always been like that. When I was a kid he cheated on my mother all the time. They used to have huge fights. In the end, my mother always took him back but made sure she got an expensive piece of jewelry for her pain and suffering. One time she opened up her jewelry box and showed me her 'affair' baubles saying, 'This ring was for Melinda' and 'That bracelet was for Carmen.' I thought he had stopped all that a long time ago. Guess not."

"It's a shitty thing for a daughter to see."

"I'll get over it. He may have been a rotten husband to my mother, but he's always been a great dad for me. I'll never forget when—"

Neville suddenly stands. "He's here. That's Der Pflug. I'll go get him."

As Neville runs off to greet the small dark-haired young man dressed all in gray, I note that it's similar to one of Eden's outfits and laugh to myself. What a day. It's barely two o'clock and I've learned my father is having an affair with a woman younger than me and the next big personality hitting the New York art scene dresses exactly like my nanny.

Moments later, Der Pflug is sipping a double espresso at our table. Neville and I take turns heaping copious amounts of praise on the young artist. He's enjoying himself and why wouldn't he? We've been telling him he's Banksy, Chuck Close and Andy Warhol rolled into one. As I lay on thick what our gallery can do for a new artist, my arms and legs start to feel funny; my whole body tingles. My heart begins to beat rapidly and suddenly I can't catch my breath and my throat's closing up. I'm trying to hold it together but within seconds feel myself swaying and then falling off of my chair.

When I wake up, something is covering the lower part of my face. I don't know where I am. A young man leans over me. He looks nice, but he's a stranger.

"Tori, you're going to be okay," he says. "I'm Jeff. I'm an EMT and I'm going to take care of you. Okay?"

I start to hyperventilate and try to sit up because nothing makes sense. Jeff gently pushes me back down.

"Try to stay still. You had a seizure. You're in an ambulance on the way to the hospital."

CHAPTER TWENTY-EIGHT

The next fifteen minutes are a blur. The ambulance comes to a stop and seconds later, I'm moved from the vehicle into the hospital on a gurney. There are lots of strange hands and faces around my body. My head is still spinning, the same way it did inside the hotel coffee shop.

They wheel me into an empty berth where lots of doctors and nurses in various colors of scrubs descend upon me. Each person seems to have their own unique job. As electrodes are attached to my skin, one of the technicians explains what they're doing. I don't care what they're doing. Why am I here?

I look around for a familiar face and see none. I want Daniel or my parents. Then, through my cloudy brain fog, I remember. My father is in a room at the Clarkson Hotel with a platinum blonde who looked about twenty-one. He's hooking up while I'm hooked up to seven machines in the emergency room.

I hear a familiar voice on the other side of the closed curtain. I turn my head. There's a nurse next to my bed tapping information into a tablet, presumably about me.

"I heard my friend, Neville," I say to the nurse. "He's somewhere here. Can you let him know where I am?" She nods and seconds later Neville pokes his head through the pale-green curtain.

I ask him what happened, but he doesn't know much more than I do. According to him, minutes after Der Pflug sat down at our table, I went pale. Then I started to shake, fell off my chair and onto the floor.

"Der Pflug held your head while I called an ambulance," says Neville. "I've explained everything to the intake people. Have you ever had a seizure before?"

"No," I whisper.

How could I have a seizure? My body truly sucks. First it was my heart, then my lungs and now this. I'm a completely defective human being.

"The ambulance was there in less than ten minutes," Neville says, panic written all over his face. "I was terrified. I thought you were going to die."

"You can't kill me that easily. Besides, who would handle Roberto if I was dead?" I say in a feeble attempt at levity.

"Don't joke. The whole thing was so scary. I'm just glad you're okay."

"Am I?"

A young, attractive man in blue scrubs opens the curtain followed by a nurse wearing the same. He tells me he's my doctor and gives me a rundown of the tests they're about to perform.

"I need to call my husband and parents before any tests," I say interrupting him. "They don't know where I am."

Then, I remember Jonah's still at the gallery. "My son," I shout starting to get up. "Where's Jonah?" The doctor and nurse gently push me down.

"Calm down, Tori," says Neville. "I already called Daniel. He's getting in touch with your parents."

I lie back on the bed.

"I also called the gallery and sent a car for Eden," Neville continues. "She's already taken Jonah home to Brooklyn and will stay with him for as long as is necessary."

I take a deep breath and let it out. As long as Jonah is taken care of, I can get through this. "Thank you," I mouth.

The nurse asks Neville to wait in the waiting room and they proceed to ask me questions about my medical history. I explain the long, tedious story of my unreliable heart and they both make notes on their tablets. They follow up with questions about other medical "events" I may have had. They ask about medication I take, food and drink I've eaten in the past twenty-four hours . . . the usual. I also let them know I use a CPAP device when I sleep to keep my airways open.

Satisfied they know every detail of my life including what I ate for breakfast — literally — I'm wheeled to another floor and attached to a whole new set of machines. When they bring me back into the ER, I'm told my husband is in the waiting room with my parents. I'm left alone while a nurse goes to find them.

When the green curtain around my bed flutters, I look up expecting to see my husband's chiseled face, but it's a woman. She introduces herself as a cardiologist on staff. She examines me and goes over the information I'd previously given. We're discussing my general heart condition when Daniel and my parents walk in. For a second, I wonder if my "event" cut short my father's afternoon activities at the hotel.

"Tori," says my mother as she races to my side and takes my hand. Even in the ER, with a bland green curtain backdrop, Marion Petrosian looks, as always, stunning.

"Hi, Mom," I say weakly, very glad she's here.

"How are you feeling, sweetheart?" she says brushing an imaginary hair from my forehead.

"Shitty." I look over at my father. "Hi, Dad."

He walks to the other side of the bed, leans over and kisses me on the forehead. "When Daniel called me, I was terrified." There are tears in his eyes and he brushes his hand against his nose to fight them off. "The doctors say you're going to be okay, thank God."

Daniel is standing behind my father, a look of anguish on his face. He steps around my father and also kisses me on my head. Then, he takes my hand as my father steps back.

"You gave us a real scare," says Daniel. "When Neville called me, I was at an audition. I ran straight out of the building and came directly here. I would have been here sooner, but the traffic was insane. How are you feeling?"

"I'm okay."

"Doctor," says my father in his usual booming authoritative voice, "do we know what caused my daughter to pass out?"

The petite cardiologist looks down at her tablet and then at my father. "Tori didn't pass out. She had a seizure. They're very different things."

She then turns to me. "Tori, you have a heart abnormality, but fortunately, it's one that can be managed. With proper care, you can live until you're a hundred."

"Do you know what caused her seizure?" says my husband.

The doctor purses her lips. "I have an idea from the blood tests and all the other data we've gathered what may have caused it, but I can't be sure."

"What do you think it is?" my mother pipes in.

"Tori," says the doctor, "you told the intake nurse you take a variety of medications every day." The doctor then rattles off the daily list of pills and potions I consume along with their dosages. When she's finished, I nod.

"Hmm," says the doctor looking back at her tablet. "Your blood work indicates twice the level of medication in your system compared to what you've told us. That increased amount could have been enough to cause your seizure. Are you taking your medication as it was prescribed?"

All eyes in the room fall on me. "Yes," I sputter. "I take them as prescribed." The doctor sees Daniel looking at me skeptically and picks up on it.

"Would you like to add something, Mr. Fowler?" she says.

My husband looks uncomfortable. "Sometimes, my wife forgets to take her meds and will miss a day or two."

"That's not a good thing, Tori," says the doctor, shaking her head, "but that wouldn't have caused a seizure. This was likely from too much medication, not too little. Do you ever double up when you forget?"

Every eye in the tiny, curtained space is on me. "I have a pill box with the days of the week on it. That's how I know if I did or didn't take them. Go look at my pill box, Daniel. Today's Thursday. I guarantee today's box will be empty but not Friday or Saturday. Since we adopted Jonah, I've become much more responsible about my medication."

The doctor speaks to us a little more and says she recommends I stay overnight for observation. I'm too tired to argue.

Before they move me to another room, my mother comes over and kisses me. "I was at the hairdresser when Daniel called. The second I heard, I literally jumped out of the chair and raced over here. I'm so relieved you're okay." That's when I notice one side of my mother's hair is significantly longer than the other. She wasn't kidding. She clearly left the salon in mid-cut.

My mother steps back and my father comes over to kiss me goodbye. "Sleep tight, kiddo. We'll see you in the morning."

My parents open the curtain and are about to leave when I ask my father a question.

"Mom was at the hairdresser when she got the news. Where were you when Daniel called, Dad?"

My father mumbles something about having lunch with an old friend as an orderly unlocks the brakes of my bed and pushes me down the hall.

CHAPTER TWENTY-NINE

The next morning, finding nothing else wrong, the hospital discharges me. The consensus of the doctors and my husband is that I inadvertently took too much of my heart medication. I suppose it's possible, sometimes I'm so distracted. Regardless, I take comfort that it was caused by a stupid accident rather than something mortally wrong with me.

It's ten thirty a.m. when we get home and Daniel insists on helping me into the house. I bristle because he's treating me like an invalid and I feel fine. In fact, I feel pretty good after getting a good night's sleep.

"Where's Jonah?" I say when I don't find him in his room.

"Eden took him to the park so you'd have some quiet time when you got home. She'll be back around two."

"I wanted to see him."

"I didn't know how long it was going to take at the hospital, so I asked her to go. Why don't you get some rest?"

"I slept for over ten hours in the hospital," I say with a modicum of irritation in my voice. "I'm fine, Daniel, really."

He nods. "You gave us all a good scare. You can't blame me for being worried."

I walk to him and put my arms around his neck. "I'm sorry. I don't mean to be so cranky. It's been a rough couple of days."

I go upstairs to take a shower. When I come down, my sweet husband has prepared lunch for me — Salad Nicoise, my favorite. We sit and have a leisurely meal together talking about a million things including me being more vigilant about my medication. I soon change the subject by telling him the latest news from the gallery.

First, I recap all the nonsense having to do with handling Roberto. Then I tell him about the new shows coming up but don't say anything about my father and the blonde. It only makes my father look bad and frankly, I don't want to talk about it. Bottom line, Sam Petrosian is a wonderful father but a lousy husband. Based on the fights I overheard between my parents when I was a kid, I'm pretty sure my father has been cheating on my mother from day one.

To keep the conversation from returning to me and my health, I tell Daniel about Der Pflug.

"He's the art world's new wunderkind," I say. "Neville is hoping to snag him for his first New York show."

"Der Pflug? His name means the plough," says my husband, holding up his phone showing me Google Translate. "Why would an artist call himself a plough?"

I laugh and shake my head. "Most artists are eccentric." It's nearly two and we hear a noise coming from the lower level. It's Eden and Jonah. I skip down the stairs to help her in with the stroller. Before the outside door is even closed, I pick my son up and wrap my arms around his little body. He smells amazing.

"How are you feeling?" says Eden as she puts her things down. She's out of her burlap sack dress now and back into her sweats. "Daniel was so worried about you."

I assure her I'm fine, that it was a stupid mistake on my part and won't happen again. I take the baby into the playroom to read him a story. As I turn the pages, his eyes close several times but he fights it. Must have been all the fresh air. Sure enough, by the end of the second book, he's out.

As I take him to his room and put him in his crib, I hear the doorbell ring downstairs. I pull down the shades in his room, turn on the baby monitor and close the door. As I get to the bottom of the stairs, I hear voices coming from the kitchen.

Two police officers from the Hamptons, an older cop in his fifties and an obvious rookie, are both sitting at my kitchen table with Daniel.

Shit.

The three of them look at me when I walk into the room.

"What's going on?" I say, trying to sound nonchalant as my crappy heart thumps in my chest.

"These officers are still investigating that missing woman from the Hamptons. You remember those other officers who were here a few months ago," says my husband.

I pour myself a cup of coffee. "I'm guessing if you're here now, you still haven't found her."

"It's still an open investigation. According to the earlier police reports," says the older cop, looking at his phone, "your vehicle was in the vicinity of Rocky Point Beach on the day the woman disappeared. Our notes show that you reported having no recollection of anything unusual happening while you were at the beach that day. Is that correct?"

"Yes. Like I told the other officers, I did see some police arrive at the beach but I was already on my way out. I was in a hurry that day."

"This has been a very challenging case," says the older cop. "Four people and a lifeguard swear they saw a woman in a bright-pink cap swimming laps in the water and then she was gone."

"I remember seeing that on the news reports," I say, taking a sip from my mug.

"The confusing thing is," the older cop says, "we didn't find her car. That made us wonder if she might have taken a cab or some other form of public transportation. The bus from town makes a stop near Rocky Point, but the driver doesn't remember her."

Shit.

"Maybe a friend dropped her off," I say, trying to appear helpful.

"We considered that after she went missing, especially with all the local press, but no one came forward," says the younger cop.

I nod. "Maybe she took an Uber."

The older cop looks straight into my eyes. It feels like he's boring a hole into my brain. "That occurred to us. That's why we've been checking additional surveillance footage and records from various car services."

There's a long moment of silence. "That makes sense," I say trying to fill the dead air with sound.

"We saw security footage that showed two different parties dropped off at the beach by an Uber that day," says the older cop. "One party was two men, and the other a male and female couple. Neither was the missing woman in the pink cap."

As I relax slightly from my heightened state of anxiety, they continue talking about other footage in the vicinity of the beach bus stop. That's when I nearly drop my coffee mug on the floor.

"From what we can tell, several people got off the bus that morning and went in the direction of the beach — four teenagers with boogie boards and a woman wearing a large floppy straw hat with a red ribbon. She was wearing large sunglasses."

It occurs to me the jig might be up and that the two officers are simply baiting me for sport. I maintain my composure, expecting them to pull out their handcuffs and take me off to the big house.

"A woman? Maybe she was the missing person you're looking for," I say, a feeble attempt to keep myself out of prison.

"No, we checked it out. According to other witnesses on the bus, the woman with the hat had a baby with her. There was no unclaimed baby at the beach that day. She must have been going somewhere else besides the beach. There are a lot of homes out in that vicinity."

I nod again and put my coffee cup in the sink.

"To be frank," says the officer, "we still aren't a hundred percent convinced the woman existed at all. There's a thing called 'group hysteria,' where people think something happened and trigger that belief in others. It gets reinforced by the group and soon is solidified in people's minds. Everyone believes something really happened, when it didn't."

"You're saying this all might be a wild goose chase?" I say. From the corner of my eye, I see Daniel looking at his watch.

"Officers," says my overprotective husband as he stands, "my wife has just been in the hospital, so if there's nothing else . . ."

"Actually there's one more thing," says the older cop. "We've asked the public for their help through TV and newspaper ads. We want anyone who was at the beach that day to search through their phones and see if they have a photo that might help us out."

"That was smart," I say, feeling ill. "You never know what you'll turn up."

"Again, officers, if there's nothing more . . ." says Daniel.

The younger cop stands and flips through his phone. He pulls up a picture and hands his phone to me. It's a close-up of a teenage girl puckering her lips while holding up two fingers, the ocean is far behind her.

"I'm not sure what I'm looking at," I say, genuinely confused. "I don't know this girl."

The younger officer reaches over and zooms in on the picture and re-centers it. "It's not the teenager we wanted you to see. Look now."

I look down at the image now focused on the upper right corner of the original picture. It's a crystal-clear side shot of a woman in a neon-pink bathing cap. Thankfully, you can't see her face.

I hand it to Daniel so he can have a look. "A woman in a pink cap," he says, handing the phone back to the officer. "She does exist."

The older cop nods. "Seems so. We wanted your wife to take a look at it to see if she remembers seeing that woman or if anything in the picture jogs her memory."

I take the phone back from my husband and give the photo a harder look. Zooming in, I want to see if I can identify any part of Sasha's features. Thankfully, you can't see her face at all, only the pink cap. I'm about to hand the phone back to the cop when I notice the partial image of another hand holding something blue near the woman in the pink cap. Something's familiar about it. I look at it again. I know what it is. It's my fucking hand when I gave Sasha the sunscreen. The picture shows a fragment of my bracelet, my grandmother's antique gold bracelet from Armenia. It's one of a kind.

Shit.

"Nope," I say as I close the picture. "I was reading the entire time I was there. Can't say I noticed much of anything."

Daniel shows them out as I brood in the kitchen.

The police are now certain the woman in the pink cap exists, but that's all. I'm the only one who knows about the bracelet and whose hand is in the picture holding the blue bottle. *I can never wear Grandma Mamie's bracelet again.*

When Daniel returns, I make up an excuse about cleaning out my closet and go upstairs to our bedroom. I dig Grandma Mamie's bracelet out of my jewelry box and slip the piece of jewelry into an empty envelope. I can't bear to throw it out, but I also can't risk it connecting me to the woman in the pink cap. Folding the envelope twice and rolling it up, I look around my bedroom until my eyes rest on an antique statue on a shelf. It's a little boy holding a bucket. I flip the statue over. There's a hole in the bottom big enough for the wad of paper containing the bracelet. I wiggle the paper inside the statue and place it back on the shelf.

No one will ever know it's there. I'm safe.

CHAPTER THIRTY

One week later at a little after seven a.m., Eden and I are in the kitchen together. I'm in my bathrobe going over documents prior to my imminent return to the gallery. Jonah is perched in his highchair while Eden, in her usual shapeless gray attire, feeds him breakfast.

I glance up from my documents and from the looks of it, more of my son's food is on the floor than in his mouth. He's making a mess and having a wonderful time doing it, which makes me smile.

"Jonah," scolds Eden when my son hurls his mashed fruit onto the floor and laughs. "Look what you've done. You're covered in peaches." Then I see her smile too and lovingly wipe his face. He squeals and throws more food on the floor as if it were a game.

I've watched my nanny closely over the months. There's no way she's faking her affection for my son. She genuinely adores him. I'm feeling pretty confident about returning to work and leaving her in charge of my most precious possession.

Daniel's footsteps trip down the stairs. He enters the kitchen wearing his gym clothes.

"Good morning," he says as he pours himself a glass of water and swallows the twenty-plus vitamins he takes each day.

"Off to the gym?" I say looking back at my contracts.

"Yup. Afterwards, I have a go-see for a new play at eleven and then my acting class is at three thirty. I should be home by seven."

"You didn't tell me you were going to be out all day. I have a meeting at the gallery at eleven thirty this morning that I can't miss. Who's going to watch Jonah?"

"Our nanny. Isn't that what nannies do?"

I hate it when Daniel's glib but keep my annoyance in check. "Normally Eden does watch Jonah but today she . . ."

Crouched over on the floor wiping up the baby's mess with a wet cloth, Eden looks up at us.

"I have a doctor's appointment late this morning. My gyno check-up," she says as she stands up and rinses the rag out in the sink. "I asked Tori about it a while ago and she said I could take off today at ten thirty."

"Well, that's just great," says Daniel dramatically, throwing up his arms. "Maybe you two could have clued me in to your plans. What am I supposed to do now? I can't miss the go-see. I'm sorry, Eden, but you'll just have to change your appointment. From now on, when you want to take time off during your regular hours, you need to get sign off from Tori *and* me."

I look at my husband in disbelief. From the very beginning, his attitude towards Eden has been absolutely dreadful. It's so out of character for him, too. He's usually cheerful and pleasant to everyone, but for some reason, not to her. He's had a bug about her from the beginning.

Eden's down on the floor cleaning again and looks up at me for help. "I guess . . . I could change the appointment. But I think I had to give them twenty-four hours' notice or they'll charge me."

I look at my nanny and put my pen down. "Eden, you most certainly are not changing your doctor's appointment."

"I booked it months ago," she says softly, while wiping baby food off of her sweatshirt. "It's hard to get an appointment there."

"Daniel, I'm afraid you'll have to miss your 'go-see' today," I say, leaving no room for debate in my voice. "I can be home before three so you can still make your class."

My husband places the glass he's holding on the counter harder than he needs to. "Fine. I'll be back at ten thirty to *babysit*," he says as he crosses the room passing Eden. "Could you wear something that doesn't look and smell like it comes from the bottom of an old gym locker?"

My mouth drops open. As Daniel walks down the hall towards the front door, neither Eden nor I speak. The door opens and closes with a bang.

I look at my nanny. "I don't know what to say. I'm so sorry. That was so rude. Daniel's behavior was unacceptable."

"It's okay," she says lifting Jonah from his chair and giving him a hug. "I didn't mean to ruin his plans."

"It's totally not your fault. My husband hasn't adjusted to his new schedule since Jonah came into our lives. He still thinks he's a single guy as opposed to a parent with responsibilities. I'll have a talk with him. Don't give it another thought."

By eight thirty, Jonah, who was up since six, has gone down for a short nap. I've got a little time before I need to get dressed for the gallery and ask Eden to help me clean out some old clothes from my closet. It's a dual-purpose endeavor. I really do need to clean out my closet to make room for the new clothes my personal shopper recently picked out for me. But I also thought it would be a great way to give Eden some of my old clothes without her feeling like it was charity. I'm not sure she's my size because she always wears such bulky things. But she's definitely no bigger than me, so my clothes should fit.

I start pulling things out of my walk-in closet handing them to her.

"I'm planning to give all this to Goodwill, so feel free to take whatever you want."

Her eyes widen and she smiles. "Really?" I nod and continue tossing garments onto my bed. I find a soft beige cashmere sweater that would complement Eden's fair complexion.

"How about this?" I say, holding up the sweater next to her face. This color would look nice on you and it goes with everything."

Fifteen minutes later, with my encouragement, Eden's sectioned off a big pile of my old clothes for herself.

"Here," I say holding up a navy-blue cardigan. "This would fit you." She nods and takes the sweater from my hand.

"This has been fun," I say with a smile, "like we're sisters going shopping. I was an only child. I never had a little sister. I always wanted one."

Eden nods and gives me another smile. I dig out more clothes from the back of the closet including some shoes. She picks out a few more items.

"Tori, the police were here yesterday. Is everything okay?"

When I hear the word 'police,' I freeze. My back is to her, so I force a smile on my face before turning around to answer.

"The police? It was nothing. Everything's fine. They had some questions about something that happened in the Hamptons last spring. Nothing to do with us. It's all settled now."

She nods. "I was in the next room reading a book and I overheard some of what they said. It sounded like a woman drowned."

I maintain my smile, which takes a lot of concentration because this topic freaks me out. "It's a sad story. They think some poor woman lost her life at Rocky Point Beach. I was at that beach the same day but left before it happened."

"I heard them say there was no trace of her, no car or anything. Don't you think it's weird they didn't find a towel, her phone or clothes?"

I don't answer, hoping to end the conversation. Back in my closet, I pull down a box containing some old T-shirts. "Eden, see if you like any of these."

Like a dog with a bone, she's not dissuaded and continues her line of questioning. "The woman who drowned must have gone to the beach by bus or cab, don't you think? That's the only thing that makes any sense."

Up on a step stool rummaging my shelves, I tug on a box and several things come tumbling down. One of them is Sasha's oversized floppy brimmed straw hat with the red ribbon.

Eden reaches down and picks it up. "That's a coincidence. Didn't the police officer say that they had a video of a woman going to the beach wearing a big straw hat with a red ribbon?"

I step down from the stool and snatch the hat from her hand. "Did he say it was red? I don't remember that. Life is full of coincidences. I'm going to keep this hat, by the way."

Once Eden leaves my room with her arms full of my clothes, I stuff Sasha's hat inside my tote bag along with scissors. I need to get that hat out of my house. It was stupid of me to keep it. That hat is concrete evidence that I had contact with the missing woman. It wouldn't be long before someone made the connection to Jonah and I could lose him.

Before I leave for the gallery, I give my little boy a kiss and remind Eden that Daniel *will* be home to relieve her so she can make her doctor's appointment.

Once outside, I walk a few blocks to a street that has several stores with large garbage bins. Stepping into an alley next to a fruit and vegetable store, I rip the red ribbon off the hat. Using my scissors, I cut the straw hat and ribbon into tiny pieces and drop a few of the scraps into the bin.

For seven blocks, I stroll slowly, dropping pieces of the straw hat and ribbon in different receptacles. Once I get rid of the last piece, I call for an Uber to take me to the gallery for my second meeting with Der Pflug.

As my car crosses over the Brooklyn Bridge into Manhattan, I congratulate myself for a successful morning. I've protected my son, fooled the cops and destroyed a piece of evidence that could connect me to Sasha.

I've also provided Eden with new wardrobe so that maybe my husband will get off of her back. When I left today she was wearing some of the clothes I gave her — a pair of black pants, a white tee and a pale-blue pullover sweater. Her hair still looked like she combed it with a rake, but I'll tackle that in the future. Hopefully, her wardrobe upgrade will put my husband in a better mood when he gets home. The last thing in the world I need right now is to have to find a new nanny. Plus, I like her and Jonah loves her.

CHAPTER THIRTY-ONE

When my Uber pulls up in front of the gallery, Neville's already standing outside the front door and comes running over.

"Where have you been?" he says, practically screeching before I'm out of the car.

"What are you talking about?" I say, closing the car door.

"Der Pflug has been here waiting for you for almost thirty minutes."

I look at my watch and grit my teeth. *Shit*. I'm half an hour late. I was so consumed with getting rid of Sasha's hat that I lost track of time.

"I'm so sorry," I say, trying to dream up a reasonable excuse when there is none. Since I had a seizure during Der Pflug's last meeting, it was important to show him we are an organized and reliable art house. "I had a last-minute babysitter issue, and then I couldn't get an Uber."

We race into our small conference room. Der Pflug is sitting at the table drinking coffee and playing on his phone.

"I'm so sorry," I say. "I couldn't get a car and there was all this construction. Tell me, how can I make this up to you?"

To my surprise, the young artist is pretty cool about my lateness. I feel Neville calming down as we all take a seat.

Over the next forty minutes, I outline how the Pierce-Woolsey Gallery envisions how his show will unfold. Then, I take him through the marketing and promotion that will go with it. The artist seems impressed and I go in for the close. Neville's sitting next to me and I can feel his energy. He's already tasting the victory of landing one of the most sought-after new artists on the New York scene.

Once we've secured our new client, I start to go over some additional details for Der Pflug's show when Anton comes into the conference room.

"How's everything going?" he says, his eyes round as he looks at both Neville and me.

I smile. "Great. We're going over the particulars right now. We've settled on a date. Der Pflug's first show with Pierce-Woolsey will be in March."

"Wonderful," says Anton, rubbing his hands together before looking directly at the artist. "I can promise you that we will make sure your show is the most exciting and talked-about event of the new season."

"I'm pumped," says the artist. "Seems like Tori has everything lined up. I feel very confident having her handle my show."

Everyone smiles as Anton places his hand on the knob of the door. "Tori, I almost forgot. I have some very exciting news for you. Do you know who Cicero Clemenza is?"

I look at him like he has two heads. Of course, I know who Cicero Clemenza is. Who doesn't? I work in the art world, not under a rock.

"If you're talking about the world-famous photographer, then yes, I do know who he is."

"Clemenza isn't just any photographer. The man's a genius. He's made a fortune licensing every shot he's ever taken. His work is on bags, books, calendars . . . even clothing. He's a marketing genius who monetizes everything. Go into any bookstore, if you can find one, and you'll see dozens of Clemenza's photo books."

Neville clears his throat and tilts his head towards Der Pflug, signaling Anton to chit-chat about Clemenza another time.

"Wait," Der Pflug says sitting up straight. "I know Clemenza's work. He does those pictures of babies inside of flowers and pea pods, right?"

"That's him," says Anton, nodding and looking at me. "Now, for the big news. Tori, remember the day you brought little Jonah into the gallery to meet everyone? Clemenza was here talking to us about doing a show. While he was walking around our space, he met your nanny and your son. Clemenza was so taken with Jonah that he took a bunch of photos of him. He wants to use those pictures of Jonah in his new book. You're not going to believe this, but he's thinking of putting Jonah on the cover."

My mouth drops open and I stare at Anton as he continues to talk. "His business manager told me he's already got several vendors who want to use the images of Jonah for a series of tote bags, mugs and baseball hats. They'll be sold in the gift shop at the Guggenheim when the Clemenza retrospective exhibit runs next year."

I scan the faces in the room while I have an out of body experience. Everyone is grinning like drunken fools. Suddenly, there's a loud scream. It's coming out of my mouth. The smiling faces in the room abruptly change from happy to she's cray-cray.

"No!" I shout as I stand up. "I won't allow my son's image to be used like that. This cannot happen under any circumstances. Who gave Clemenza the right to take a picture of my child without my permission? He's exploiting my son. I won't have it!"

There's a pall over the room. The new expressions on everyone's face tell me they are all uncomfortable.

"I believe," says Anton, clearing his throat, glancing over at Neville and back to me, "your nanny told Clemenza that it was all right to take some pictures of your son."

"My nanny," I shriek. "Since when does a nanny get to decide something like that? If Clemenza uses a single image of my son for anything, I will sue him for everything he's got. Am I clear? You tell him that, Anton."

My outburst has left me out of breath and exhausted. It takes a lot of energy to be so angry. I've just made my crappy heart work extra hard and for what? The room has gone eerily silent. No one knows what to say after my tirade. Der Pflug finally breaks the silence as he stands.

"I think it's best if I get going. I have another appointment in Midtown," he says as he walks to the door.

Neville stands. "We can go over the rest of the details another time. I'll have the contracts sent to your business manager."

"Let me think about it," says Der Pflug as he walks through the open door. "I'm not so sure this gallery is the right place for my show. I'm sensing a bit of toxic energy here."

A second later, the artist is gone and all eyes fall on me.

"What the fuck was that?" shouts Anton, obviously furious. "What kind of normal person reacts that way? Most people would be thrilled that a world class photographer like Clemenza wants to photograph their child. Instead, you have a fucking fit in front one of our most important potential clients and screw up the whole deal."

Neville has his head down. He looks like he's going to cry. "Der Pflug was already on board with us," he says. "We would have been the envy of every gallery on the east coast. I don't understand what came over you."

I look into both men's eyes. Everything is all screwed up. Over ten years of trust and love working together has evaporated in seconds. From their perspective, my outburst was an unexpected and unnecessary tantrum that just cost them a huge important show.

I can barely explain it to myself. All I know is that at that moment, I was a mother lioness protecting my cub. There's no way I can allow Jonah's picture to go into books or be on merchandise for a museum's gift shop. Anyone could see it and recognize him. I could lose my son. If I let Clemenza use his image, I might as well post Jonah's picture in *The New York Times*.

I look at Anton and Neville. They're waiting for me to say something. Clearly, they think I'm a lunatic, a fanatical, overprotective shrew of a mother. If they knew the truth, they'd understand.

"I'm sorry. It caught me by surprise," I say meekly, my head starting to spin and a wave of heat passing over me. "I don't want my son's image plastered all over key chains and drink coasters."

Neville and Anton lock eyes on each other. They appear to be communicating telepathically. Neville turns and faces me.

"Tori, we could understand if you didn't want your son's image used by Clemenza," he says gently. "That would have been fine. It was your delivery and manic temper tantrum that was disturbing. You behaved like a four-year-old having a meltdown. You were screaming and stamping your feet. It was highly unprofessional and frankly, unpleasant for those of us in the room."

Was I stamping my feet? I don't remember doing that. But truthfully, I don't remember anything from those few minutes. It's all a blur. I only know I couldn't risk losing Jonah.

The room is really spinning now and I grip the table to hold myself up. It's too late. A second later, I feel myself falling and everything goes black.

CHAPTER THIRTY-TWO

When I wake up, I'm in a strange room with curtain around it. Through a gap in the curtain, I see a window. It's dark outside. My mother and father are standing over me, concerned looks on their faces.

"Where am I?" I say.

My father sits on the edge of my bed and takes my hand. "You're in the hospital, honey. You passed out at the gallery. Neville and Anton called an ambulance. You don't remember?"

"Where's Daniel?" I whisper.

My father pats my hand. "He's on his way, honey. He had to wait for your nanny to get home to watch Jonah. I told him to bring the baby here and that we'd look after him, but he didn't want to. Do you know what happened?"

"I remember feeling dizzy at the gallery, but that's all. Dad, what's wrong with me? Why does this keep happening?"

A tall, thin man with a receding hairline and glasses stands in the doorway.

"Perhaps I can help answer that question," he says, introducing himself as my cardiologist. "Given your history, and your previously diagnosed heart condition, we ran just about every test we have and . . ."

In a nutshell, the tests revealed a good news/bad news scenario. I did indeed have this sucky heart that didn't pump right. In an extreme situation where my blood pressure shoots up due to excitement, fear, anger or all of the above, it could trigger a cardiac event.

"I think that may have been the cause of today's episode. The man who brought you to the hospital told the intake nurse you had been very upset and visibly angry shortly before you passed out."

I look at my worried parents and feel so stupid. If they knew what I'd done, and how I've lied to keep my son's real identity a secret, would they still love me? I decide my father would, not sure about my mother.

"Do you remember being extremely distraught before losing consciousness?" the doctor asks me.

I nod.

My father grasps both of my hands. "What was making you so upset, sweetheart? Does it have to do with Daniel?"

"No," I say immediately to disabuse him of any negative feelings about my husband. My father's never been fully on board with Daniel. He always thinks the worst of him. "Daniel had nothing to do with why I got angry. It doesn't matter now."

"There are things in life that upset us and get us angry," says the doctor. "Most of us power through it and get on with our day. In your case, these fluctuations are not well tolerated. It's important you maintain as much calm as possible or you could be looking at an even more dangerous situation.

I let out a sigh.

"I'm serious," says the doctor, shaking his head ever so slightly. "This is no joke. You could have a heart attack and die if you're not careful."

"We'll make sure she stays calm," says my father.

During the doctor's warning speech, I'm thinking — *Good luck with me staying calm, Mom and Dad. What would you think of me if you knew I stole a baby and passed him off as your grandson?*

But instead I say, "So, what's the good news?"

"The good news is that there are several things you can do to mitigate this from happening again."

The doctor walks me through all the good habits I need to commit to: religious use of my CPAP device, and maintaining a cool composure in difficult situations. He goes through the usual stuff — diet, exercise, minimal drinking, blah, blah, blah. Then he prescribes a new medication he thinks might help.

"If you follow all these guidelines, there's no reason you can't live a good long life. Remember, you're not like other people. I'm afraid that's not the hand you were dealt. You need to follow strict rules or I can't guarantee you'll be around next year."

The doctor leaves after I agree that Daniel and I will meet with him in two weeks to go over my compliance. Since my father can't go more than two hours without a cup of coffee, my parents hand me my phone before running to the hospital coffee shop. Seconds after they leave my ER berth, my phone rings.

"Darling, how are you?" says Neville.

"I'm okay. Listen, I'm so sorry for losing it today. I can understand if you don't want me at the gallery anymore."

"Don't you say another word. Friends don't abandon each other when they're not well. Anton and I both agree that the most important thing now is for you to get better."

"I ruined everything with Der Pflug."

"Yes, you certainly did. I don't think the young artist will be back, but who cares? There will be other shows, but there won't be another you."

I smile. Neville's being awfully sweet considering how psycho I was during that meeting.

"But," he continues, "Anton and I insist that you to take some more time off to get well. We only want you back at the gallery when you're ready. Okay?"

I feel so much better after Neville's call. Still by myself and missing my son, I sit back and open the app on my phone to view the baby camera in Jonah's nursery. When the picture comes into focus, I see Eden sitting on the floor with Jonah. She's making a plastic train move around him and adding in all the right train noises. My son is eating it all up. A smile creeps onto my face as I watch her scoop him up and sit with him in the rocking chair. She plays peek-a-boo. He loves that game and never tires of it.

Viewing my son and seeing him so happy sends endorphins flying through my body. Within seconds, I feel infinitely better. I'm still smiling when Daniel pulls the blue curtain back.

"You look better than I imagined," he says, worry in his eyes. "What did the doctors say? I wanted to get here sooner but had to wait for Eden to get home. She had her phone off because of her doctor's visit and forgot to turn it back on. I knew we should have made her change that appointment."

"Let's not start that again. It wouldn't have made any difference. Basically, the cardiologist said I need to follow the program, no deviations. Period."

Daniel's response is very firm and he reminds me how he kept warning me to follow the rules.

"You're always so cavalier about your health. You forget to take your meds half the time and you never check your blood pressure. You're supposed to do that every day."

He's right, so I tell him what I think he wants to hear.

"Daniel, from this day forward, I promise to be a model patient."

CHAPTER THIRTY-THREE

One morning a week later, I'm home alone with the baby when Neville calls. We talk and agree to wait until after the Christmas holidays to discuss my return to the gallery. I plan to use the next few months to get my life together and spend some more time with my son.

Eden is off today and Daniel has already left for the gym. The note he left on the kitchen table said he has two auditions this afternoon and won't be home until five. When Jonah takes his nap, I'll have time to tackle my last remnant of Sasha.

I give Jonah a bath, dress him, and put him in the stroller. It's a sunny and reasonably warm October day as I head outside through our lower-level entrance.

I've got an appointment at one p.m. with All Tangled Up, Inc. They're a "do everything, problem solving" tech company. According to their ad, they can wire your house, fix your hard drive, recover a lost document and, hopefully, bust into a phone when you don't have the password — no questions asked.

We take an Uber over to Williamsburg and pull up in front of an old brick building. At first I'm not sure I'm in the right place. I'm about to call them when I see *All Tangled Up* in small letters printed on a glass window. I look in through the glass. Five young men in their twenties and thirties sit in front of computers. Piles of equipment and wires are stacked up around them.

I open the front door and push the stroller in. The place screams 'hipsters only.' The men are so engrossed in what they're doing, that no one looks up or acknowledges our presence.

I clear my throat. "Excuse me?"

A young man turns his head. "Can I help you?" he says.

"I have an appointment with TJ."

"That's me," he replies as he looks at his phone. "You must be Audrey? The one with a phone problem, right?"

"Yes," I say as I push the stroller next to TJ's desk and take a seat. I used a phony name. I can't have loose ends pointing back to me.

I explain to him that my cousin passed away suddenly and I was her only living relative.

"Her phone's locked and I need to find out if there's anything important on there. You can understand."

He looks at me thoughtfully. "Hey, no judgements here. You do what you gotta do. I have to warn you, sometimes when people do this, they don't like what they find. Are you prepared to find out something about your cousin that you may not want to know?"

I nod. "I need to get into that phone. I want closure. I don't expect to find anything radical or disturbing."

"People never do," TJ says, shaking his head as he takes the phone from my hand and plugs it into a power source.

For the next twenty minutes, Jonah sits on my lap, while I watch TJ press different buttons on the phone attempting to unlock it. He sighs several times and comments on how this particular phone is "stubborn." I wonder if it truly is or if TJ simply doesn't know what he's doing.

Finally, he stops and looks at me. "I'm not sure what's wrong, but this thing won't budge."

"Please, you've got to get it open for me."

He lets out another sigh. "There's one more thing I can try, but if that doesn't work . . ."

I hold Jonah closer and bite my bottom lip, my eyes glued to TJ until he lets out a yelp.

"Now, that's what I'm talking about. Got it," he says, all smiles.

"Nice one, man," says one of the other men in the room.

Thank God for TJ.

"Now, what is it that you want to find on this phone?" he says as he continues to play with it.

"I'd like to see my cousin's email, texts as well as any voicemail messages and phone calls placed and received."

He nods and plays around with the phone. "Huh? That's really strange."

"What's strange?" I say, leaning forward.

"There are no voicemail messages and no record of any calls being placed or received."

"That makes no sense," I say. "What about her email?"

He messes around with the phone again and shakes his head. "The email account on this phone was never set up."

"What about her texts? There have to be texts."

He takes a moment and looks up at me. "It looks like your cousin didn't send or receive any texts."

"I don't understand," I say, thinking out loud. "Why would someone have a phone if they weren't using it?"

"Did *you* ever send your cousin texts?" he says, peering at me.

"No, I always communicated with her on her house phone."

"Maybe she had two phones and used this phone only for the internet," says TJ. "Let me check her browsing history." Jonah is squirming now and so am I while we wait.

Finally, TJ turns to me. "I hate to tell you, Audrey, but there's no browsing history on this phone either. Your cousin or someone else wiped it clean. It's on factory settings."

"Why would she do that?"

"I don't want to speak ill of the dead, but usually with stuff like this, the person was hiding something. Maybe your cousin had a secret she didn't want anyone to know about."

I leave TJ with more questions than before I arrived. Sasha's phone being empty was the last thing in the world I expected or understand. Who carries around a charged phone but never uses it? I grab an Uber back to my house, mulling over the turn of events. The one positive thing is that Sasha's phone being blank means there's no possible connection the police could trace to me.

Jonah and I are safe.

CHAPTER THIRTY-FOUR

Several weeks later, I dig through my bedroom closet looking for the perfect outfit to wear for lunch with my father. Leave it to him to get us a reservation at Chez Marchet. It's currently one of the most difficult restaurants to get into ever since one of New York's top food critics called it 'a morsel of heaven on earth.' One thing's for sure — my father is a force. When he wants something, he gets it.

I throw six more dresses onto my bed and let out a long and apparently loud groan. Seconds later, I hear the sound of Daniel's footsteps coming down the hallway. He pokes his head into our bedroom, both of his eyebrows raised.

"Everything okay?" he says.

"Yeah, fine."

"It sounded like you were in here slaughtering a cow."

I giggle. *Do I really sound like that?* I put my hands on my hips. "The problem is, I've got nothing to wear for lunch at Chez Marchet today."

Daniel sees several dozen garments strewn around the room and shakes his head. "You have more clothes than days to wear them. First world problem, I guess."

He sticks his hand into the largest pile and pulls out a relatively new black-and-white designer dress and holds it up.

"How about this one? You wore it when we went to that concert at the Met a few months ago. You looked amazing in it. People couldn't take their eyes off of you. I know I couldn't."

I feel myself blush and my anxiety level plummet. Daniel always has a calming effect on me. I can be spinning out of control and a few choice words from my husband take me from a hundred down to two. When that happens, he calls himself 'the Tori Whisperer.' Sometimes, he truly is.

I smile and reach for the dress in his hand. "That's perfect. Thank you."

He pulls his watch off his wrist and holds it up. "While you're out, would you drop my lucky watch off and have the battery changed?"

I nod as he drops it into my black bag. He adores that thing. The watch was a gift from the cast of the play he directed during his senior year in college. There's an inscription on the back:

With Love,
The Cranbury Players

"The restaurant is only a few blocks away from my father's jeweler. I can take it in before lunch and pick it up after. I might do a little shopping at Bergdorf's when lunch is over, but I'll be home by four. I want to take Jonah out for a walk before it gets dark. Want to come with us?"

"You've got a date," he says before he turns and heads towards the door. "Don't forget about my battery."

Later, I'm standing in front of my bedroom mirror putting on a pair of gold drop earrings. Eden comes into my room carrying Jonah on her shoulder and stands behind me. My son is nearly nine months old, and still crawling. He tries to push himself up whenever he can. Pretty soon, we'll all be chasing him around the house.

"You look amazing," says Eden, switching Jonah to her other shoulder. "That dress fits you like a glove."

"Daniel picked it out for me," I say with a bit of bravado while looking at Eden's reflection in the mirror. She looks a lot better since I gave her some of my old clothes. At least you can see her shape now. She's much thinner than I'd thought. Her hair is still a disaster, but at least Daniel's stopped complaining about her now that she's out of her sweats.

I take Jonah from her and give him a kiss.

"Be a good boy. I expect to get an excellent report from Eden when I come home," I say, kissing his neck a half dozen times. "When I get home, Daddy and I are going to take you to the park."

Adjusting the belt on my dress, I grab my black bag and walk down the hall to Daniel's office to show him how I look. As I reach for the office doorknob, Eden calls out from the other end of the hall.

"He already went out," she says. "He said he had an appointment with his diction coach."

I wonder why he didn't mention the coaching session to me. For a man who doesn't have a job, he's awfully busy. I tell myself it's better he's out doing something constructive than sitting around the house wallowing in self-pity. As he often reminds me, an actor's life isn't easy. Guess what? Neither is being an actor's wife.

I jump into a cab and head across the bridge into Manhattan. I'll have just enough time to stop at our jeweler's on East 56th Street to drop Daniel's watch off before I meet my father. I can walk to the restaurant from there.

My parents have been shopping with this jeweler for years. The proprietor knows me as soon as I walk in.

"Tori, what a pleasant surprise. Looking for something special for yourself today? How's the baby? Your father was in here not too long ago and told us your son's about ready to walk."

"Any day," I say as I smile and dig around in my bag for Daniel's lucky watch. I can't find it. It's not in the bag. I take everything out and place all the contents on the jewelry case counter. I check every pocket, but still no watch.

I saw Daniel put his watch into my bag. I took the bag downstairs and got straight into a cab. During the ride, I pulled out my mirror to check my make-up. The bag tipped over slightly. I didn't see anything fall out. But it must have.

Panicking, I sift through the contents of my bag for my taxi receipt.

"Is something wrong?" says the jeweler.

"I think I lost my husband's watch." I find the receipt and dial the phone number printed on it. There's a recording telling me to leave a message. *Shit.* I leave a quasi-hysterical message about Daniel's missing timepiece saying I'll give whoever returns it a thousand dollars. After I hang up and try to compose myself, a pit forms in my stomach.

He'll never forgive me. He wears that watch to every audition for luck. It can't be replaced. What have I done?

My whole body is in pins and needles mode when I walk up to the front door of Chez Marchet. Taking in a few deep breaths, I feel the crispness in the air as it goes down my throat and into my lungs. I won't mention the watch to my father, he's already so worried about me. Besides, there's nothing he can do. And, there's another important conversation I need to have with him. I don't want to get distracted by Daniel's missing watch. Hopefully, the cab driver will find it and claim his thousand-dollar reward.

I enter the beautiful French restaurant. It's full of antique tin, white tile and flowers as far as the eye can see. The hostess leads me to my father's table. His face is stern as he scours the menu but changes completely when he sees me. His broad smile and the sparkle in his eyes whenever he looks at me is always so healing. I feel better already.

Someone will return the watch.

"Right on time, my girl," he says as he leans over and gives me a kiss.

We do our usual small talk for a few minutes before we order. Once the waiter leaves, Dad looks me in the eyes.

"Okay, so tell your old man, how you're really doing? You've given your mother and I quite a few scares over the last few months. You haven't seemed yourself since Jonah arrived. Maybe you could use more—"

"I'm fine," I say before he finishes his sentence. "Jonah has nothing to do with it. He brings me more joy than anything else in my life."

My father presses his lips together and nods. "I can understand that. I have a daughter that I feel the same way about. Your mother and I just want to be sure you're all right. Is Daniel doing enough to support you?"

I start to defend my husband, but my father shushes me. "I don't care about Daniel. I do care about you and my grandson, though. You've ended up in the hospital twice. Do you really want Jonah to grow up without his mother?"

I roll my eyes.

"I'm serious, Tori. The doctors have all said you could die if you don't follow the rules."

I spend the next fifteen minutes promising I will not detour from the advised medical program in any way.

"I swear to wear my CPAP, eat properly and do everything the doctors tell me."

Satisfied, my father changes the subject and asks me for the latest details on Jonah. I show him a picture of my son standing by himself holding onto the coffee table.

My father's eyes twinkle. "He's one smart kid. You can tell just by looking at him. You know something? In this picture, Jonah looks a lot like you did at that age."

It's wishful thinking on his part but nice to hear nonetheless. When my father finishes gushing about his grandson, I change the subject to the one I really want to discuss.

"Remember the first time I passed out and went to the hospital?"

"Of course. It was terrifying."

"Where were you when you got the message?"

My father pauses. That's a tell. My father is never at a loss for words.

"I believe I had a business appointment," he says slowly.

I let out a sigh and stare directly into his eyes. Obviously, he's not going to give it up easily, so I opt for the direct route to expedite things.

"Dad, I saw you going into an elevator at the Clarkson Hotel with a platinum blonde that day. I was meeting an artist there for coffee. You kissed that woman in the elevator."

My father looks down at his half-eaten plate of food but says nothing.

"I thought all that stuff was over," I say softly. "Mom doesn't deserve it. You promised her you stopped."

CHAPTER THIRTY-FIVE

After a tense end to our lunch, I kiss my father goodbye. He's late for an appointment and hurries off. I wait alone for my Uber feeling a mix of sadness and disappointment in him. He's always been there for me, but I realize now, he hasn't been there for my mother. That explains why she's always been so brittle, her anger simmering beneath her calm and collected surface.

While I wait for my car, I call the taxi company again upping the reward to five thousand dollars. It's a ridiculous amount of money, I know, but worth every penny if I get the watch back. I can't even imagine telling him it's gone.

"Five thousand for a Bulova?" says the dispatcher. "You know you can buy that same watch for about two hundred bucks."

"This one has sentimental value," I say and he assures he'll call as soon as he hears something.

I get home to Brooklyn much earlier than expected. After losing the watch, I have no appetite for shopping. No amount of retail therapy is going to solve my problem today.

My Uber pulls up in front of our townhouse at two forty-five. As I get out of the car, I look up and the sun is still shining. It's a perfect fall afternoon for our family outing in the park.

I pick up the mail as I walk into the house and head straight back to the kitchen. Everything's quiet and I remember it's still Jonah's nap time. I place my bag on the kitchen counter and sit on a bar stool sifting through the mail. Most of it's junk. I'm about to toss the envelopes and circulars into the trash when I notice one looks different. It has no return address, only my name and address typed on the front. It's postmarked 10022 — Midtown Manhattan.

I tear open the envelope. There's a single sheet of white paper inside containing six typed words, all in caps:

THE TRUTH WILL SET YOU FREE

The message startles me and I push back from the counter, nearly toppling over on my stool. My heart goes from zero to a thousand and there's a loud screeching noise in my ears. *Someone knows. Someone knows about Jonah.* I feel myself hyperventilating. A little voice in my head tells me to calm down. But I can't. The noise gets louder and my breathing becomes more erratic.

I consider who might have sent this and ultimately decide it is not some benign entity. This message is a harbinger of more shit to come.

Gripping the edge of the cool marble counter to maintain my balance, I try to slow down my breathing. No wonder I'm nearly hysterical, my day has been loaded with trauma: the lost watch, my father's affairs and now this. I try to wrap my head around the laundry list of incoming missiles when I hear a noise from upstairs.

Slowly trying to maintain my balance, I get up from the stool and walk over to the bottom of the stairs.

"Daniel? Eden?" I say loudly. There's no answer so I go up. First, I go to my son's room to check on him. His door is closed. I open it as quietly as possible.

The room is still and I tiptoe over to his crib on the other side of the room. He's asleep and snoring ever so slightly. I kiss him on his forehead and walk out into the second-floor foyer.

I look down the hall. My bedroom door is ajar.

"Daniel?" I say as I push the door open. The room's empty, just as I left it this morning, my clothes still scattered on our bed. I do a quick search for the watch, hoping maybe it had fallen out there. No watch. I go into the bathroom, wash my face and look in the mirror. The cool water on my overheated skin feels good and I take a moment to review the situation.

Someone sent an anonymous letter threatening me and my son. But what's their endgame? If that person believes I've committed a crime, why don't they go to the police? Why the mysterious note?

I deliberate for a few seconds, and eventually understand the implications.

My son is the bargaining chip. The sender of the letter wants something from me. In return, they'll keep my secret. I wish I could tell Daniel or my father about this. They'd know what to do. But I can't, not ever.

I take a last look in the mirror, throw my shoulders back and go looking for my husband.

"Daniel?" I call out.

I hear a door open from the floor above. "I'm up here," he shouts. "Be right down." I hear the baby start to cry and go to his room. As I pick him up, I hear the stairs creak from above. When I go out into the foyer with the baby, Daniel is coming down the stairs from the third floor. He's barefoot and dressed in jeans and a T-shirt.

"What were you doing up there?" I say, getting a whiff of Jonah's dirty diaper.

"You know Eden likes to draw, right?"

I nod. *Yes, I do. But I didn't know you paid attention to her hobbies. You barely acknowledge her when she's in the same room. Hmm.*

"She had one of her charcoal drawings framed and asked me to hang it in her room," he says.

"And, did you?"

"Mission accomplished," he says as he walks towards our bedroom.

I follow him.

"Still want to go for that walk?" he says, stretching out on our bed. "I'm going to lie down for a few minutes until you're ready to go."

I take Jonah to his room, change his diaper and get him dressed in something warmer for our outing. With my son in my arms, I climb up to the third floor and knock on Eden's door. There's a rustle on the other side before she opens it.

She's wearing a pair of my old jeans and the jade-green cashmere sweater I'd given to her. Even with those awful dark-framed glasses that do her no favors, the green of the sweater brings out the color of her blue-green eyes. For the first time I notice that her eyes are quite pretty. Her hair is still a semi-matted disaster but overall, she's a bit improved.

"Did you have a nice lunch with your father?" she says smiling.

"Yes, we had a very good time. The food was incredible."

"What did you have?"

My mind is a million miles away. *I've lost my husband's prized watch. My father regularly cheats on my mother. And, I have a stalker who's threatening me and my son.*

I smile because I swear, if I don't, I'll cry. "I had steak fritte with wilted spinach. It was delicious and creme brulée for dessert." I walk around her room looking at the walls bouncing Jonah on my hip. There's a medium-sized framed charcoal picture hanging over her bed. It's of two little girls playing together on a see-saw.

"Is this the picture Daniel hung for you? It's good," I say, admiring her moderate though undeveloped talent. "Have you ever taken art classes?"

"Nothing formal. I love drawing. It relaxes me."

I stare at the picture and then look at my nanny. "Daniel's all thumbs and not the least bit handy. The fact that you got him to hang a picture for you is a minor miracle."

Eden laughs. "He measured, hammered in the nails for the hook and it was done."

I remind her that Daniel and I are going out for a walk with the baby and that she should prep something for dinner.

Carrying Jonah down to the second floor, I pop my head into my bedroom.

"Wake up, sleepyhead," I say to my groaning husband. "Time to go. Meet me downstairs."

"Five more minutes," he mutters and puts the pillow over his head.

Down in the kitchen, I pack a bottle and some Cheerios for Jonah's walk. I pull out the drawer where I keep the sandwich bags, and that's when I see it — the only one we have. Our hammer.

How did the hammer get down here if Daniel was using it to hang a picture on the third floor? He didn't have it with him when he came down the stairs. Then, he went straight into our bedroom. So how did it get down here into this drawer?

CHAPTER THIRTY-SIX

A few mornings later, I'm sitting at the kitchen table drinking a second cup of coffee while Jonah plays happily in his highchair. I'm still mulling over the hammer conundrum. My eyes are on my son, but inside I'm worrying about my growing list of problems. I needed time to think, so I gave Eden the day off.

First, I have to find a replacement for my husband's watch. I can't let him know it's gone. He'll never forgive me and it will add fuel to the narrative that I'm losing it. Next, and even more critical, I have to figure out who sent that threatening letter.

I'll have the house to myself today to think. Daniel's leaving in thirty minutes for a session with his trainer and then has an audition reading somewhere in Manhattan for an Off-Off-Broadway play. With any luck, he'll be gone all day.

While I wait for my husband to come downstairs, I sing a few of Jonah's favorite nursery songs to him. Despite me being consistently off key, he always enjoys it. I leave him in his highchair making a big old mess while I scan websites for used Bulova Classic watches. It can't be a new one, Daniel's was beat up. He'd notice if it was new.

I'm bidding on a watch on Poshmark when an energized Daniel bounces into the kitchen ready to 'seize the day' as he so often annoyingly says. He's pumped about his afternoon audition, but truthfully he always thinks he's going to get it. How he manages to stay so upbeat despite all of his professional disappointments, I'll never know. If I had been kicked to the curb as much as he has, I'd be reduced to a puddle of goop.

"I have a good feeling about today," he says. I've heard this same comment a thousand times, but I cheer him on anyway. You never know. His tenacity being intact despite getting very little positive reinforcement tells me that acting must truly be a calling for him.

He pops a piece of buttered toast into his mouth, pours himself a cup of coffee and looks around.

"Where's Eden?" he says.

"I gave her the day off, remember? She went out about forty minutes ago. I think she was meeting her boyfriend."

"Do you have my lucky watch? I want to wear it to my audition today."

The irony of him calling it his 'lucky' watch hasn't escaped me. He's had this good luck talisman for at least fifteen years and his acting career hasn't exactly taken off. I wonder when this luck is supposed to kick in.

"Right, your watch. Unfortunately, the jeweler didn't have the right battery and had to order it. He hopes to have your watch ready by next week — supply chain issues."

"But I have a bunch of important meetings this week."

"I know, sweetie, it couldn't be helped. We'll have it back soon. I'll even go into Manhattan and pick it up for you."

He shakes his head, mutters something about how his day is ruined, downs the rest of his coffee and heads out the door.

I clean up Jonah, put him in his playpen and turn on some kiddie music. Once he's playing with his toy xylophone, I go back online to bid for the watch. While I'm simultaneously bidding on several, I call the taxi company to see if anyone found the original. No one has turned it in. After all this time and the insane size of the reward I offered, it's not likely to turn up. I'm on my own on this.

After an hour scouring the internet, I score an identical Bulova watch being sold by some guy in Bay Ridge, Brooklyn. I close the deal, and make arrangements for someone to pick it up and deliver it to me. It should be at my house by noon. If all goes as planned, I'll bring it to a local jeweler here and have it engraved. If I slip the engraver an extra hundred bucks, they'll do it overnight. First problem, almost solved.

Waiting for my package to arrive, I focus on that scary cryptic letter and who could be behind it. I make a list of people who could possibly have seen what happened at the beach. There was no one sitting near us. And, how could they know my name and where I live in Brooklyn? None of it makes any sense.

After an hour brainstorming, interrupted by a few games I play with Jonah, I come up with a shortlist of possibilities.

First, there's Sasha, but she's dead. It can't be her. Then there's Chloe the masseuse, but I didn't get the vibe she knew anything. It could have been a bystander on the beach, but who and how did they trace me here? There's also Eva the cleaning woman at my parents' house. She'd know how to find me in Brooklyn, but how could she know about the baby and the beach? I told her I adopted a baby. Why would she think it wasn't true?

I'm about to hurl my pen across the room when the doorbell rings. It's the watch delivery. I tip the kid, take the box into the kitchen and examine the contents. The watch and watchband are identical to the one I lost. *Finally, a little luck is running my way.*

I get Jonah wrapped up to go out, put him in his stroller and walk about seven blocks to a little place that I once used to do some engraving work for the gallery. I wheel the stroller into the tiny shop. The quaint sound of a little bell jingles as I enter.

Within seconds the owner comes out from the back to greet me. I remind him of the other projects I've previously sent to him from the gallery and he gives me his full attention.

"This time it's a personal job for me," I say, handing him the watch along with a card that lays out how the inscription should look.

With Love,
The Cranbury Players

"I need these words engraved on the back of this watch exactly the way I've shown you," I say. "It has to be on two lines and written in this script font. And, I need it by tomorrow."

The man starts to protest the fast turnaround when I hand him a hundred-dollar bill followed by a second. "It would be a personal favor to me if you could have it done by tomorrow."

He nods as he puts the bills into his back pocket and assures me it will be ready first thing in the morning.

I feel so much lighter when I push the stroller out of the shop. With a little ingenuity, I solved my own problem and my husband will never know. A little sneaky, but what's to be gained from telling him I lost his watch? It would only reinforce the notion that I'm unstable or, at the very least, fragile and forgetful.

It's sunny but also a breezy late fall day. I zip up my jacket and adjust the blanket in Jonah's stroller to make sure he's warm. Relieved about the watch, I stop at this amazing Italian produce, cheese and bread store and load up on tons of nibbly things. I'm feeling so relieved that I've decided to splurge. Daniel and I will have a Mediterranean picnic dinner with a bottle of red wine tonight.

By the time I get home it's nearly three. Jonah is asleep in his stroller. I pick him up carefully trying not to wake him. I place him in the portable crib in the family room next to the kitchen and put the groceries away.

As I place the last item in the fridge, there's a ding from my phone. It's a text from Daniel.

Audition went great, this could be the one. Having a drink with an actor I met there. Be home before seven.

I've heard those words before. But maybe this time he caught a break. Wouldn't that be nice. I'm daydreaming about how important a win would be for Daniel when my phone dings again. It's a text from a number I don't know. I'm about to delete it without looking at it when a voice in my head stops me.

With the phone in my hand, I sit down at the kitchen counter, scroll to the message and click on it.

DO I NEED TO SAY IT MORE CLEARLY? THAT BABY ISN'T YOURS. YOU STOLE HIM AND NOW YOU'RE GOING TO PAY FOR IT.

CHAPTER THIRTY-SEVEN

My phone falls from my hand onto the marble counter and bounces onto the floor. I'm literally frozen and unable to process what's happening to my body as I slump to the floor. This hits me harder than the first message because this one is more threatening and to the point. I start to tremble and my breathing is off. I look over at the crib; Jonah's moving, he's awake.

Heading into a full panic attack, my maternal instinct commands me to calm down. I can't pass out or crawl into a ball when there's no one else here to take care of my son. After a few minutes of square breathing, mind wins over matter and I manage to get up. The first thing I do is get a glass of water and take the medication in my purse.

A few more minutes pass and Jonah starts to cry. He wants me. I'm feeling almost normal again and go over to his crib. He stops fussing as soon as he sees me. When I have his soft body in my arms, I feel nothing but pure love for him. Squeezing him gently, I tell him how much. We go over to the bookcase to pick out a few of his favorites to read and then sink into the big comfy armchair.

I must have dozed off because I'm awakened by Daniel leaning over us. He picks the baby up from my lap and carries him across the room bouncing him as he goes.

"How's my big boy? Were you good for your mom today?"

"He was perfect," I say. "On another note, I have some good news. The jeweler called, your watch will be ready tomorrow."

A smile spreads across my husband's face. I look over at the clock. It's six thirty. "And, I've got a little treat for you. I was out with the baby today and stopped in at Tramonti's Salumeria."

Daniel has a deliciously evil look in his eye. "You naughty girl. What did you get? Tell me you got prosciutto and those little stuffed olives I'd give my left arm for."

Half an hour later, Daniel and I are having a feast in the kitchen when front door opens and closes. Eden steps into the room in an oversized jacket and a pair of my old jeans. She's wearing a pretty blue-and-white scarf around her neck.

"Looks like quite a feast," she says, looking at all the food covering our kitchen table.

"Join us," says Daniel. I stare at my husband. Only a few weeks ago he was hinting about getting a new nanny. Now, he wants her to pull up a chair? Was it because I gave her some decent clothes so she doesn't look as much like a street urchin? Honestly, I'll never understand men.

Eden smiles. "It's tempting, but my boyfriend and I just had dinner. I couldn't eat another bite. I think I'll go up to my room now. I can take Jonah up with me and put him to bed."

By nine, Daniel and I also go upstairs. He's got an early audition followed by a modeling job and wants to get a good night's sleep. While he's in the bathroom brushing his perfect set of white teeth, the letter and text from my stalker is on my mind.

I need to talk to someone. Carrying this whole thing around by myself is eating me up. I weigh my options of which there are few. I can't tell my husband or any of my friends. Daniel would hate me for lying and it would only give lift to the idea that I'm not stable. I can't tell Neville and Anton, not after how crazy I've behaved at the gallery. I definitely can't tell my parents that the grandson they adore and set up a trust fund and private school account for isn't their grandson. Telling them I stole him off a beach like a loaf of bread and then lied about it wouldn't land well at all. And obviously, I can't go to the police unless I'm prepared to be arrested.

I hear Daniel gargling the way he does every night. From experience, I know that's the last part of his nightly bathroom ritual. He comes out of the bathroom and sits on his side of the bed and swings his legs up.

"Take your pills?" he says, looking over at me. Daniel going over my bedtime checklist has recently become our nightly ritual.

"Yes."

"Including the ones for your anxiety?"

"Yes."

"Good. Remember what the doctor said. You have to follow all the rules, not just some of them when you feel like it. If you want to continue being Jonah's mother for the next seventy-five years, you've got to do exactly what they tell you."

I nod and reach for my CPAP device on the nightstand. I put the damn thing on my face, turn it on and immediately feel the comforting rush of air. When Daniel hears the machine go on, he reaches over and rubs my arm. Minutes later, he's asleep.

I lie there in the dark, thoughts swirling as I examine every possible angle of my dilemma. The reality is, I can't fight an enemy if I don't know who they are or what they want. The text said 'pay for it'. But what exactly does that mean? With money? With my life? With Daniel's life? Do they want to take Jonah from me?

The last thought sends terror right through me. I don't care about money or even my life so much. But I do care about Daniel's and will never under any circumstances let anyone take my son. Thinking about all these terrible possibilities gets my heart racing and I begin to cough. Sitting up, I pull the CPAP off and gasp for air.

Daniel flips on the light and faces me. "Are you all right?"

He runs to get me a glass of water and then instructs me to sip it slowly.

"Better," he says as he takes the glass. I nod. "What happened?"

"I don't know. My heart started to race and . . . I don't know."

Daniel fluffs up my pillows and hands me the CPAP again. I put it back on and he tucks me in.

"Let's try and get some sleep now," he says as he crawls onto his side of the bed.

Sleep? Easier said than done. Someone is threatening my family and I can't tell a soul or I'll end up in prison.

CHAPTER THIRTY-EIGHT

In the morning, Daniel's up and out early. After his audition, he's got a half- day of modeling work for a mid-priced men's clothing catalog. Thankfully, he gets occasional catalog work to make him feel like he's earning *some* money. At the end of the year, what he earns from modeling is peanuts, but it keeps him sane.

I get up early to play with and feed Jonah. We have a wonderful but messy breakfast together. When Eden, back in her gray sweats, walks into the kitchen, I hand my oatmeal- and peaches-covered child to her.

She smiles as she takes him from me. "You're wearing your breakfast again, I see."

Jonah gives her a big peachy smile that makes me smile.

"I've got a bunch of errands to run today. I'll be gone for a few hours," I tell Eden. "Would you give him a bath? He's got peaches in his ears. Also, I think his laundry needs washing."

"Of course," she says as she carries my son towards the stairs looking down at him as she walks. "C'mon little man, let's go have a bath. Then, I'll read you some of your favorite stories. And after that . . ."

I hear her chattering as she ascends the stairs and her voice trails off. Now, it's my turn to get cleaned up and do what needs to be done. I run upstairs, wash my face, run a hairbrush through my blonde hair, noticing the dark roots are showing. Keeping one's hair blonde when your real hair is practically black requires a lot of maintenance and commitment. I text my colorist to see if there's any way she can squeeze me in today.

Slipping on my jeans, I throw on a sweater, glide some gloss across my lips and sail down the stairs.

"I'm leaving now," I shout out as I open the front door. "Be back in a few hours."

There's a little chill in the air when I get out on the street. I throw the shawl I have in my bag over my shoulders and begin the twenty-minute walk to the engraver's. For the entire journey, I fret about the watch. What if it doesn't look the same? Will Daniel notice it's different?

It's nearly ten thirty when I arrive at the shop. The same man I left the watch with is on the phone with a customer. He smiles at me and points to a chair in the corner. I take his smile as a good omen and sit down.

When he finishes his call, he greets me. "Mrs. Fowler, so nice to see you again. You've come for the watch."

"Yes," I say all breathy. "It's ready, I hope."

He nods and reaches into a drawer behind the counter and pulls out a plastic bag with the watch inside. He removes the watch and places it on a black cloth pad on his counter and flips it over.

With Love,
The Cranbery Players

It's perfect, exactly the way I remember it. Now, Daniel will never have to know I lost his precious watch. I thank the engraver several times.

"You have no idea," I say as I leave the shop. "You've saved my life and my marriage."

For the next few hours, I run errands and return home around two. Jonah's asleep in his crib. Eden is beside him in the rocking chair reading a book.

"Has he been asleep long?" I whisper.

"About half an hour," she whispers.

"You don't have to stay with him while he sleeps. Use the monitor."

She smiles as she closes her book. "I don't mind. I like listening to him snore. It's adorable."

Her devotion warms my heart. I've seen other nannies in the park jabbering with each other and not paying attention to the children in their care. Eden is the opposite. Note to self: give her a raise next month and a nice bonus for Christmas.

Two hours later, I'm in the living room reading a magazine when Daniel returns from his shoot. He always looks extra fabulous after a modeling session because I suspect he's wearing a little make-up. I can tell he's feeling good when he walks in the door. It's the perfect time to give him his 'lucky watch.'

"Good day?" I say, walking over to him and giving him a kiss.

"Great day."

"It's going to get even better," I say as I hand him his watch and hold my breath.

He unwraps the plastic and smiles as he holds it up. "I missed you, buddy," he says speaking directly to the face of the watch. He flips it over and his face goes from one of joy to confusion. He looks at me with an accusatory stare. "This isn't my watch. What's going on?"

Shit. Be calm. Stay Cool. Play dumb.

"What do you mean?" I say, glancing down at my magazine and flipping the page in an attempt to diminish the importance of his discovery.

"This is *not* my watch."

I take the watch from his hand and examine it. "It looks like your watch to me. Besides, how many Bulova watches have an engraving from the Cranbury Players on the back?"

"That's the problem," he says staring at me. "The engraving on this watch spells Cranbery with an E. I was the director of the Cranbury Players which was spelled with a U. It was spelled C-R-A-N-B-U-R-Y. No E. What's going on here, Tori? Where's my watch and where did this thing come from?"

I'm trapped like a rat. My brain searches for some kind of logical and sane answer, but none comes. I've got nowhere to go. I can either come clean or pretend to pass out. I opt for a fainting spell.

I crumple to the ground, careful not to hit my head. My eyes are shut, but I squint to see what's going on. Through the tiny slits in my lids, I see Daniel rush over to me. I guess I'll have to tell him the truth eventually. I'm hoping the fainting buys me a little sympathy.

"Tori," he shouts as he kneels by my side and sits me up. I make my eyes flicker open slowly as if I had been momentarily unconscious. "Are you all right?"

"Yes," I whisper. "Help me up to a chair." He lifts me and gently places me on the couch. "Can you get me some water?" He nods and runs out of the room.

I've got only seconds to figure a way out of this jam. Nothing comes and my window for creative excuses is closing fast. With nowhere else to go, I decide to tell the truth.

Daniel comes back and hands me a glass of cold water. My mouth is very dry and the water tastes good. "Are you sure you're okay?" says my husband, sitting down next to me.

"Yes," I say as I sit back on the couch. "Daniel, there's something I need to confess . . ."

He listens without saying a word. I tell him the whole story about losing the watch peppered with how sorry I am. "You fainting just now, was that real or fake?" he says.

I think for a moment. The fainting bit was pretty psycho, so I decide not to give that part up. "No, that was real, I was genuinely lightheaded."

It was kind of true. When Daniel started hammering me, I did feel sick to my stomach. I just enhanced the moment with a little fall to the floor.

The room is silent and I hear Eden's footsteps coming down the stairs. "Somebody wants to see his daddy," she says, smiling as she walks into the room holding a freshly changed Jonah. The baby smiles and reaches his arms towards Daniel.

Both of us say nothing and only look at our nanny.

"What's wrong?" she says, her eyes wide.

"It seems," says my husband taking the baby from her, "that my wife has a big problem with the truth. Did you know about her scheme to replace my watch?"

Eden looks at me and then back at Daniel. "I'm sorry. I don't know what you're talking about."

"Didn't think so. Tori is the mastermind of her web of lies."

Our nanny looks extremely uncomfortable, so I jump in. "Eden, why don't you take Jonah upstairs to the playroom? Daniel and I have a few things to discuss."

For the next five hours, we go round and round about my health, my lying, my confusion and my inability to take responsibility for things. It's feeling very one-sided. He's got the upper hand and I notice he's blowing a few things way out of proportion. I start to get mad.

"Okay, so I lost your freakin' watch. I admit it," I say. "I only tried to hide it because I knew you'd lose your mind. I figured I'd replace it and we could avoid all this drama. You're acting like I murdered someone."

Daniel shakes his head as he walks across the room towards me. "Get your head screwed on straight. This lying has got to stop."

CHAPTER THIRTY-NINE

At seven in the morning on Thanksgiving Day, I'm still lounging in bed making lists of all the things I need to do before my guests arrive. I'm hosting a small group this year: my parents, my mother's cousin and her husband visiting from Boston, Eden and us. It's Jonah's first Thanksgiving and I want it to be really special.

Daniel's asleep next to me in bed. I'm listening to the sound of his soft rhythmic snoring when I hear Eden's voice calling me from the hall.

"Tori, come quick. It's Jonah."

I can't tell if her tone implies panic or danger. I leap out of bed and run into the hall.

"Where are you?" I shout down the hallway.

"In Jonah's room. Hurry."

My adrenaline kicks in, which is exactly what I'm not supposed to ever let happen. I tear down the hall to my son's room imagining him bleeding or dead. His door is half closed and I push it with force. It swings open and slams into the door jam on the wall with a bang. My eyes dart around the room looking for my dead child but land on Eden's smiling face. *Why is she smiling when my son is dead?*

She's holding up her phone. I look over at the crib. Jonah's gone. *Someone has kidnapped him. Why is she still smiling?*

"I want you to see this," she says, pointing across the room at the toy chest. My eyes follow the direction of her finger and I let out a gasp.

"Oh, my God," I say. Jonah is standing next to the chest by himself and starts walking towards me.

"His first steps. He's not even ten months old," says my nanny, getting teary. My eyes flood with water as my son attempts each new step, concentration written all over his face. Eden is filming the whole thing as Jonah lands in my arms.

"You did it," I say to my smiling son. "Aren't you the clever one. I wonder what the percentile is of babies who walk before ten months. C'mon, let's go show Daddy what you can do. He'll be so surprised."

I carry Jonah down the long hallway to my bedroom, Eden trailing behind. Daniel is still asleep and I gently nudge him. "Daniel, wake up. You need to see something." He grunts, rolls over and opens one eye. "You'll want to open both eyes for this. Trust me."

He pushes himself up on his elbows and sees Eden standing behind me. The expression on his face is a mix of bewilderment and sleepiness. "What's going on?"

I smile. "Watch and be amazed."

I lower Jonah until his feet touch the floor and then carefully let go.

"Jonah, go to Daddy." It's as if he understood my words completely, because my son walks directly to Daniel. After ten seconds, Jonah gets to the side of the bed with a big silly grin on his face. He gazes up at his father for approval. Daniel has a smile from ear to ear and jumps out of bed, picks up Jonah and swings him around the room.

"What a big boy you are," he says. "You took your first steps on Thanksgiving Day. Now, the whole family has something to be really thankful for."

"Wait until my parents see him go," I say, still brimming with pride.

Eden has been filming the whole time. "I got it all," she says with a smile. "Every bit, including his first step. Sorry to wake you up, but I knew you wouldn't want to miss it. It was thrilling to watch him go for it."

"Thank you so much for alerting us and getting it all on video," I say.

We watch Jonah do a half dozen more walks across the room, improving each time. Finally, he's tired and Eden picks him up to give him a bath. She also offers to be our videographer for the day.

I'm truly touched how much she enjoys Jonah's milestones the way Daniel and I do. Some nannies just go through the motions for a paycheck. Not her, she really loves kids.

"Eden, since it's Thanksgiving Day, I wanted to say that I'm so very thankful for you. You're like the little sister I never had. We hope you stay with us for a very long time. Don't we, Daniel?"

"Yes, that would be great," he says flatly just before Eden leaves the room with the baby.

It's been nearly two weeks since Daniel and I had our big, uncomfortable talk about the missing watch, among other things. The outcome? I agreed to get a full physical and go back to my sleep doctor for another evaluation. While I do have heart, sleep, anxiety and mild depression issues, not everything that's happened is related to that. Most of my anxiety comes from trying to tie up all the loose ends regarding Jonah's "adoption." Unfortunately, a medical doctor can't help me with that. No one can, it's my secret and mine alone to bear.

Five hours later, I look around the Thanksgiving table. Jonah is sitting on my mother's lap playing peek-a-boo. Everyone is laughing because my son is surprised every single time she uncovers her eyes. It's amazing how much a single baby can captivate a room full of adults.

My mother has totally embraced being a grandma. She spends half of her time shopping for Jonah and the other half visiting him. He's not even one yet, and yet he's one of the best dressed children in Brooklyn — courtesy of Grandma Marion.

After we have pies for dessert, my mother's cousin and her husband say goodnight. Eden takes Jonah up to bed while I put away all the perishable food. My parents and Daniel move the party into the living room. Ten minutes later, when the kitchen is reasonably clean, I join them with a bourbon in my hand.

"Do you think you should?" my husband says, looking at the healthy pour in my glass.

"It's a holiday," I say as I take a sip. His eyes lock on mine.

My father leans forward in his chair. "Daniel has told us about some things that have gone on around here."

I look over at my husband and squint. *What did he tell them?*

"Tori, let me ask you something," says my father, "are you deliberately trying to kill yourself? Is it your wish to leave Jonah without his mother?"

What exactly is happening here? We were having a really nice day. This feels like an ambush.

My mother also leans forward and looks at me. "He's right, darling. Remember what the doctors told you? You've got to slow down. You're not like other people. You need to take extra care with yourself."

I place my glass on the end table. *What the hell did Daniel tell them?*

As the poison arrows start sailing in my direction, I try to deflect and diminish all of their complaints. It's no use. Daniel has obviously laid out everything so succinctly that my feeble excuses sound stupid and pathetic.

Daniel faces my parents. "Sam. Marion. You need to know the whole truth, the one that Tori won't tell you."

Shit. What the hell is he about to say? Does he know the truth about Jonah?

Daniel continues as I hold my breath. "Your daughter wheezes every night, all night, even when she's wearing the

CPAP. She's blacked out in public on more than one occasion. She forgets commitments and loses things constantly. And, her shortness of breath is getting worse. I've tried to get through to her, but she won't listen to me."

"She," I interrupt, "is in the same room. I can hear you, Daniel."

My father clears his throat, gives my mother a sideways glance and faces me. "Don't bite Daniel's head off, he's concerned about you. He's right to tell us what's going on."

Pigs must be flying over my house, because that's the first time my father has ever agreed with my husband.

My father stands and paces around the room. "We've got to get control on this situation. Obviously, you're not capable of doing it yourself, Victoria. To be honest, you're acting like a teenager. From now on, I'm getting involved. I will go with you to all of your doctors' appointments."

They all begin to scold me like a five-year-old who didn't put away her toys. From the looks on their faces, it's clear none of this is negotiable. I'm exhausted, so I reluctantly surrender. After agreeing to let them all be more hands-on with regards to my health, everyone smiles and it becomes Thanksgiving again.

CHAPTER FORTY

At eight thirty that same night, I'm still in the living room being grilled when our doorbell rings. I volunteer to answer it to get out of the inquisition I'm in. Looking through the glass window on the sides of my front door, I see a young man holding a large bouquet of flowers.

"Tori Fowler?" he says when I open the door. "Special Thanksgiving delivery. These are for you."

They're beautiful and I wonder who sent them. I give the delivery man a tip and bring the large assortment of orange, yellow and deep red fall flowers into the kitchen and place them in the sink as I untie the wrapping paper. There's a card attached to the outside of the paper. I open it.

> *WHAT A TANGLED WEB WE WEAVE*
> *WHEN FIRST WE PRACTICE TO DECEIVE*

My legs buckle and my fingers grab for the counter so I don't fall. The flowers drop from my hands into the sink. Holding on so I don't end up on the floor, I take a couple of deep breaths.

Someone knows. This isn't a coincidence.

While gripping the marble counter, I look up at the dark kitchen window over the sink and see my reflection. There's a look of terror on my face.

"Tori," shouts Daniel from the living room. "Who was it? We're all waiting for you."

"I'll be right there," I shout, trying to compose myself and bring my soaring heart rate down. "Someone sent us some flowers." I pick the stems out of the sink and examine the card a second time. They're from Brooklyn Blooms, a florist here in Carroll Gardens. I've used them myself. I slip the card into my pocket, planning to call them in the morning when they open. I have to find out who sent these flowers.

There's nothing more I can do now so I carry the arrangement into the living room and place it on a side table. "They're from Anton and Neville wishing us all a happy Thanksgiving. Wasn't that sweet of them?"

"They're lovely," says my mother. "Now, sit down, Tori, we'd like to finish our conversation. We don't want to belabor this, but are we all on the same page?"

"Yes, Mom."

"And, you'll do all the things we outlined in terms of taking better care of yourself?"

I nod. You can't fight city hall and deep down, they're right. I know they're only acting tough because they love me. I do need to be healthy and strong for Jonah.

"I'm all in," I say. "As of now, I'm turning over a bright new shiny leaf."

I see smiles on my parents' and Daniel's faces. My father gets up, crosses the room and gives me a hug. Even now in my forties, whenever my father hugs me, it makes everything better. Mom's not a hugger but given this pivotal moment, she follows his lead and wraps her arms around me, too.

"Remember, I'm your mother and I'll always protect you," she whispers into my ear. "That's what mothers do. We protect our children, no matter what. I promise, everything will be all right."

The next morning at nine a.m., I call Brooklyn Blooms. The woman at the flower shop tells me my order was a phone-in.

"It was super busy yesterday when they called that one in, what with the holiday and all," the store manager explains as she looks through her system for the order. "It looks like the person who placed that order used a Visa gift card for their payment."

"You have no record of who they are? You just send out flowers without knowing who's sending them?"

"Hey, I just work here. If someone pays for a flower delivery, we send 'em. Most people have no problem with receiving flowers."

"What about the message, didn't you find that strange?"

"We get all kinds of messages to go with the flowers, some are triple X-rated. You wouldn't believe the kind of crazy messages people send. I don't have time to pay attention to what the cards say. Do you have any idea how many deliveries we make on Thanksgiving?"

"Please, this is really important."

"I'll admit," says the store manager, "I thought that message was a little odd, but I figured it was some kind of inside joke. I remember one time two years ago—"

"Do you remember if it was a man or woman who placed the order?" I say getting agitated.

"I'm pretty sure it was a woman."

"Did she say anything else? Did you get a phone number?"

"I can't give out that kind of information."

"Please, I have to find out who sent them. I think I'm being stalked."

I must have hit a chord. Thirty seconds later, the store manager gives me the phone number that came in on the caller ID when the order was placed.

As soon as I hang up, I call the number. It's a recording. The number's not in service. Another dead end and I feel like the walls are closing in on me.

CHAPTER FORTY-ONE

For the next couple of months, as promised, I become a model patient. I comply with *most* of my doctor's advice — exercise, eat right (most of the time), not drinking too much (most of the time) and I wear that hideous CPAP religiously. I still occasionally take a sleeping pill. After a good night's sleep, I wake up feeling a hundred percent better so it's worth the teensy little risk.

Christmas came and went and it was extra special because it was Jonah's first. Eden went home for the holidays to see her family for the entire week. Honestly, I missed her while she was gone. Not because I had no one to help me with Jonah. I enjoy taking care of him myself, it wasn't that. I missed her being around. Since she's been with us, we've become friends. We laugh at the same things, tell each other funny stories, share little secrets. Of course, she's also wonderful with my son, which makes me like her even more.

Unfortunately, Daniel still hasn't completely warmed up to her. I'm not sure he ever will. He seems better with her now — I think. We don't talk about it anymore. He and Eden have established an unspoken détente, so I've decided to leave well enough alone.

By the time February 1st rolls around, I've got an increasingly fuller plate. Daniel's finally landed that Off-Off-Broadway role he wanted so badly and I'm thrilled. His play opens in early April and runs for two weeks. Rehearsals started the last week in January and now he's almost never home. He's got something going on every day — a read-through with his director, costume fitting or running lines with another cast member. And of course, he's got his personal trainer sessions. I miss him being around the house, but it won't be forever. He needed a plum part in a play to help his sagging self-esteem. I can't wait to sit in the audience on opening night and cheer him on.

Jonah's first birthday is also coming up and my mother has taken over the planning of the celebration, which suits me. I'm not the party planning type. Organizing the birthday party of the century keeps her busy and at the same time makes her so freakin' happy. From the details she's shared with Eden and me, it's going to be quite an event. She's got a clown and a ukulele player who sings kiddie songs. She's ordered an obscenely expensive cake in the shape of a merry-go-round that spins and plays music. Imagine that. The whole thing is being catered by this amazing farm-to-table eatery in Brooklyn Heights. She's also arranged for two waitresses and a bartender.

My only job was to create the guest list, which had to be submitted to her right after the Christmas holidays. She had invitations custom made and mailed them herself. Basically, all I have to do is show up with my one-year-old.

The big news is that I've heard back from Neville and Anton. They must really love me because they want to give me another chance at the gallery.

"You gave us such a scare when you came back last fall," says Neville on the phone in early February. "Obviously, it was too soon. Between your seizures and your behavior, we didn't know what to think. But honestly, you seem so much better now and God knows we need you. The gallery is literally falling apart without you."

"I doubt it's that bad," I say, secretly hoping it is.

"We want you to come back, but only if you feel you're up to it. That said, we can't have any more incidents."

I assure him that I'm feeling great and my doctors have adjusted my medication and given me the green light to go back to work. We agree I'll return to work on March first for a test run starting with only two afternoons a week. In the meantime, I'm doing a little work for them from home to get back in the swing of things.

Jonah's birthday party is a huge success. Fifteen kids ranging in age from one to four along with fifteen sets of parents are invited. All in, we're hosting forty-five people. Jonah got his first taste of cake and not surprisingly, loved it. Who doesn't like cake?

My mother works the room like a dinner club comedian, joking and gushing with pride over her grandson. In return, she receives a litany of compliments about the wondrous birthday event she's organized.

Eden is an incredible help with all the kids at the party and takes videos of everything. I'm quite touched by the present she made for Jonah. She knitted him a navy-blue sweater and hat. They're adorable and must have taken her many hours to complete. She's also given us a charcoal sketch of him that she drew herself. She's really quite talented. I'm going to have it framed.

It's been three months now since I last heard from my stalker. While I know it's magical thinking on my part, I'm pretending it's all over. I try to convince myself that maybe the cryptic messages had nothing to do with Jonah. Maybe it was someone I crossed swords with at the gallery. Artists can be very temperamental and bitchy. Sometimes they don't like it when I have to be direct and tell them bad news.

It's nearly ten o'clock in the morning. I'm sitting at my desk in the family room poring over the plans for a new artist installation opening at the gallery in May. Daniel's at the gym and Eden's upstairs getting Jonah dressed so I can take him to a Mommy and Me tumbling class at eleven thirty.

The doorbell rings. Stiff after sitting still for so long, I groan as I stand and walk to the door. When I open it, there's no one there. A thin package addressed to me sits on the top step.

I look down at the return address as I walk back to the kitchen. It's unfamiliar to me, just a PO box number. I nonchalantly open the packet and a card spills out onto the floor. As I bend over to pick it up, I freeze. It's a hundred-dollar gift certificate for Body Therapy by Chloe in the Hamptons. I look inside the packet. There's nothing else in there and nothing written on the gift certificate. *What the hell does this mean?*

Is my stalker back or is this much more innocent? Maybe Chloe pulled my address from my Visa to do a promotional mailing? Does Visa give out that kind of information? Everyone knows that companies buy and sell personal data all the time. It's possible that's where this came from . . . or not.

My heart is racing again, and I take several deep measured breaths to slow it down like the doctors have shown me. It doesn't work. I feel a full blown panic attack coming on as Eden comes down the stairs with Jonah dressed for our outing.

"Are you all right?" she says looking at my face. "You're completely white."

I need to find out who sent that gift certificate.

"I don't feel very well," I say. "I think I should . . ."

"Do you want me to call someone?"

"No. That's not necessary. I just need to lie down, that's all. I've been spending too much time going over plans for the gallery, I guess. Would you take Jonah to his tumbling class today?"

"Of course. I'd love to."

Half an hour later, Eden and Jonah head out the door, giving me a couple of hours to myself. I review all the interactions I've had with my stalker, hoping to discover some pattern or commonality.

First there was the letter with a Manhattan postmark and the biblical quote: 'The truth will set you free.' The second point of contact was the text message and then the third was the note on the Thanksgiving flowers that said: 'What a tangled web we weave when first we practice to deceive.' I google both quotes to see if there's any connection. I'm desperate.

After several searches, I get nothing. The tangled web quote was written by Sir Walter Scott and published in 1808 in Scotland. It means when you tell lies or act dishonestly, you create problems and complications which you can't control. *Yeah, well, it's a little too late for that.*

I move on to the Bible quote: 'The truth will set you free.' I google the hell out of this one but see no connection between the two messages. All I know is, someone is calling me out as a liar. But who?

With nowhere else to go, I pick up my phone to call Body Therapy by Chloe in the Hamptons but stop before the call connects. If Chloe's behind all the craziness, I'll be tipping my hand. She was the only person Sasha came in contact with, at least that's what Sasha told me. But why would Chloe do all this? She barely knew Sasha, or at least that's what I've been led to believe. If Chloe thought I did something wrong, like stealing a baby, why didn't she go to the police? Why send all the mysterious and obtuse messages? What's her endgame?

I ponder this for several minutes and then it hits me — money. It's no secret my father's a very successful man. It's also no secret that I'm the apple of his eye. It doesn't take a genius to figure out my father would do anything to protect me, including paying off a blackmailer. Money's the only thing that makes sense.

I look at the clock in the kitchen. I've still got a few minutes before Eden and Jonah return. I decide to take a chance and call Chloe. The way I figure it, if she knows something, she knows. What do they say, better the devil you know? I want to know who my devil is.

I punch the number of the massage salon into my phone. It rings five times. A woman answers and I ask to speak to Chloe.

The other end of the phone goes silent.

"Hello," I say again. "May I speak with Chloe, please?"

"Are you a client of hers?"

"Yes, I was in to see her last summer."

"I guess you didn't hear. Chloe's no longer with us."

I didn't expect that answer. She must have sold her business. "That's too bad. I really liked her. She did wonders for my back. Do you know where she went? Maybe you have a phone number for her?"

"I'm sorry. I guess I wasn't clear. Chloe died two months ago."

My mind tries to wrap itself around that tidbit of information. I didn't expect that at all. First Sasha and now Chloe. Is this some kind of conspiracy playing out?

"Oh, my God, I'm so sorry to hear that. She was lovely. She didn't drown, did she?"

There's another moment of silence before she answers.

"No. Why would you say that? Chloe was in the city seeing a Broadway play and was hit by a bike messenger. She never regained consciousness."

I hang up the phone in a puddle of tears and lie down on the couch in the family room. Some tears are shed for Chloe, who actually seemed like a nice person. The rest are for me and my son because now I have nowhere to go and no idea who's sending the nefarious messages. Chloe was my last link to Sasha.

I feel trapped. Someone has me in their crosshairs, and there's no one I can tell and no one who can help me. If I call the cops and tell the truth, they'll take Jonah away for sure. If I don't call the cops, some unknown entity is threatening to expose me. If that happens, I'll lose my son.

When Eden comes home with Jonah, she finds me curled up into a ball on the couch. I don't blame her for calling Daniel. I was a mess and wouldn't tell her why. Seeing Jonah's innocent face only made me cry harder.

CHAPTER FORTY-TWO

I was supposed to return to work at the beginning of the month, but I just couldn't do it. Emotionally, I'm a basket case. After hitting a dead end when I learned about Chloe's death, I start to unravel and end up in bed for a week. Thankfully, Neville and Anton didn't argue when I asked them for more time. Right now, I don't want to talk to anyone and only rally occasionally to hold Jonah. On some level, I'm aware how my behavior looks, but I don't care. Eden has been bringing me food and tea throughout each day. She's also been doing all the heavy lifting in taking care of Jonah and managing the house.

Daniel comes to talk to me several times a day. His face wears a worried look every time he enters the room. Thankfully, he's held off calling my parents, partly because I've begged him not to and partly because he's afraid I'll spin out. I don't want my parents to see me like this. They'll be so worried and disappointed in me.

I guess Daniel's hoping I'll eventually snap out of my funk on my own. He repeatedly asks me what's wrong. I just shake my head and start to cry. Obviously, I can't tell him. I can't tell anyone and it's eating me up from the inside.

Lately, my heart's been beating in all kinds of irregular ways. I feel it from time to time but try to ignore it. The only thing that brings happiness is when Jonah comes in to cuddle or when I watch him playing on the baby monitor app on my phone.

There's a knock on my bedroom door. My eyes are closed, but I recognize the crisp sound of my husband's footsteps.

"Tori, I want to talk to you," he says softly as he sits on the edge of our bed on my seventh day of solitary confinement. "How can I help you, if I don't know what's wrong? I've been lying to your parents all week. I took Jonah over to see them yesterday. I had to make up excuses about your absence saying you were doing work for the gallery. Your father didn't buy it, that was pretty clear."

"He'll get over it," I mumble.

Daniel clears his throat. "Maybe, but I won't. I think you should see a therapist. This has gone on for too long. I don't know why you can't tell me what's bothering you. I'm your husband."

I open my eyes and look up at his face filled with anguish. I want to tell him, really I do, but I can't. I can never tell.

"Give me another day to get myself together," I say softly, closing my eyes again. "I'll be fine, I promise."

"I'm afraid you don't have another day. Like I said, your father didn't believe my excuses. He just called. He's on his way over."

I groan and roll over on my stomach.

"If you don't want him to see you like this you'd better get dressed. He'll be here in half an hour," says Daniel before he leaves the room.

I want to get up. I really do, but my body feels so heavy. I reach for my phone and check the baby monitor again. I've got a camera in every room of the house except the bathrooms. I try a few different locations until I see the image of Eden and Jonah playing with some toy cars on the floor in the playroom. Jonah is jabbering but not with words I understand. I can't wait for the day when he calls me 'mommy.'

From upstairs in my room, I hear the doorbell ring. It's followed by my father's bellowing voice echoing off the walls as he enters the foyer of the house.

"Tori," he shouts as he climbs the stairs. Within seconds he knocks on my door and peeks his head into my room.

"What's going on? Why are you still in bed? It's nearly one o'clock in the afternoon."

"I think I have a bug, but I'm feeling better. Probably need another day of rest."

My father eyeballs me. It's the same way he used to look at me when I was a kid and he didn't think I was telling the truth. I turn away because I'm afraid he'll know I'm lying.

"Look at me, Tori," he says loudly, the timber of his voice filling the room. "Enough is enough. We've talked about this before. You must follow your prescribed regimen to the letter. Answer me truthfully, have you been taking your medication?"

"Yes."

"Have you been avoiding certain foods as well as alcohol?"

"Yes, Dad."

"Have you been wearing your CPAP every night?"

"Yes."

"Then, what's the problem? Daniel tells me that nanny of yours has been taking care of Jonah full time this past week. Your mother is frantic. You need to get up now and take care of your son."

I'm so tired of lying. I haven't slept all week and I feel like shit. My father's pleading eyes filled with love give me the strength to sit up and swing my legs off the bed.

"I'll take a shower now. I feel a little better. I'm sorry to have worried you and Mom."

My father nods and leaves the room saying something about making an appointment for me with *his* cardiologist.

I get into the shower and let the hot water run over my head. I'm not sure how long I stand there, but since my fingers and toes look like prunes, I must have been in there for a while. The water is therapeutic and as I step out of the tub, things seem clearer.

I can't fight an enemy when I don't know who they are or what they want. My only choice is to ride this out and deal with it as it happens. I dry myself off and feel infinitely better having some sort of plan. It's not perfect, but it *is* a plan. I need to get back to my life and my family.

I get dressed, comb my wet hair into a ponytail and join my father, husband and Eden in the kitchen. She's feeding Jonah a snack in his high chair. He squeals and extends his arms towards me when I enter the room. His unconditional love lifts me and I go to pick him up.

"Wait," says Eden wearing her usual sweatpants ensemble. "He's covered with mashed pears. Let me clean him up or you'll get it all over your clothes."

"I don't care," I say, flashing my first smile in a week. I lift my little boy into my arms, and hug and kiss him several times. Just the body contact with Jonah sends my endorphins flying.

"I'm glad to see you're up," says my father, with a look of satisfaction and relief. "I called the cardiologist. You've got an appointment with him, four weeks from today. It was the earliest I could get you in because he's on vacation. He's the best damn heart doctor in New York."

Jonah's squirming to get out of my arms and onto the floor. I place him down and as I let go he takes off. It wasn't long ago that we all marveled at his first few clumsy steps. Now, he literally runs around the house.

"I almost forgot," says my father as he fishes something out of his pocket and hands me a child's red hat. "My assistant knitted this for Jonah. It's starting to get cold out. Don't want my grandson getting a chill. He'll look like a million bucks in it."

Satisfied they have both fixed my problem, Daniel walks my father out on his way to his rehearsal. When the front door closes, I sit cross-legged on the floor in the living room with Jonah and Eden. We're building castles with blocks. After a few minutes, I notice Jonah goes to her much more often than to me. He presents her with each block from his basket and she adds it to the structure. He only brings them to me when Eden encourages him to do so.

A pang of jealousy floods through me as Jonah hands her one of his stuffed bears and gives her a kiss. *Does he like being with Eden more than me?* I shake my head. *Stop it. Of course he goes to her. I've been an absentee mother for a week.*

"Tori, what are you doing?" screams Eden, holding Jonah on her lap and staring at my hands.

I look down. Blood is trickling from my left forearm where I've deeply dug my nails into my skin. I pull my arms apart and wipe off the blood. Flustered, I make up a dumb excuse.

"Oh my God. I was thinking about a problem at the gallery and didn't realize I was pressing on my arm so hard. I guess I need to trim my nails."

Eden's eyes are round and I know what's going through her mind. She's thinking I'm unstable. If she only knew the real reason I'm so on edge, she'd really think I'm nuts.

"Please don't say anything to Daniel about this scratch," I say. "He'll read more into it, and I don't want to worry him."

She nods tentatively and takes Jonah upstairs to change him before they go out for a walk. I rub my face with my hands. *What's happening to me? I've turned into this paranoid person, someone I don't know or like.*

Half an hour after Eden and Jonah leave, I'm in the kitchen wiping down Jonah's highchair when I hear a ping on my phone. There's another text message from a number I don't know.

I open it. There's no message, only a video. I click on it. It shows Eden pushing Jonah in a baby swing at our local park. The video is from today because Jonah's wearing the new red hat my father gave him when he came by earlier.

Someone is watching my son at the park right now.

CHAPTER FORTY-THREE

I try calling Eden, but there's no answer. I text and call a second and third time. It's cold outside, but there's no time for a coat. I pull on my sneakers and run out my front door as fast as I can towards the park. All I know is, whoever's been contacting me is watching my son at this very moment and wants me to know. My maternal instinct kicks into overdrive and I can't physically feel my feet moving, but they are.

The park is four blocks away. I race down the sidewalk imagining the worst. *Someone is going to hurt my son and possibly Eden. Someone's trying to take him away from me.* The terrifying thoughts propel me and I pick up more speed, not remotely feeling the cold wind slam into my thinly clad body.

I run as fast as I can towards the corner and make a left. Then, another block and I make a right. As I turn the next corner, I plow straight into Eden pushing Jonah in his stroller. I stop to bend over and catch my breath.

"Are you all right?" I gasp, feeling the cold air claw at my lungs as I check my son strapped into his stroller. "Is Jonah okay? Did anyone bother you?"

I quickly assess both of them. Jonah's tucked into his stroller nice and warm, a blue plaid blanket covering him.

Eden looks normal with the exception of the confused expression on her face as she stares at me.

"Jonah's fine," says Eden, peering at me now. "Where's your coat? It's freezing out."

I can't tell her the truth. But clearly, I've got to tell her something or this is all going to blow up on me. I show her the video on my phone.

"I got it less than ten minutes ago. It came from a number I don't know. I was scared," I say, still out of breath. "I didn't know what it meant. I tried to call you. Why didn't you pick up? You have to pick up when I call."

"I'm so sorry. My phone was in my bag and there was some noisy construction work going on near the park. That's why we came back so soon. I didn't hear it ring."

"You've got to keep it on loud. I need to be able to reach you at all times. Did you see anyone near you taking pictures?" Eden shakes her head. "Someone took this video. Think, Eden. Who else was in the park?"

Her forehead wrinkles. "There weren't too many people there today probably because it's cold out. It was mainly a few regular nannies that I always see there."

We start to walk back to my house and I feel my heart slowing down from its frenzied beat minutes earlier. I'm sweating and the cold wind against my wet body makes me shiver. "What about any men? Did you notice any strange men lurking around?"

I push the stroller as I interrogate her.

"I didn't see any men alone. There were one or two men playing with their kids but nobody alone."

We arrive at my house and I help Eden get the stroller inside on the lower level. After we shut the door, something occurs to me.

"You mentioned construction work before. How far away was it? Could someone have taken the video I showed you from where the work was being done?"

Eden purses her lips. "I guess so, there were a couple of guys using jackhammers breaking up some pavement on one side of the park. I don't think they could hold a phone and take pictures while they were using that kind of equipment. Besides, how would they get your phone number?"

I can't tell her how, so I brush it off. "I don't know, but there are ways to get phone numbers."

I call my husband to tell him what happened. When it goes to voicemail, I get a little hysterical. Then, I remember he told me there's a strict policy at all rehearsals for phones to be turned off. With nothing left to do, I leave him a message.

"Daniel, somebody took a video of Jonah and Eden at the park today and sent it to me anonymously," I say. I fill in more details and tell him to call me as soon as possible.

As I boil some water for tea my heart is still beating faster than it should. Of course it is. Someone is stalking me and my son.

Eden goes to her room and I sip my tea and play with Jonah in the playroom. Focusing on him helps, but I keep drifting back to that video. I wish Daniel would come home and put his arms around me. All I can think is that things are escalating and I've still got no way out.

Daniel finally walks through the door at five carrying a pizza, a smile on his face. When I see him smiling, after what I've been through, I get angry. He's been out at rehearsal having a grand old time unburdened by anything. Meanwhile, I've been shouldering everything.

Stop it, Tori. He doesn't know. Give it a rest.

Before he hangs up his coat, I'm on him. "Something really scary happened today. Did you listen to your voicemail?"

He turns around, one eyebrow raised. "What do you mean?"

I explain what happened and show him the video of our son and Eden in the park. He starts to laugh.

"This isn't funny," I screech, my hysteria returning. "Some crazy person was photographing our son today. He has my number." My husband laughs even harder and I become infuriated. *Does he not get it?* I'm starting to lose it when Daniel places his hands on my shoulders. The simple touch of his skin against mine has an instantaneous calming effect. I feel myself relax, but only a little.

"Honey, I'm so sorry. I didn't intend to upset you. We're using these cheap throwaway phones in the play for a scene. I was walking past the park on my way to the gym and I saw Eden with Jonah on the swings. My iPhone's battery was dead so I used the phone from the play to take a video and sent it to you."

"What? *You* sent it?"

"I'm sorry. I totally forgot you wouldn't recognize the number or who it was from," he says, putting his arms around me. "I see now why you were so alarmed. It was totally my fault. I thought you'd get a kick out of seeing the video of Jonah on the swings."

I let out a few big breaths and slowly feel myself calm down. For the past couple of hours, I was on the brink. Now, it all turns out to be a stupid mistake.

"Don't do that again," I snap. "You scared me half to death and then I scared the hell out of Eden. I'd better go upstairs and apologize to her. She must think I'm insane."

"An apology is a good idea if we don't want to lose her."

"You're an Eden fan now?"

"I wouldn't say fan, but she's grown on me. And, as you always say, she's really good with the baby."

"How's rehearsal going?" I say, trying to change the subject as I walk towards the stairs. "Only two weeks until opening night. It's a shame that my parents will be out of town that week at a wedding in California. They won't be able to make it."

"I knew that. Your mother mentioned the wedding months ago. As long as you're there, that's all that matters."

"You couldn't keep me away," I say as I start up the stairs.

I knock on Eden's door and beg for forgiveness. She accepts my apology and even lets me off the hook for freaking out on her.

"I would have reacted the same way if I'd received a video like that," she says.

The next day, things go back to normal. Still, with all the stress I've been under, I'm unable to sleep more than an hour or two each night. After being mostly awake for three consecutive nights and unable to function in the morning, I dig out my sleeping pills. *Just two or three until things calm down. I'll use my CPAP. Everything will be fine.*

CHAPTER FORTY-FOUR

Two weeks fly by and it's April already. Thankfully, there have been no new incidents or scary communications from my stalker. Tonight is opening night for Daniel's Off-Off-Broadway play. It's a small house, which means less than ninety seats. According to Daniel, the playwright and director are both 'up and coming.' He's convinced his two-week-long run in the drama will lead to bigger and better roles. I've got my fingers crossed and am sorry my parents will miss his big night and see my husband shine. He's such a good actor.

It's three thirty p.m., and I'm standing in my walk-in closet trying to decide what to wear to the opening when Daniel comes into the bedroom. He's holding up a blue pinstripe suit and I notice his face looks weird.

"You were supposed to get my costume dry-cleaned?" he says with an accusatory stare.

"What?"

His eyebrows knit together and he speaks in a short staccato. "I handed this suit to you last week. I asked you to get it dry-cleaned before opening night. You said you would."

Feeling like a caged rat, I have absolutely no recollection of him asking me to do that. I stare at him, trying to recall the conversation. I've been taking sleeping pills over the past few weeks. Sometimes, I'm still groggy the next day and forget little things. My eyes lock in on his angry face. Before I can stop myself, the words tumble out, "Are you sure you asked me to—"

"Seriously? You're kidding me, right?" he says, his voice getting more pissed off with each word. "I have to be at the theatre in ninety minutes with this suit. It's got a big fucking stain down the front of it. How am I supposed to go onstage in this?"

Oh, my God. How could I have let him down on his big night? "Maybe you could use one of your own suits for the play," I say. "You have a nice blue one."

My comment only enrages him more and he starts shouting, "Every guy in the show is supposed to wear the exact same blue pinstriped suit. It's a plot device, the sameness of all the men. I can't just swap it out for any old suit from my closet. You've totally screwed me this time."

"Maybe I can get the stain off," I say meekly.

He looks at the stain and laughs, and not in good way. "I already tried," he says. "I see what's happening here. Your career with the gallery has gone way off track, so now you're trying to sabotage mine."

Part of me thinks if the suit was so damn important, he should have taken his precious costume to the dry-cleaner himself. It's not like he has a real job. But, given the out-of-control hostile look on his face, I don't point that out. Instead, I reach for the suit in his hand.

"Give it to me. Maybe I can get the stain off with some soap and water."

He pulls it away from me. "And then what? I'm supposed to go onstage with a big wet stain on the front of my jacket?" he says with a snarl. "You know what? Don't come tonight. I don't want you there. You obviously don't take my career seriously. I guess that's what happens when you're born with a silver spoon stuck in your mouth. Careers don't matter that much, when you have all the money in the world handed to you."

"If you would just let me try to get the stain out," I say reaching for the suit a second time, "I'll dry it with my hairdryer."

I thought that was pretty good suggestion. But as I watch him shake his head with exasperation and contempt, it's clear he doesn't agree.

"Don't come to the theatre tonight. I mean it. I don't want you there," he says as he stomps out of the room.

Five minutes later, I'm still standing in the doorway of my closet trying to figure out what had just happened. Did I really forget to have Daniel's suit cleaned for one of the most important nights in his professional life? Maybe the sleeping pills I've been taking have affected me more than I thought? I've forgotten a few other things, too. Am I a horrible, self-absorbed person? It's because I've had a lot on my mind.

I tally up all the mistakes I've made over the past few weeks and it's not a pretty picture. Last week, I forgot I'd given Eden an afternoon off. It was right after lunch. I was reading Jonah a book in the living room when she came waltzing down the stairs in one of my old outfits. Her coat was draped over her arm.

"I'll be back at six in time to give Jonah a bath and put him to bed," she said, standing in the doorway putting her coat on.

"What do you mean?" I said. "Where are you going?"

A puzzled look crossed her face. "The other day I asked you if I could take the afternoon off to spend some time with my boyfriend. You said it was fine. We were in the kitchen, don't you remember?"

I totally didn't. I wanted to say, "No, I don't remember saying that. You can't go because I have a hair appointment in forty-five minutes." But the part of me that was screwing up lately didn't want to let on that I'd forgotten something else.

So, I played along, pretending I did remember our conversation but had just momentarily forgotten. The minute Eden left the house, I was on the phone to my hairdresser. After ten minutes of groveling, she gave me another appointment.

What the hell is wrong with me? First I forgot about Eden, and now Daniel's suit. There were a bunch of other things I forgot, too. But forgetting Daniel's suit was pretty unforgivable. This play is all he's talked about for months. How could I do that to him?

Since I was no longer welcome at my husband's big opening night in New York, I put the dress in my hand back in my closet. When I step out, I hear Daniel's muffled voice downstairs. I walk over to the railing and look down the staircase. Eden is standing by the front door holding Jonah while Daniel gathers his things to bring to the theatre. He's got a garment bag and several tote bags filled with who knows what.

"Wish me luck," he says to Eden as he walks across the foyer and kisses Jonah on the head.

"Break a leg," says Eden. "I'm sure you'll be great."

"Let's hope so," says my husband as he walks out the door.

I step back from the banister, tears in my eyes. This was supposed to be an amazing night for both of us. I've had this date circled on my calendar for months. Feeling very sorry for myself, I try to think of ways I can make it up to him.

By five thirty, I've finished feeding Jonah his dinner when it hits me. I am going to Daniel's play tonight. I've got a ticket and I'm not missing my husband's opening night in New York because he had a hissy fit. I'll sit in the back and keep a low profile. He won't even know I'm there. Besides, he won't stay mad at me for long. He never does. By the time the show's over, he'll be over it. If I don't go, I'll never get this night back.

I take Jonah upstairs and change my clothes, putting on the black dress I had selected earlier. With my son in my arms, I find Eden in the laundry room folding clothes. Since I'm fairly certain she heard the fight between Daniel and me, I keep my plan to myself in case something goes wrong.

"I'm going out for dinner with a friend in Lower Manhattan," I say. "We may go to a movie after. I should be home by eleven." She nods but says nothing. She definitely heard the argument and probably wants to stay out of it. Smart girl.

It's nearly seven when Eden, balancing Jonah on her hip, holds open the front door for me. I kiss my son good night and walk out of my house to the waiting Uber.

As I get into the car I have mixed feelings. I'm excited to see Daniel in the play. But I'm also nervous he'll still be angry that I came when he specifically told me not to. I've done stupid things before. Why stop now?

CHAPTER FORTY-FIVE

On the way into Manhattan, we hit a ton of traffic. At seven forty-five my car pulls up in front of The Lobby, an experimental theatre in the West Village. I present my ticket. There's no assigned seating and I head towards the back row.

My plan is to sit quietly and leave right after the play is over. In a day or so, when Daniel cools off, I'll tell him that I was actually there on opening night to see his brilliant performance. I'll tell him how proud I was and things will go back to normal.

The attendant takes my ticket and hands me a paper program. I find a seat in the back on the end of a row for a quick getaway and settle in. While I wait for *Ten Men in Blue* to start, I thumb through the program reading all the biographies. There's one about the director, the playwright, the costume and lighting designers. Next is the cast, in order of appearance. For a small show, there are over twenty people in the play.

I read one at a time savoring each actor's resume waiting until I come upon Daniel's. I'm three quarters of the way down the list but haven't come to his yet. I read faster to get through them and finally I get to the end. Daniel's name isn't there.

As the lights start to dim, I flip through the pages, scanning the words for his name. It's getting dark in the theatre. I use the light on my phone and look through the pages again, when an usher comes by and asks me to turn off my light. I comply.

Why isn't his name there? Did I miss it? Maybe it's a printing error. Daniel must be so upset. His first big New York show and they left his name out. Maybe they can get new ones printed for tomorrow night. I won't say anything to him about it. He must be devastated.

The curtain opens and I sit back in my chair to watch the two-act play. It's an odd little drama that I'm not sure I completely understand. I've seen Off-Off-Broadway before. Some of it's good and some, not so much. This play unfortunately falls into the latter category, but I won't tell Daniel that. He's worked too hard. The only words he'll hear out of me will be 'brilliant,' 'amazing' and 'spectacular'.

The lights come up at the end of Act One and I've yet to see my husband on stage. There are many men in blue pinstripe suits but not him. Since there are still more characters listed in the program that I've not seen yet, I assume he's only in Act Two.

During a brief intermission, I treat myself to a glass of white wine before taking my seat. Act Two commences and the plot gets weirder by the minute. I'm on the edge of my seat waiting for Daniel to walk onto the stage. Then, the play ends and the actors take their curtain call. While they're bowing, I'm flipping out. The cast takes a second curtain call to thunderous applause, but my husband's not up on the stage. He didn't appear in this play at any time.

Did something happen to him? Maybe he was in an accident on the way to the theater? Or was he so mad at me that he skipped out on his own play? No, he wouldn't do that. He's a professional. This was his big break. He told me there would be talent scouts here tonight. He wouldn't miss out on that. Would he?

As the crowd gets up from their seats, I ask one of the house ushers if they know Daniel and where he might be. The people working there don't have any information about the cast and suggest I speak with the director. They tell me he'll be out to greet people in a few minutes.

I wait and soon a small thin man in a black T-shirt with two sleeves of tattoos struts into the room. Several other people race over to him and tell him how much they enjoyed the show. Since I hadn't seen this man on the stage, I assume he's the director.

Waiting off to the side until the adoring crowd dissipates, I walk over to him.

"Excuse me," I say, putting out my hand to shake his. "The play was amazing. Really well done. I'm Tori Fowler. Daniel Fowler is my husband."

He looks at me with a blank expression.

"Daniel Fowler," I say, already starting to feel sick. "He's a member of your cast but I didn't see him performing tonight. Did something happen to him before the show started?"

The director squints at me and takes a step backwards. "I'm not sure I know what you're talking about. There's no one named Daniel in the cast."

"Wait," I say, rummaging through my bag for a picture of him thinking maybe Daniel uses a different professional name. I pull out a wallet-sized headshot of Daniel and hand it to the director. "That's him. That's my husband, Daniel."

The man shakes his head again as he hands the picture back. "I'm sorry, I don't know him," he says as he tries to disengage from me. As he starts to flee, he suddenly turns back. "Wait a minute, let me see that picture again."

I pass it back. He studies it and nods his head. "I remember him now. Daniel Fowler, yes, Daniel. He auditioned for the play several months ago, but we didn't cast him. Too handsome for the part. Pretty good actor, though."

Mortified, I slither out of the theatre barely able to hold up my head. A million questions and fears swirl around me as I order a car. I can't make any sense of it.

I'm numb when the car arrives and still trying to piece it all together. My husband went to rehearsals every day for months but was never cast in the play. He talked endlessly about the impact this production would have on his career, but he never got the part. Daniel was lying to me the whole time. But why?

I crack open the window of the car to let in some fresh air and try to make some order out of what I've just discovered. Let me get this straight. Daniel was never in the play, never went to rehearsal on all those days he went out. I review all the many conversations we had about the show. That's when it occurs to me he may have deliberately picked the fight with me today. He had to prevent me from going to the theatre and finding out his secret.

The fight was planned so I wouldn't learn the truth. Which also means he never asked me to have his suit cleaned. He made that up so I wouldn't know about his lie. But why would he lie about this? And if he did, what else has he lied about?

The driver is heading southeast across Manhattan towards my house in Brooklyn. I'm in the back seat shaking, feeling a mix of fear, anger, confusion and utter disappointment. I wonder, will Daniel be at home when I get there? I don't want to see him. I won't know what to say to him and I definitely don't want to hear any more of his lies, not tonight.

All I want to do right now is run away. If it weren't for Jonah, I'd tell the driver to keep going until we got to California. All I know is I don't want to go home. I'm not ready to talk to Daniel. As we near my street, I tell the driver to drop me at a bar a few blocks from my house. I need a drink and I need to think.

At one a.m., the bartender announces, "Last call," so I order one more dirty martini. It's my third . . . or fourth. I lost count. All I do know is I'm numb and that's what I was aiming for.

At one thirty, I finish my third or fourth martini and slide off the bar stool and out the door. Considering all I've had to drink, I'm amazingly steady on my feet, or at least I think so. I walk the two blocks to my house without incident.

When I get inside and up to my room. Daniel is sitting on the bed.

"Where have you been? I almost called the police," he says through gritted teeth.

I stare at him in my boozy haze before I speak. "I went to the theatre. You weren't in that play. I talked to the director," I slur as I sit on my side of the bed. "You lied to me about everything. What the fuck is going on?"

The next twenty minutes are fuzzy, but essentially Daniel confesses that he lied because he was so embarrassed he didn't get the part. He says something about wanting me to think he was making progress on his career.

"Then what was your plan going to be, Daniel? How were you going to explain to me why you weren't in the play? Where the hell did you go every day?"

He looks at me sheepishly, which usually softens my heart but doesn't this time. "I went lots of places. I'd go to the gym, the library or take a walk in the park. Remember when I saw Eden and Jonah in the park and took a video of them?"

I nod, my eyes half open. "Let me get this straight. You did all this so I wouldn't know you *didn't* get a part in a fucking play?"

Tears well up in his eyes. "I didn't want you to stop loving me. I wanted to be successful so you could be proud of me."

I'm not sure if it's the booze or the tears in his eyes but the next thing you know, I'm fucking comforting him. I'm pathetic. Before I know it, my arms are around him and I'm telling him everything is going to be okay.

"Promise me, no more lies," I say, my head bobbing slightly.

Once we sort ourselves out, I peel off my black dress leaving it on the floor beneath my feet and go into the bathroom. I brush my teeth and take my nightly sleeping pill, but only just one tonight.

I go back into the room and Daniel's snoring softly. How is he able to sleep so easily after perpetrating such a fraud? I drag myself over to my side of the bed. There's a glass of ice water on a coaster and a single sleeping pill next to it.

As I reach for the glass and pill, I stop. Did I already take a pill? I can't remember, so I pop it in my mouth.

My CPAP is also on the nightstand. With all I've had to drink tonight, I definitely need to put that thing on whether I like it or not. I place my phone next to me and loop the device over my head and turn it on.

Climbing into bed next to my husband, I review all that happened over the past twenty-four hours. It's hard to keep my thoughts straight. I'm groggy from all the martinis, but at least I know now things are right again between Daniel and me. I didn't realize how fragile he was. He's a big strapping man, physically strong and handsome, but inside he's a scared little boy.

As I drift off to sleep, the gentle hum of my CPAP churns and I gratefully give in to my overwhelming exhaustion.

CHAPTER FORTY-SIX

THE OTHER WOMAN

It was no accident when we met two years ago. Let's just say I put my thumb on the scale to make it happen. I knew he'd be there because I arranged it. Most people make things more complicated than they need to be. I like to cut through the bullshit and get things done. Give me any task and I'll get it accomplished so fast it will make your head spin.

It was important that he and I meet in a completely organic way, one that wouldn't raise his suspicion. It had to be a very normal, everyday moment. I looked in the theater trades and found there was audition for a play that he'd be perfect for, a real juicy role. It didn't take much to appeal to his ego and convince him to go. It did, however, require a ruse.

I looked up his agent and called him, pretending to be his agent's new assistant. I figured if the request came from the agency, he'd definitely show up at the audition, no questions asked. Actors are easy to manipulate because they need so much constant validation.

"This is Jason Fried's assistant," I said in my most professional voice. "Jason would like you to go to an open call tomorrow. There's a new play going into production at the

Imperial Theater. Jason thinks you'd be great for the part of the son and . . ."

The next day, I'm wearing an extremely short, skin-tight, red dress that shows every one of my hard-earned curves. I sit in a large rehearsal room on the West Side of Manhattan leaning back against the wall. I've got a script in my hand and am pretending to go over my lines for my audition. He sits several chairs away looking over his dialogue.

"You auditioning for the part of the son?" I say in a collegial sort of way.

"That's what they tell me," he says, pretending nonchalance while glancing down at his own script. "I'll bet you're going for the part of the sister."

"Oh, yeah. Why is that?" I say, my blue eyes looking up into his.

He smiles. "Because the sister is supposed to be hot and that's exactly what you are."

I smile back and lower my eyelids. It is almost too easy. We chat amiably for thirty minutes, killing time by trading bad audition war stories. Of course, all of mine are made up, but he doesn't notice. While we talk, he grows on me. He's handsome but he's also charming and surprises me when he makes me laugh. When I planned this, I didn't anticipate liking him. As our conversation continues, I realize that I'm flirting with him — for real.

When they call his name, I wish him luck and part of me means it.

"Good luck to you, too," he says as he heads for the audition room door. Halfway across he spins around. "Grab a coffee after?"

Another smile spreads from one side of my face to the other and I nod. "Sounds good, break a leg," I shout as he walks through the open door and disappears.

I wait for nearly ninety minutes until he comes back into the large hall. The second he enters, his eyes scan the perimeter looking for me. That one gesture gives me the confidence that I've hooked him and my plan is going to work.

I wave to him. "How did it go?"

He smiles and shrugs. "How do any of them go? You know how it is. Seems great while you're in there, you're killing it, but then someone else gets the part."

"Tell me about it. It can be so demoralizing. These casting directors have your whole life in their hands. I must be nuts for pursuing acting. If only I'd been born rich, then I could just be happy."

"Not necessarily. I know plenty of rich people who aren't that happy."

We head out of the hall for a coffee. When we get outside, I suggest we go for a glass of wine instead. He looks at his watch, nods and ten minutes later we're sitting at a bar on Ninth Avenue drinking Negronis.

By the end of the night, much to my chagrin, I'm actually falling for him. That isn't part of my plan. Yet, there's something about him that's so intoxicating. He's supposed to be my pawn, not my partner. This is my first complication.

In person, he's even better looking than he is in pictures. Nothing prepared me for the kick in the gut I got when I first laid eyes on him. I almost scrapped the whole thing. But my plan's been too long in the making, and I have way too much invested.

Whether I like it or not, I can't help myself. Eventually, when I think he can handle it, I'll let him in on what I'm doing. I won't tell him everything up front, that would be too much. I'll dole it out a little bit at a time so he can digest each bitter morsel. He won't fully understand the scope of it at first.

I'll be asking a lot of him. Given that, I can't dump it all on him the first day. He'll surely run, despite my slinky dress and mouth that's open and willing. I start slow with a little tease, a suggestion, a what if — to gauge his reaction.

At first he thinks I'm playing a silly game between lovers. We're both laughing. Nothing is real, we're fooling around. I keep it going and we both giggle, adding crazy dimensions like actors doing improv.

Despite the playfulness of the conversation, I've got a long way to go with him. We're not on the same page yet, but we will be. He talks about theater, the craft of acting and the Tony Awards while I'm masterminding a major coup. It would have been so much easier if I hadn't fallen for him. Now, I have to take it slow or I'll scare him away. I need him to make all this happen.

The truth is, without Daniel, my plan won't work. I've got to snare the fish so he can't get off the hook. That way, he'll do whatever I ask him. And, it will be a lot.

That first day, we end up standing on the corner of Eight Avenue and 55th Street in each other's arms. He kisses me and we're both oblivious to the hundreds of people passing by us. Now I have a dilemma. Having a genuine romantic entanglement with Daniel versus the fake one I had originally planned on could blow everything up. I'm playing with fire now.

He kisses me again and my legs go weak. My usual steely mind turns to mush. Seconds later, I find myself making modifications to my plan to accommodate my feelings for him. Sometimes, you find love in the most unexpected places. You've got to grab it when you can.

"You make me so crazy," he says before he kisses me again. "I have to see you tomorrow and the next day."

"Anytime, anywhere," I say as I kiss him and press my body into his.

After that first day, there was no turning back. I fell hard for Daniel. It may have been the biggest mistake of my life, but I made it and chose love.

CHAPTER FORTY-SEVEN

After our first encounter, Daniel and I start meeting almost every day. It's easy for him to get away because he's always out taking classes or going to auditions. And, his wife works about fifty hours a week at some art gallery. She doesn't have her eye on the ball.

My small walk-up studio apartment in Williamsburg becomes 'our place.' He starts keeping clothes and toiletries there and tells me how my place feels more like home to him than the palace in Brooklyn Heights he lives in with his wife.

We're in bed one afternoon eating Chinese food. He holds up a pork dumpling with two chop sticks and gently places it in my open mouth. It's good and salty and I wipe the grease from my lips as I chew.

"No more," I say as he holds up another in front of me. "I can't eat another bite."

I snuggle into him and he snaps open a fortune cookie. Little crumbs fall from the cookie onto the bed.

"I'm so sorry," he says. "I'll clean it up."

He starts to get out of bed and I pull him back. "Forget it. Who cares about a few crumbs?"

He laughs and shakes his head. "Tori would have had a fit. No eating allowed in our bed."

"No eating in bed? The finest hotels in the world offer breakfast in bed. That's one of life's great pleasures."

"Not as far as my wife is concerned," says Daniel. "She's got all sorts of crazy sleeping problems and needs her bed a certain way. Last year, before we got married, we did a prenup. She joked about eating in bed being grounds for divorce."

I giggle. "She sounds kind of rigid."

"She can be quirky and occasionally demanding."

"What else did your prenup say?"

"Most of it was boilerplate," he says, taking a sip of wine and refilling my glass. "Basically, if we get divorced, I'm not entitled to anything she owned prior to the marriage."

"Like what?" I say, sitting up straight and taking a sip from my glass.

"I have no claim on the house or her trust fund or any art, jewelry or furniture that she had."

"Sounds like everything. Not a great deal for you."

"If we get divorced, I'll get a small lump sum of twenty-five thousand dollars to help me re-establish myself in a new apartment, but that's all. Tori's father is used to getting what he wants. He wouldn't budge on that. If I wanted to marry his daughter, I had to sign."

I get up, put on a silk robe and sit on a wooden chair next to the bed and face Daniel.

"What about if you had children?" I ask. "What would happen then?"

He smirks. "That's a whole different story. Tori really wants kids. You might say it's her reason for being. Our prenup states that if we have children and get divorced, I'll get a monthly stipend until the youngest is twenty-five."

"How much?"

"Ten thousand dollars a month. Tori's father wanted to make sure I'd have the 'proper living quarters for when his grandchildren stayed with me.' The old man knows how little actors make."

I take another gulp of my wine. "What if you didn't get divorced? What if you have a kid and then your wife passes away?"

"In that situation, I guess you could say, I hit the jackpot. If Tori and I have a couple of kids and she dies, I inherit everything as the father of her children. There would be certain money earmarked for a separate trust fund for the kids. But I'd get the house, everything in it as well as Tori's personal investments."

"Hmm," I say.

"But none of that matters. Tori and I've tried to get pregnant and it's not happening. She's got all sorts of health issues, and some are pretty serious. Doctors think the odds of her getting pregnant are slim to none. Regardless, she's focused and determined. She wants to try an IVF program."

"I hear that works for a lot of people."

Daniel shakes his head. "The doctors aren't hopeful. Because of her condition, there are all sorts of complications for her with IVF. Tori's brought up the idea of adoption, but I'm not so sure I want to go that route."

I stare at him. "If you adopt, does the prenup recognize the adopted child the same way as if you had your own?"

He thinks for a moment and nods. "Yes. An adopted child satisfies the prenup. If we adopt and divorce, I'll get my monthly ten-thousand-dollar stipend. If Tori passes away, I'd inherit her estate."

"I see."

"But I'm not going to have children with her now. I want to be with you. You and I are all that matters now. I'm going to ask her for a divorce."

"Hmm."

"Open another bottle of wine?" he says, getting out of bed. His naked sinewy body glides across the room, making me lust for him even more. We're so good together.

He hands me another glass of wine as I mull over all the information he just shared with me. After learning about the structure of his prenup, I can hardly think of anything else.

This could be so much bigger than what I had originally planned.

Three months later, Daniel and I are madly in love. I never thought two people could feel this much, but we do, we really do. He's my soulmate.

* * *

For the next few months, I amend my plan. I've decided that Daniel and Tori must have at least one baby together.

"Don't you see, sweetheart?" I say as we lather each other up in the shower. "All you have to do is have one baby with her and then you can get divorced. We'll be set financially. Ten thousand a month is a lot of money."

After a bit of convincing, Daniel agrees to go forward with the IVF program. He and Tori sign up and both go through a battery of tests. After a couple of months, Daniel tells me the doctors don't think it's going to work. I don't understand all the medical jargon. It seems the combination of Tori being in her forties and her other heart issues makes a viable pregnancy a long shot. Plus the hormones and other medications she'd have to take aren't good for her.

They try harvesting eggs and all that jazz, but nothing takes. Each time it fails, I'm as disappointed as Tori, maybe more. After one round, the doctors give Tori and Daniel bad news. Daniel shared that conversation with me.

"As we told you before we started, Mrs. Fowler, you were never a good candidate for in vitro fertilization for a variety of reasons," said the director of the fertility clinic. "We normally wouldn't have accepted someone like you, but your father has been a very generous donor. You and your husband were so committed that we thought we'd give it try. But, in good conscience as your doctor, we can't allow you to continue. The drugs are dangerous for you."

Daniel tells me he's exhausted and disappointed but glad it's over. He talks about getting divorced again. I shush him and take him in my arms. Pulling my head back from his shoulder, I look into his beautiful eyes.

"Daniel, I have to tell you something. I'm pregnant."

CHAPTER FORTY-EIGHT

As the words tumble from my lips, the look on Daniel's face is priceless. At first he looks stunned. Then he squints at me and smiles.

"You're putting me on, right?" he says, examining my face, searching for the hidden truth. "You're not serious?"

I smile back at him. "I'm deadly serious. Daniel, you're going to be a father. We're going to be parents. Isn't that amazing?"

It takes a few minutes for him to take it all in and process what this development would mean. I sit quietly, giving him time and wait for him to speak.

"I'm going to be a father? That would never happen with Tori. I always thought I'd make a great dad."

"You will. "

We laugh as we lie in bed together, our bodies intertwined, talking about what it will be like to have a child. We make fantasy plans about future trips to theme parks and trick or treating. After fifteen minutes, we're both quiet as reality sets in. "What are we going to do? I'm married," he says. "If it were just you and me . . . but it's not."

I sit up and look at him. "I'm having this baby with or without you, Daniel. I want you to know that. I want this baby more than anything."

"I know," he says softly.

"Do you love her? Do you love Tori even a little bit?"

"Not the way I love you."

"Then, what's the problem? Tell her you want a divorce."

"It's not that simple. What would we live on?" he says, getting up and pulling on his shorts.

"We'll live the same way we live now. You move in here with me and then . . ."

"What do we do for money?"

"I could get another job making more money and you . . ."

Daniel puts his head in his hands and paces around my small studio. "This is very complicated."

"We love each other. That's all that matters."

He looks up at me. "Don't be naive. I make almost nothing. Practically everything I have has been bought and paid for by my wife. She pays for my clothes, gym membership, trainer, headshots, acting classes. I live for free in her house, use her car and she even gives me two thousand dollars a month for pocket money."

On some level, I suspected something like this. But when he lays it out in black-and-white terms, I get his point.

"What about all the money you earn acting and modeling? That's something."

He shakes his head and laughs. "Do you know how much I earned last year from modeling? Thirty-six hundred dollars. How far do you think we'll get on that? Babies are expensive."

He continues pacing, only now his hands are clasped behind his neck. I had no idea he earned so little. I didn't expect it would be a lot because he didn't work that much, but it's far less than I had imagined.

"Maybe you could get a job?" I say softly.

"I could, but it would mean giving up my dream. I wouldn't be able to go to auditions. I've worked for too many years. Things are finally starting to click for me."

"You could work off hours like a lot of actors do."

He's still pacing. I know what's going on in his head. He's trying to balance his love for me and our unborn child with his lifelong dream of being an actor.

We don't speak for five full minutes, which feels like an eternity. I've got a pit in my stomach. Is he going to turn his back on me and our child and go back to her?

"We don't have to make any decisions right now," I say. "Let's take some time to digest the baby news. It's a lot. Tonight, let's just enjoy the idea of our child."

He smiles. I offered him a temporary 'get of jail free' card and he's taking it. He climbs back on the bed with me and we lie in each other's arms musing about popular baby names.

* * *

Over the next five months, Daniel and I talk incessantly about the coming birth but never about the entire situation. On the few times I bring it up, he changes the subject. I do love him, but I can see now how much he enjoys the trappings of his marriage. Can't say I blame him. It must be nice to live a life of luxury without having to work for it. Who wouldn't want that? I'd like that, too.

At my six-month obstetrician appointment, Daniel comes with me and gets to see the ultrasound and the baby's heart beating. It's a wonderful moment for both of us. When the doctor tells us it looks like a boy, Daniel's chest puffs up and he smiles like I've never seen before.

"I always wanted a son," he says as we walk out of the doctor's office.

"I wanted a boy, too," I say as we wait for an Uber. "Now that we're into the home stretch, have you given any more thought to what we're going to do?"

"I've given it a lot of thought but not come up with any great answers."

While Daniel's still high from seeing the ultrasound, it feels like the right time to introduce my solution.

"I have an idea of how it could work out for us," I say as I rub my protruding stomach. "You'd keep your income from Tori and we'd be together with our son."

"I'm listening."

People often say 'the plan is simple.' My plan definitely wasn't simple. It was complex, dangerous and required meticulous preparation and long-term planning. Everything had to work perfectly. If one thing was out of place, the whole scheme would fall apart. We both had to fully commit and make no mistakes. And, once we started, there would be no turning back.

"We both agree that our primary goal is for you to divorce Tori and marry me. Then, we live happily ever after with our son."

He nods.

"The secondary goal is that you continue to receive money from the Petrosians so you can keep your acting career going."

"In a perfect world, yes. How would it work?" he says skeptically. "Tori's father isn't going to give me money if I dump his daughter and marry you."

"He will, if we do everything right."

As I lay each part of my plan out, I watch Daniel's face contort ever so slightly. He tries to interject reasons why it will fail, but I insist he let me finish before he passes judgement.

I have it all figured out. We do absolutely nothing until after I have the baby. Then, when the baby is four or five months, we put our plan into action.

CHAPTER FORTY-NINE

The next few months go by quickly as Daniel and I prepare to welcome our little boy into the world. Daniel's with me in the birthing room and helps me through a very long labor. But it's all worth it when I see my baby's face for the first time. He's gorgeous but looks like neither of us, and we don't care, he's ours.

The three of us leave the hospital and Daniel drives us to my Brooklyn studio. A crib and a changing table along with all the other necessary baby supplies are already there. The baby is sleeping in his car seat when we walk into the apartment. I close the front door and notice everything is so quiet. It's the first moment we are alone together and it's magical.

"Daniel," I whisper. "We're a real family now."

He smiles, takes the baby from my arms and sits in a chair gazing down at our newly born son. There's so much love in the room that I can physically feel it. I love this baby so much. My body is now flooded with maternal feelings that I didn't know I had. There's nothing I wouldn't do to give my son a good life.

In order to spend more time with me and the baby, Daniel tells his wife that he's got a modeling job out of town for a few days. Tori's so busy with her gallery that she doesn't question it. He repeats this charade several more times over the next few months to give us some family time together.

I remind him that we have a timeline and soon need to implement our plan. I work out the last details and go over everything with him.

"Let's go over the legal stuff one more time," I say to him. "If you and Tori adopt a baby but later divorce, you'll get a ten-thousand-dollar monthly pay out until the child is twenty-five. Is that absolutely ironclad?"

"Yes," he says with full confidence, "I had a lawyer look at it before we got married. It was a concession Tori's father made after I balked at the whole prenup thing. If Tori and I have a kid, no matter how it happens, adopted or otherwise, that clause kicks in. I will also get joint custody."

I didn't know anything about the baby payout prenup clause when I first met Daniel. But, when he told me, it was instantly clear there was a way to exploit it. We could have everything we both want — our son, and money to live on as well. Daniel could continue his acting career and I'd get to live the life I've always deserved with my child.

Even with all of my meticulous planning, there's still a whopping wild card — Tori. Will she bite? We'll set everything up so that it's something she can't resist. But what if she does resist?

"How do you know she'll go for it?" I ask Daniel in all seriousness as I pick up the baby and hold him close to me.

He laughs. "You don't know her. She has a one-track mind. The only thing she wants in the whole world is a baby."

"I get it, but in order for this to work, everything has to go exactly to plan, including Tori taking the bait. No deviations."

"I know her and where her head is right now. Just last week, we signed up with two adoption agencies and did all the paperwork," he says, putting his arm around me. "When they told her it could be years before we got a baby, I thought she was going to lose her mind. When we got home, she started looking into adoptions from other countries. She began talking about 'black market babies' and how to get one. She'll take this bait."

I have to trust his judgement on this. "Okay, so she takes the bait. There's still another possible problem," I say. "Our plan is that you'll file for divorce after a year based on irreconcilable differences related to Tori's dubious mental and emotional state."

"That's the plan."

"Then, you'll petition the court for full custody."

"Correct."

"But how can we be sure that she'll be mentally and emotionally incapacitated?"

"You have to trust me on this one, too. Tori is a medical train wreck. She's got over a dozen health problems, some very serious, and she doesn't take care of herself at all. Now, add in her occasional outbursts of paranoia along with occasionally drinking more than she should. You've got a recipe for a very unsuitable parent."

With the baby in my arms, I look into his eyes. "Let me be very clear. I cannot lose my child to her, not even for part of the time. Do you understand? Joint custody is not an option. You must get full custody. We need to do whatever it takes to ensure that. If we need to turn her into a raving lunatic, then that's what we do."

* * *

When the baby is two and a half months old, I tell Daniel it's time to start prepping before we put our plan into action. We wait for the first warm-ish spring day and drive with the baby out to the East End of Long Island. Destination — the Hamptons, near the Petrosians' summer home. We're scouting locations for the first part of our plan. He takes me to Rocky Point Beach and shows me where his wife always likes to sit.

"This is her spot. She hates being in the sun, so she'll always sit here to get shade from that tree," he says, pointing to a large tree off to the side.

I nod. The location is good. Next, we walk down to the water so I can get a look at the beach and the adjacent jetty. Daniel carries the baby in a front harness and waits as I walk up and down the entire beach getting the lay of the land.

I climb up onto the jetty and walk all the way out. I traverse the rocks until I get to the end where it juts out into the sea. From there, I can see everything below. I take note that the beach on the other side of the jetty can't be seen until you get right up to the rocks and look over. It's the perfect spot.

I've already checked the ocean current records for this part of Long Island. This section is usually moderate. Regardless, I can handle it. Having been a champion swimmer in high school and a lifeguard, I still have a very strong stroke and can hold my breath for an inordinate amount of time. It's a skill I don't use much but will be pivotal in carrying this whole thing out.

I walk through the sand back to Daniel. The baby is awake now and blinks both eyes every time the wind blows into his face.

"So?" Daniel says. "What's the verdict? Will this location work?"

I smile. "I think it could."

"Think?"

"It will work. I can handle the beach part. My biggest concern is if the bait will attract the big fish."

Daniel smiles and kisses our son on the top of his head. "Don't worry about that. One thing I know about Tori Petrosian is her obsession with becoming a mother trumps everything else. There's nothing she wouldn't do to have a baby. Nothing."

We check out a bunch of other sites in the Hamptons that will be a part of our plan — Airbnb locations, a local masseuse, bus schedules and a few other assorted places we need to be familiar with. Once we've got all that squared away we return to the city and wait. Our plan can't happen until it's warm enough for her to go to the beach. I also want to wait until my little boy is weaned off of my breast milk.

For the next few weeks, there's much to do. I've got to get some equipment and need to accumulate props like wigs, colored contacts, waterproof body make-up and a hot pink bathing cap. In the meantime, Daniel's organizing several weekends in the Hamptons for Tori. We're hoping it works the first time, but if not, we'll try again.

Long before we put our plan in action, we do some dry runs and test everything out. We time things making sure we can get from point A to point B at precisely the right moment. I practice with the props. I slather my body with waterproof olive/tan make-up and put on brown contact lenses and a long black wig. For extra oomph, I color in my eyebrows, making them very pronounced, place a fake beauty mark next to my eye and glam up my lips with bright-red lipstick. Looking in the bathroom mirror, even I don't recognize myself.

"Are you ready?" I shout from inside the bathroom.

"Bring it," shouts Daniel.

Slowly, I open the bathroom door and step out into the main room wearing a one-piece bathing suit, a big floppy brimmed hat and oversized dark sunglasses. I peek at him over the glasses.

His mouth drops.

"What do you think?" I say, removing the sunglasses.

"I think you look really hot."

I shake my head. "Seriously, what do you think? Would you recognize me?"

"No. You've transformed yourself," he says, walking up close to me and peering at my face. "You've taken my blue-eyed girl with fair skin and turned her into someone who could be Middle Eastern or Mexican. It's amazing."

"If the father of my child and the man I sleep with doesn't recognize me," I say with a smile, "then neither will your wife. I think we're ready."

CHAPTER FIFTY

The day finally arrives. Tori thinks Daniel's in California on a shoot. As a little added insurance policy and to prime the pump, I called Tori yesterday afternoon pretending to be the adoption agency giving her an update. It wasn't good news. The message I left said that the 'timeline for getting a baby was probably much longer than the agency had originally anticipated.' I figured that message would give Tori more of an incentive to do what we wanted her to do. Our plan can work, if we do everything right, no mistakes.

Daniel and I are staying in a hotel fifteen miles from the Hamptons. We've rented two cars. One we're using now to drive out to the Hamptons. The other we leave in a lot a mile down the road from Rocky Point Beach to use later.

Not wanting to take a chance we'd run into anyone, we wake up early. For a few minutes, we lie in each other's arms knowing what we are about to do is going to change our lives forever. We won't be together like we are now for quite some time. It's the way it has to be and we've accepted that. The end justifies the means. It will all be worth it when it's over.

I go into the bathroom while Daniel feeds our son. Thirty minutes later, I emerge a raven-haired, dark-eyed bombshell with a dark complexion. I put on a beach cover-up along with my sunglasses and floppy hat and parade in front of Daniel. "How do I look?"

"Amazing. A totally different person. Are you ready to do this?"

I nod and pick up the carrier containing my son along with my beach bag. Daniel helps us to the car and we drive east towards Rocky Point Beach. We've practiced this several times before so I know exactly where to go — the shady spot by the tree.

It's early, around eight a.m. when Daniel drops me in town near the bus stop. There can be no record of our car anywhere near that beach. I get out of the car and walk around to the other side to grab the carrier from the back seat. Before I do, Daniel, still behind the wheel, rolls down his window.

"I love you," he says. "You can do this."

For a minute, I have second thoughts. "What if Tori doesn't take our son? What if she calls the cops? What if they put him into the foster care system? What if . . ."

"We've already talked about this. I'll be here watching her. If it looks like anything's gone wrong, I'll run down onto the beach like I'm surprising her. I'll take control of the situation and . . ."

"But what if . . ."

"Trust me, she will take the baby. There's no doubt in my mind. She'll believe she's doing the noble thing by giving the baby a great life with all the trappings that money can buy."

I nod and take a deep breath as I reach into the back seat for my son. As soon as I close the door, Daniel pulls away and heads to his perch where he'll watch the whole event take place.

After he leaves, I wait for the bus and take it all the way to Rocky Point. It's a little before nine when I arrive at the beach. The lifeguards aren't on duty yet. That's how we planned it. The fewer people to notice me and the baby, the better.

I walk slowly through the sand on the nearly empty beach, my eyes fixed on the shady spot to the right. It's a nice, clear, dry day and very pleasant for sitting out on the beach. I get to the shady spot, place the baby carrier on my oversized beach towel and call Daniel.

"I'm in place," I say. "Now we wait."

"I love you," he says before he hangs up.

That's our last communication until it's all over. I take my phone and clear it of everything, putting it back to factory settings so there's nothing to trace. I place it in a pocket in my diaper bag. My nerves are on end, so I pick up my son and sing to him to calm myself.

Time goes so slowly while waiting for Tori to appear. Daniel swears she's a creature of habit and will be here between ten thirty and eleven. It's ten fifteen. I look back at the parking lot to see if there are any signs of her. Every few minutes a few more people saunter down the beach bringing towels, coolers and umbrellas.

I'm looking out at the water and don't hear her when she approaches.

"Excuse me, I hope you don't mind, but this is the only part of the beach that has any shade and I . . ."

I spin around, my heart beating so hard while trying to look calm and relaxed. "It's a free country," I say, testing out my subtle faux Czech accent. "Help yourself, as long as you don't mind the noise."

For a second, I can't believe I'm actually talking to her. I've only seen her from afar — across a park, on the other side of a restaurant, but we've never spoken. After all this time, it's kind of surreal.

She puts her towel down about twenty feet from me. After a little time passes, I'm about to strike up a simple conversation to get the ball rolling. As luck would have it, she starts talking to me first. Even better. We trade comments back and forth until she offers me a piece of gum. I take it, it's the friendly thing to do and that's what I'm trying to foster . . . a friendship of sorts.

After a suitable amount of time shouting back and forth, I say something about my throat getting scratchy from all the yelling. That's when Tori suggests, as I hoped she would, that we move our towels next to each other so we don't have to scream. I agree wholeheartedly and she moves her stuff over near me. We continue chatting for over an hour, our conversation covering a million topics. I share little fabricated tidbits about my past; how I'm all alone in the world and how my son's father doesn't know the baby exists.

As we talk, I get to know her, too. She's different from how I thought she'd be. She's nice. I didn't anticipate that. She and I surprisingly have a lot in common. I like her. I didn't think I would, but I do. I'm starting to feel a little reticent, but I remind myself that liking her is irrelevant. Tori has everything I want and deserve. Daniel and I have worked too long and hard to mess this up now simply because I kind of like her.

The moment passes. I feel my heart harden and am relieved. After an hour or more of girl talk, I go in for the kill. I ask her if she'd watch my baby for a few minutes while I take a dip in the water. She agrees.

I stand up and put on my hot-pink bathing cap, one she'll be able to see from where she's sitting. As I put the goggles on my head, I thank her for watching him. I tell her I'll back in a few minutes and walk towards the water without looking back.

There are a fair number of people at the beach now, but nobody's paying attention to me. I walk into the water up to my waist and dive in. It's cold but it feels good. I turn my head to look back at the beach, but Tori's too far back for me to see anything more than a dot. But she'll be able to see my pink cap.

I look over at the lifeguards. There are three of them and they're watching a bunch of kids and not focused on me, which is a good thing. I start doing my laps across the stretch of the beach. My stroke is strong, swimming feels so natural to me.

I get to one end of the beach, flip over, turn around and go back the other way. I do that five times. On the last lap, I take a huge breath and quietly go under.

CHAPTER FIFTY-ONE

I'm down in the water now going deep and swimming alongside the jetty. In the weeks leading up to this day, I had gone to the YMCA pool near my apartment and practiced holding my breath. After two weeks, I was confident I'd be able to do the swim and even practiced at Rocky Point on one of the dry runs Daniel and I did earlier.

The compass on my waterproof watch tells me exactly where I am. When I get to the end of the jetty, I carefully swim around it, mindful of the current so it doesn't push me into the jagged rocks. It's relatively calm that day, but there is still an undertow. I easily maneuver the tip of the jetty and start my swim back towards shore on the other side of it.

I'm gliding now, letting the waves help me into shore. While under water, I remove my pink bathing cap and the wig underneath it. While pumping with my legs, I turn the cap inside out, roll the wig up into it and squash it into a small ball. I swim with both legs and one arm as I stuff the wig and hat down the front of my suit.

I'm in the final stretch. All I have to do is swim as far from the other beach as possible. When I get close to shore I make a hard right and swim east. I can feel my breath is almost done and my lungs start to constrict. Only a few more stokes and I can stand up. I see the sand beneath my feet and push my legs down waiting to feel the ground beneath them.

Instantly, my legs push me up and my head pops out of the water as I gratefully take in the air my lungs crave. After several breaths, I get out of the surf as fast as I can. I run quickly down the beach away from the scene of my crime. There's no one on this side of the jetty. From where I'm standing, I can't see anything on the other side. I'm blocked by the rocks. I have no idea if anyone has noticed that I've gone under yet, but I can't hang around to find out. I've got to stick to the plan.

I get out of the water and continue walking east along the beach. After nearly a mile, I turn left in a section with no bathers and walk through the sand dunes towards the road. Before I get to the main highway, I see the gray rental car in the brush. The keys are hidden on top of the left rear tire and a fully charged phone is in the glove compartment.

I find the keys, let myself into the car and turn on the phone. I have to know what happened.

I dial the number of Daniel's new burner phone. It rings once, twice and then three times. I start to panic but thankfully, he finally answers.

"Are you okay?" he says.

"Yes," I say, still out of breath. "What's happening? Where's our son?"

"He's fine. I'm looking at him right now through my binoculars. He's with Tori. She's looking around trying to figure out what's going on in the water."

"Someone saw me go under?"

"Seems that way. The lifeguards are in the water looking for you. Where are you now?"

"I'm in the car where we left it."

"You need to get out of there. I'm here. I'll call you as things happen. Now, go."

I'm supposed to go to the hotel Daniel and I had been in the night before. He's in a spot where he can view everything that's happening on the beach from a distance. If anything goes wrong, if he sees Tori talking to the cops, he'll step in. I want Tori's money, but I won't lose my son to get it.

I drive west towards our hotel, hitting typical East End traffic. My heart is beating a million miles a minute and I'm stressing out over why Daniel hasn't called again. It's been nearly thirty minutes since the last time we talked. I pull over and text him.

What's happening? Why haven't you texted me?

I'm not driving one more inch until I know my son is safe. I'm listening to the radio to distract myself and gnawing on the nail of my right thumb when his text comes in.

Everything going to plan. Police arrived. Tori walked right past them with the baby. It's exactly as I predicted.

I let out an audible sigh of relief. My son is all right. I text Daniel again asking for more details, but he doesn't respond. I wait for ten minutes, still nothing. Another five and finally I hear the ping of a new text.

The eagle has landed. Tori just called me and said 'the adoption agency has a baby for us and she's picking him up today.'

As I hang up I puff up my cheeks and let out a huge breath. I can't believe we've pulled this off. We've still got a long way to go and many steps left to take, but this is good. Today was the most speculative part of our entire plan and it worked. I smile, put the car in drive and continue on to the hotel to meet up with Daniel.

That night, he arrives at the hotel with two bottles of champagne and some food he picked up at some overpriced gourmet shop. We spend the night in our room making love basking in the cleverness of our plan.

"I knew it would work," he says as he takes me in his arms. "Tori's so predictable, I know how she thinks. She figured she's solved two problems. She gets a baby and she's kept an orphaned child out of foster care."

I kiss Daniel on his chest and look up at his face. "We have to make sure she doesn't change her mind."

"Not a chance," he says. "She's already told me a hundred lies about how she got the baby. She's also informed her parents that they're grandparents. She won't change her mind now. She's in way too deep."

This night is our last one together for a while. As far as his wife knows, Daniel's flying in from California tonight to meet his new son. As much as it kills me, he and I have to stay apart for a while. It's part of the plan.

* * *

For the next several weeks the only time I see my son is when Daniel takes him out alone for a walk. We meet in a special place in a park in Brooklyn. It's close enough for Daniel to walk to, but not so close that Tori might see us. I live for these outings and am so thrilled to see my little boy looking happy and well nourished.

"Trust me," says Daniel when he observes the worry on my face. "Tori has a lot of issues, but being a good mother isn't one of them. If anything, our baby gets too much attention. Not only from Tori and me, but her parents are over every other day bearing gifts and taking turns feeding and holding him. Our child is never put down."

I smile. He knows that's what I want to hear. It's torture being away from my son, but it's the only way.

"It won't be for much longer," Daniel says. I nod, knowing we're about to embark on the second stage of our plan.

Two days later in the late afternoon, I climb up eight steps and stand in front of a gleaming heavy antique wooden door. There's a large ornate brass knocker on it. I take one last breath and reach for the knocker letting it bang on the wood several times.

The door opens. A blonde woman in an expensive looking outfit holds the door. She smiles at me. "You must be Eden. We've been expecting you. I'm Tori."

CHAPTER FIFTY-TWO

After I secured the nanny job, the next six months proved to be more challenging than I expected. Keeping up the physical disguise took some work. I've got naturally strawberry-blonde hair, an extremely fair complexion and light-blue eyes. Without make-up, I look a little washed out, which works in my favor. To be less of a threat to Tori, I constantly bleach both of my eyebrows blonde, making me look even more bland. I wear clothes that are unattractive and oversized, use absolutely no make-up and do nothing with my hair. Sometimes, I don't even brush it.

One might ask how I was able to turn my child over to another woman. The answer — it's complicated. After being assured by Daniel that my son would receive the best care, I considered the fact that I'm technically with my son nearly every day, all day. I actually spend most of my time now taking care of my little boy. For all of Tori's talk about 'dying to be a mother,' she's quite happy to pass 'her' baby off to me, so she can pursue other things like her job at an art gallery or go to a hair appointment.

To be fair, she does spend a fair amount of time with the baby. She's very loving to my son, which has been a huge relief. I was worried she wouldn't take good care of him, but she's rather devoted. In fact, when it comes to the baby, he gets the best of everything. He receives the finest organic baby food, clothing practically spun from gold, and his nursery furniture is all imported from Italy. His playroom is stocked with every book and toy ever made. In short, my son wants for nothing.

The hardest part about living in the house with Tori, Daniel and *my* young son is keeping my mask permanently on. I'm careful not to look at Daniel in that way lovers look at each other for fear she'll notice. I've instructed Daniel to do the same. Instead, we've concocted a whole scenario where he constantly finds fault with me to throw Tori off track. It helps that Daniel's a good actor. He's perfected being a meanie to me in front of her. Sometimes, he's so good, he almost has me convinced he dislikes me. Ironically, it's Tori who always comes to my defense.

As far as my baby is concerned, I pour as much love into him as I want. I dote over my/her son's every move, and it only delights Tori more.

"Eden," she says out of the blue one day, "I'm so grateful we found you. You may be the best nanny in America. All the other mothers are jealous."

Sometimes, I'm aware Tori's watching me from across the room when I cradle the baby. I sing to him and hold him in a way that only a real mother could. Tori loves it, she laps it up. What working mother wouldn't want a nanny who gives two hundred percent to her kid?

As the weeks and months go by, Daniel, Tori and I get into a rhythm. In a weird way, we're like a family, except Daniel and I are the only ones who know who the real parents are. I become so used to being the nanny that sometimes I forget we're putting on a play. I have to remind myself that nothing about our life right now is real.

I manufacture a pretend boyfriend to make it appear that I have a quasi-normal life outside of my world with them. I also make a point of frequently talking about my made-up family and siblings in the Midwest so Tori doesn't suspect anything.

It's not easy maintaining this facade twenty-four seven, but I do it for my son. Very soon, Daniel and I will leave this place. We'll be able to start our lives with money in the bank. He can pursue his acting career and I can be the mother to my son that I've always wanted to be.

Tori's parents are also completely devoted to my son. They're constantly showering him with love and gifts and he seems to really like them. He lights up whenever the Petrosians visit and especially likes the father. I've also gotten to know the older man and like him as well. He's short on social graces but long on charisma. I understand his appeal. My son and the old man have really bonded. Even Tori notices how taken the baby is with her father.

"Dad, do you see how Jonah perks up when you come into the room? Look at him smiling at you. He can't take his eyes off of you."

"He's a smart kid," says the old man, grinning as he bounces my son on his knee.

Aside from the play-acting I do as a nanny, this pretend period is also hard on Daniel and me. I miss being in his arms, our legs tangled, our bodies one. Sometimes, he whispers to me when we pass in the hall.

"I love you. How much longer?"

I smile at him without saying a word and keep walking. We've come too far to let our guard down now. We're so close. And it's not total abstinence. We do meet privately whenever we can. He'll tell Tori he's got an audition or a session with his trainer and we meet in my studio apartment and make love.

"Stay strong," I remind him as we get dressed to return to our phony roles in Tori's house. "Soon, we'll be together and then we'll have it all."

Daniel seems more resolute after our meetings, but I worry about him. If one of us is going to crack, it won't be me, it will be him. For all of his bravado and outward strength, if it weren't for me holding the line, I think he would have abandoned the ship a long time ago. I won't let that happen. I've been planning a version of this for too long and given up too much to stop now. I'm taking it all the way home and there's still much to do.

Along with Daniel, I've helped facilitate a number of Tori's 'unhinged' and forgetful episodes. For someone with all of her medical issues, Tori's brazen recklessness with her health is somewhat staggering. That particular aspect of her personality is what we've been able to exploit. Her weakness will be her undoing. She can be very needy and sometimes self-indulgent but still, there are things I like about her. She's often warm and has a good sense of humor, but it doesn't change my mind.

Shortly after I arrive on the scene, Tori singlehandedly alienates several clients and her bosses and ends up unconscious in the hospital — twice. We had a hand in it. We 'helped' her lose and forget things, but it's her own erratic nature that lands the plane for us. Everyone, including her parents, thinks she's on shaky ground.

It's finally nearing the end of the line. I'm waiting for the right moment for Daniel to ask Tori for a divorce. He thinks we have almost enough incidents documented to swing the court in favor of him getting full custody.

Using a fake name, Daniel met with an attorney and showed him his prenup. I wanted to get one more definitive legal opinion. I had to be absolutely sure that Daniel is guaranteed his monthly financial stipend if he gets full custody.

"The lawyer's sure?" I say, sitting on a park bench next to the man I love, the baby in the stroller in front of me.

"Nothing's a hundred percent, Sasha. The attorney said we definitely had a legitimate case."

I look up at the blue sky and let out a loud exasperated sigh.

"Having a legitimate case and winning one aren't the same. I've told you that. I'm willing to do anything, but I cannot lose Liam."

We go round and round on this topic for an hour and both reach the same conclusion. Though small, despite Tori's behavior, there's still a slight chance she could get joint custody. Sam Petrosian has a lot of money. I couldn't live with that scenario.

We sit in silence, mulling over our next move. I think about everything we've done to get to this point. It can't all have been for nothing.

"There is one other way," I say, looking into Daniel's eyes while rocking the stroller with my hand.

"What's that?"

I take in a breath. What I'm about to suggest will take our plan to a whole different level. I've got to present it just right, or he'll run.

"Anyone who knows Tori, including her parents, knows that she's a train wreck. Frankly, it's amazing she hasn't killed herself already. You want that person to be your son's caretaker? She's reckless. She might leave Liam alone in the bathtub? Or forget about him entirely and go out for the day. She's not grounded in reality. You know it's true."

"Tori would never hurt or neglect Liam."

"You don't know that. We're his parents. We have to protect our son, don't we? How many times has she almost killed herself? What if the next time she goes off track, we help her along a little bit? She'd simply expire by her own hand. Given her history, nobody would think there was any foul play."

Daniel grimaces and starts to get up. I have my work cut out in order to convince him this is the only path forward. I place my hand on his arm.

"Sit down and hear me out. If Tori kills herself, you'll be the grieving widower left to take care of your motherless son. Everyone will feel sorry for you. You'll also inherit Tori's entire estate. We're talking millions of dollars instead of a paltry hundred and twenty thousand a year for getting custody in a divorce. Daniel, you'd get the whole enchilada, the house, the stocks, the art."

"I never signed up for murder. This is going too far."

I laugh. "*This* is going too far? I hand over my infant son to a total stranger on a beach, fake my own drowning and live in your house posing as a nanny. That wasn't too far for you?"

"But murder is . . ."

"Daniel, listen to me. It's so clear to me now what we have to do. It's the only way. You and I both know that Tori will eventually kill herself anyway. I can't wait around for that to happen, it could be years. I want us to be together as a family now. Tori just needs a little push."

He's not completely sold on the new plan, but over the next couple of days I get him on board. Thank God one of us is steering this ship.

Originally, Daniel only told Tori he got the part in that play as an excuse to get out and be with me. Rehearsals conveniently happened whenever I had time off or was out for a long walk with the baby. We made sure the opening night happened when Tori's parents were planning to be in California. Our plan always was that he'd pick a fight with her on the night of the play's opening. That way, she wouldn't go to the theatre and discover he wasn't in it. We could keep our secret meetings going with each new play or acting job he said he had.

But our plan backfired. Despite the strategically timed fight on the day of the opening and his angry demand that she not go, Tori sucked it up and went anyway. I can only imagine her confusion and embarrassment when she realized he wasn't there, and never had been.

That night at the theater could have been the end for Daniel and me. But fortunately, crazy Tori went out after the play and got herself tanked up on martinis in front of witnesses. Her behavior that night becomes the opportunity we had been waiting for and we go for it.

After Tori comes home trashed, she pops a few sleeping pills in her mouth and unwittingly drinks six or seven more pills that Daniel crushes and dissolves in her bedside ice water. She always drinks a tall glass of water before bed. She was so drunk she couldn't taste anything in the water. After that, there's only one more step. Once Tori's in dreamland, Daniel will turn off her breathing machine.

Tori knows that sleeping without her CPAP is extremely dangerous. We're talking stroke, heart attack and so much more. Take away that device, throw in half a bottle of gin and six or ten sleeping pills and she could easily flatline.

That night, I wait in the nursery for Daniel to complete his tasks. As I sit there, I visualize him turning off Tori's machine and pouring any of the remaining water/pill mixture left in her glass down the drain — like we planned. He'll take her sleeping pills out of her nightstand drawer, remove the cap and place the open container in her hand. To make her look like she was out of her mind, he'll also scatter several pills in the bed sheets. Then, he'll tuck her in for the night or I should say — for the last time.

I hear a noise and look up. Daniel appears in the doorway of the nursery. My son is nearby sleeping in his crib. Daniel comes over and sits down on the single bed next to me.

"Are we good?" I whisper softly, not wanting to wake the baby.

"It's done."

"You turned off the machine?"

He nods and kisses me, a long soulful kiss. "In the morning, I'll turn it back on before I call the police, just like we planned."

CHAPTER FIFTY-THREE

THE WIFE

I'm half asleep but coughing and sputtering in my dream. My face is really itchy and I raise my hand to scratch it. My arm feels so heavy that I can't get it up to my face. I'm not fully awake but somehow vaguely aware it's taking longer than it should to move my arm. The idea of opening my eyes seems beyond my ability.

I lie there for several moments before slowly forcing one eye open. There's a little daylight in the room and I look over at the clock. It's six in the morning. I turn my head a fraction more to see if Daniel's awake yet. That slight turn of my head unleashes an excruciating stabbing pain in my temples. As I lie still trying to cope with that pain, I remember the martinis from the night before. Why did I do that to myself? I don't even like gin.

It takes me another minute, and then I remember — my husband lied to me. He wasn't in the play he'd been talking about for months. That also meant he hadn't been out running lines with other cast members for his 'big breakout role' either. This play wasn't the 'turning point' in his career that he had proclaimed each time he walked out of the house to go to rehearsal. He lied to me about everything.

I pull the cotton sheet over my face. I pretend that if I lie still the pain will go away faster. But what's ailing me is more than just a physical pain in my head. I also ache from my heart.

My throat is dry. I need water. Without opening my eyes, my hand searches the top of the nightstand for the thermal container of water I always keep there. I grasp it, pull the CPAP mask off of my face and bring the cup to my lips. It's empty. Shit. I have to get out of bed after all.

Pushing myself to a sitting position, I reach over and turn off my CPAP. The room wobbles as I stand. With my cup in one hand, I slowly walk to the bathroom to get some water.

After draining the cup twice, I take a good look at myself in the mirror. Horrifying is an understatement. When I got home last night, I apparently neglected to wash my face. Remnants of the previous night's make-up lingers on my skin. There are big black splotches of mascara under both eyes.

I splash some cool water on my face and scrub it with a washcloth. Thankfully, my head throbs a little less now. Then I wonder, where the hell is Daniel? Did he come home last night? After what he did, I'm not sure we can repair our relationship. Some things are unforgivable and this may be one of them. Then I remember, Daniel was here. We talked and he cried and I comforted him. What was I thinking?

I sit in front of my vanity mirror for some time replaying the events of the previous night. I can't remember a lot. Between those awful memories and my wretched headache, I nearly forget that I'm hosting a big important luncheon for the gallery today. The thought of going out and putting on a game face right now is daunting. I feel awful and my marriage is crumbling before my eyes.

I can't let Neville and Anton down, not again. That would be the end for them and me. It's nearly eight a.m. and I'm supposed be at the gallery at ten fifteen and then over to the restaurant by eleven fifteen to get everything ready. I'll have to think about Daniel later.

Somehow, I manage to go up to the third floor and knock softly on Eden's door to remind her I'm going out soon. She doesn't answer so I slowly open it. She's gone and her bed hasn't been slept in. She often sleeps in the baby's room, and I go to look for her there.

As I'm leaving her room something catches my eye. Eden's sketch book is open on a chair, surrounded by some of the clothes I've given her. She's never shown me any of her drawings except for the one she gave us of Jonah. She says she's too embarrassed to share her work. I decide one little peek can't hurt.

I flip through dozens of sketches of landscapes and portraits of people in the city. I recognize one scene, from a park near our house. As I turn the pages, it strikes me that she's quite good and not the novice she pretends to be. There's a sketch of the front of our house, drawn perfectly to scale.

Halfway through the book, I come across a picture of an infant. It's Jonah. I flip several pages and they're all of my son when he was quite tiny. I stop to think how much Jonah's changed. As I look at the portraits of my son, it occurs to me something's not right, but I can't put my finger on what it is.

With my head still pounding, I close the sketch book and drag myself back downstairs to my bedroom to get some Tylenol. As I cross through my room, I pick up my phone to check on Jonah. Opening my video baby monitor app, the nursery looks fairly dark and quiet. Jonah's not awake yet. Good. I need some recovery time.

I sit on my bed for several minutes trying to make sense out of my husband's behavior. He told me he was embarrassed his career was stalling and that's why he did it. But still, how could he lie to me so often for so many months if he really loved me? His excuse doesn't justify his actions and I'm really angry.

Suddenly, there's a noise on my phone and I look at the app. The morning sun now partially illuminates Jonah's room. The white wooden railing of his crib is now visible. Something moves on the bed next to the crib. It's Eden, she's going over to him.

I hear her whisper to my son, "Everything will be perfect."

I watch her on my phone, but she says nothing more. *Everything will be perfect?* The phrase rings a distant bell, but I don't know why. My addled mind is still a fog. Though pieces of a puzzle are moving around in my head, they make no sense. Something tells me to go back up to Eden's room and have another look at the sketches of Jonah.

Back in her room, I flip open the sketch book and stare at my son's portraits for nearly a minute. Then, it hits me. All the early portraits of Jonah show a faint strawberry birthmark between his eyes. I scroll through old photos on my phone until I find the picture I took of Eden on her first day with us. She's holding Jonah on her lap. They're both smiling and there's no sign of his birthmark. That had disappeared before she came to work for us. So, how did she know about it and why is it in her drawings?

CHAPTER FIFTY-FOUR

In a matter of hours, I've got to pull off a massive luncheon for the gallery. While the birthmark in the sketches strikes me as really odd, my head is splitting. With no bandwidth left to decipher what the pictures mean, I go back down to my room to shower and dress. I'll ask Eden about the sketches after the event is over.

Forty minutes later, I'm ready to leave the house. The Tylenol has kicked in and I head downstairs to the first floor. Jonah's in his highchair having breakfast. He smiles when he sees me talking earnestly in his own unique but indecipherable language.

"Good morning," Eden says as she places some scrambled eggs on his tray. "Leaving already?"

"Yes," I say as I pick up my bag and keys. "Today is the big lunch event for the gallery. Maybe you can take Jonah to the park today? I have a few meetings after the lunch, probably won't be home until five."

She nods as she gives Jonah some sliced bananas.

"Did you see Daniel this morning?" I say as I gather my things.

"Haven't seen him. He must have gone to the gym early."

"Probably," I say as I walk down the hall towards the front door. "See you tonight."

The entire ride into Midtown I obsess about Daniel's web of lies. Part of me is surprised he hasn't contacted me this morning. He has to know how angry and hurt I am. Now that I'm sober and can think straight, his lame excuse last night is all the more insulting.

I stop at the gallery, pick up what I need and head over to the venue. For the next four or five hours I have to be a hundred percent focused on gallery business. The meet and greets go well, and there's a good press turnout. Neville and Anton appear pleased and I congratulate myself for pulling it off despite the horrendous revelations from the night before.

As the main course is being cleared, I duck into the ladies' room. It's an old-school bathroom that has a separate seating area with chairs and mirrors for primping. I glance in the mirror on my way out. My hair needs some smoothing so I take a seat. While running a comb through my unruly mane, I check my baby monitor app to see what my little angel is up to. That always makes me happy. The first room that comes into focus is the playroom cam — no Jonah. I switch to the nursery cam, also no Jonah. When I try the kitchen camera, my little boy is in his swing, a big smile on his face. He loves that swing. I see Eden over by the sink making a hot cup of something. I watch Jonah swing back and forth for a few seconds while applying a fresh coat of lip gloss.

I'm about to turn off the app and go back to the lunch when I hear Daniel's voice coming from the baby monitor.

"What do we do now?" says my husband off camera.

"We knew this was a possibility. We try again," says Eden, stirring her drink.

"The doctors said excessive drugs combined with alcohol and not wearing her CPAP would be a recipe for disaster," says my husband. "She should have had a massive heart attack or a stroke or something. Tori *should* be dead right now."

"But she's not," says Eden, taking a sip from her cup.

"Maybe it's a sign."

"Don't be ridiculous," says Eden. "There was always a chance she'd survive."

"Maybe we should leave while we can. Let's just get out of here now," says my husband.

In the swing, Jonah has his arms outstretched reaching for Eden. She goes to him.

"Come to me, sweetheart," she says as she picks up my son, hoists him onto her shoulder and faces Daniel, who is now visible. "After all the planning we did. Fuck. I almost died that day at the beach. Fuck."

What are they talking about? Eden almost died?

"We'll have to try again, that's all," she says, cuddling my son. "We didn't give her enough. Next time we give her more, a lot more."

I watch my husband walk towards our nanny and put his arms around her and Jonah.

"Don't you see," he says, "we've been granted a reprieve, a second chance. Nothing happened. There's been no crime committed. You and I can walk out of here today and start over."

"Are you fucking kidding me? After all we've been through, you want to stop now? No. There's way too much money at stake."

"I don't care about the money anymore," he says. "I love you and our son. Let's pack our clothes, get in the car and start some place new, far away from New York. We can go to California or even Mexico."

"How's that going to work, Daniel? The minute Tori realizes we've taken the baby, she'll call the cops. We'll be charged with kidnapping."

Daniel shakes his head. "She won't call the police. Tori thinks she stole the baby from a Czech woman at the beach who drowned. She could go to jail for that. Technically, we're within our rights to take him. He's one hundred percent ours. A DNA test will prove that. You're Liam's biological mother and I'm his father, so what crime are we committing?

Tori never legally adopted him. She just pretended she did. He's our son, not hers."

I'm sitting in the restaurant bathroom having an out of body experience. My stunned silence is broken when someone from our lunch pops their head into the bathroom to tell me dessert has been served. I mutter something to get them to go away while I continue to watch the app.

"Sasha," says my husband, "I'm begging you. Let's leave now before Tori comes home."

I see Eden pull away from Daniel. Her face contorts in anger. "You promised me we'd get it all, every penny. Now, you expect me to walk away with nothing? Tori gets to keep everything? What do I get?"

"I can withdraw twenty thousand dollars from our joint account today to get us started," he says. "I'll get a job. We'll start over and raise our son."

"And Tori keeps all the money? Why does she get everything?"

I listen as they debate whether to leave New York with my son or to make a second attempt on my life. During their discourse, bits and pieces start to come together for me.

Eden is Sasha and the drawings I found with the birthmark were done before I met her. It sounds like she wore a disguise at the beach the day we met because she mentions something about wigs, colored contacts and nearly drowning. Daniel knew where I always sit at the beach. She made sure she got there first so I never suspected anything.

I don't quite understand all of what they're saying because it's out of context. It sounds like their intention all along was to set me up. They were sure I'd take the baby. Daniel knew the most important thing in the world to me was to have a child. He knew I'd do anything for one. He was right.

"Tori doesn't get everything. You have the only thing she cares about," says Daniel, looking down at the baby. My husband wraps our nanny in his arms again with the baby in between them. "Sasha, I love you and Liam more than anything. Let's get out of here now before it's too late. Don't you see? We've been given another chance."

There's silence for a moment until Eden/Sasha finally speaks in a loud whisper and shakes her head. "All right. We'll go. I guess we're going to be poor for the rest of our lives."

"But happy," says my husband as he kisses her and looks at his watch, the Bulova I bought for him. "You pack up Liam's things. We've got to be out of here in an hour or we run the risk of running into Tori."

With that last comment, they're gone from the screen while I'm left in shock. Staring at my reflection in the mirror, I feel every nerve ending in my body all at once. Everything I ever thought about my marriage and family is wrong. Up is down and down is up and the sky is definitely not blue.

There's a knock on the ladies' room door.

"Tori, are you in there?" says Neville from the other side of the heavy wooden door.

Shit — the luncheon. The gallery's public relations lunch seems so insignificant after what I just learned. I stagger to the door and open it. Neville reacts in alarm when he sees me.

"Oh, my God. You're white as a ghost. Do you need me to get you to a doctor?" he says.

"I don't feel very well. It might be something I ate. I think I should go home."

"Of course, everyone's leaving now, anyway. The event was a smashing success, you've outdone yourself. Go home and rest. We'll talk about it tomorrow."

I race to the front of the restaurant sick to my stomach. I've got to get home immediately to stop them from leaving with Jonah. I call a pricey limousine service that can usually get a car to me anywhere in the city within five minutes. I'm quasi-hysterical when I call, but the dispatcher assures me he's got a driver two blocks away.

A minute later, I'm sitting in the back seat of a limo headed to Brooklyn.

"There's a hundred-dollar tip in it for you if you can get me there in twenty minutes," I shout as I start to call my father and ask for his help. I'm about to send the call when I suddenly stop. What am I going to tell my father? The grandson he adores isn't his grandson? That I stole him from his mother and now she wants him back? That my husband and my nanny tried to kill me and failed? I can't prove any of that.

If Sasha and Daniel are telling the truth, and I reluctantly believe they are, legally they are my son's parents. I never adopted Jonah. I took him. I don't have a fucking leg to stand on.

CHAPTER FIFTY-FIVE

SASHA/EDEN

After putting all the baby's clothes and supplies in the car, I'm in my room cramming as much as I can into three small bags. Daniel's already packed up the playpen along with Liam's favorite toys and put them in the trunk. Liam is sitting on my bed playing with his toy dinosaur, oblivious to the chaos around him.

Daniel says we need to be out of here in ten more minutes so we have time to get to the bank before it closes. We've got to get the money today before Tori realizes we're gone and have taken the baby. I thought I'd be getting millions. Now, I'll have to settle for a paltry twenty grand. Guess the joke's on me.

"You almost ready?" Daniel says, panting as he carries several boxes. "We've got to go now."

I nod and hold up a finger.

"I'll put Liam in the car," he says. "Hurry up."

I finish packing and zip up my bag, walking out of my bedroom for the last time. Daniel's waiting for me in the running car. I place my luggage in the trunk and get into the back seat with the baby. Liam is already asleep in his car seat by the time we pull away from the curb.

"What are we doing about Tori?" I say. "She'll freak out when she sees we've left with the baby. She might call the police."

"As soon as we leave the bank with the money, I'll send her an email explaining the situation. I've already written it."

We pull up in front of the bank and Daniel goes in leaving me in the car. Ten minutes later, he emerges.

"Did you get it?" I say as he gets in.

"Yeah. Twenty thousand. Enough to get us started."

He starts the car, drives a few blocks and pulls into an empty parking spot to send Tori a message. He reads it to me before he hits send.

Tori, I know this will come as a shock and I'm sorry to tell you this way. Bottom line — Eden, who you also once knew as Sasha, and I have been in love for some time, long before she came to live with us. The piece of information that will be the most difficult for you is that Jonah is Sasha's and my biological son. I can't explain anything more than that. We've decided to start fresh as a family somewhere far away. Given the circumstances of how you "acquired" Jonah, I think it's best if we leave the police out of it. I'm sorry it ended this way. For the record, you were a good mother.
Daniel

"This isn't the way it's supposed to end," I say, tears in my eyes. "I'm supposed to have the house, the money and the baby. It should all be mine."

"Sasha, it's over. I just sent the email, she knows. It's time to move on."

I burst into tears as Daniel pulls away from the curb.

He keeps talking, trying to calm me down. "We have our baby and we'll get our own house one day. I promise. We'll make our own money. You'll see. Everything will be fine."

I snort and roll my eyes.

"It will all work out," he continues. "I'll get some modeling jobs and maybe then we'd have—"

"Don't you get it?" I say, screeching at him from the back seat, waking up the baby. "This was my only chance to have what's rightfully mine. Now, my son won't get his legacy."

As he drives, Daniel turns his head around to look at me. "What the hell are you talking about? What legacy?"

Liam starts to cry.

"Are you so blind?" I shout, tears running down my cheeks. "Haven't you ever noticed the resemblance between our son and Sam Petrosian?"

Daniel swerves around another car and quickly turns his eyes back to the road.

"What are you talking about?" he says as Liam wails in the car seat next to me.

"Tori's father is my father. Sam Petrosian is my father. I'm the result of one of his many affairs. Tori's my half-sister. She's the one who got everything — money, education and all of our father's love while I got nothing."

Daniel twists his head around to look at me and we lock eyes. He's confused. A long loud horn sounds and he turns his head around, jerking the steering wheel after nearly sideswiping a truck.

"Watch out," I yell to his narrowed eyes glaring at me in the rearview mirror. "You're going to kill us."

"You set me up from the beginning," he says, disbelief in his voice. "Our meeting at that audition, it wasn't an accident, was it?"

"Don't you see? I got nothing. I grew up in a trailer park. My mother died of cancer when I was a teenager because we had no money for her treatment. My father never knew I existed. Tori got everything."

Daniel's driving recklessly and scaring me.

"Watch the road," I shout while trying to comfort the baby. "At first, I only wanted to take you away from her. To prove that she couldn't have everything. I didn't plan the rest until later. After I fell in love with you, I realized I could have it all — you, the money and her family. I wanted to know my father. You were my way to get close to him."

Daniel turns around to yell at me while pressing his foot down on the gas pedal. "How can you say you love me when you've been manipulating and using me all this time? You convinced me to kill for you."

"Stop screaming and slow down," I shout as Liam gets hysterical, "you're scaring the baby." Daniel faces front but keeps driving fast. "When you told me you'd signed a prenup that paid out only if you and Tori had kids, it got me thinking. Then, I learned that Tori was a medical mess who couldn't get pregnant, and things became so clear."

"You're sick, you know that? I can't believe I let you talk me into everything."

"You don't understand. I only wanted what I was entitled to. Tori doesn't take care of herself. She wasn't going to live long anyway. I figured if you and I got pregnant and you and Tori adopted our baby, it was the perfect set-up. When I moved into the house and spent time with my father and the baby, I wanted things to stay that way. You don't know how much being with my father means to me. You see how he dotes on our son. He feels the connection. He adores Liam. I wanted him to adore me too."

"You used me for some twisted family revenge."

"Don't put it all on me," I shout. "You went along with it. I'm not the one who gave her sleeping pills and turned off her breathing device."

"I did it for you and Liam."

"It could have worked out if you hadn't gotten cold feet. If Tori died, as the nanny, I'd stay in the house to take care of the baby. After an appropriate amount of time, you and I would get married. The Petrosians would still see their grandson, and I'd be able to develop a relationship with my father. He'd be grieving and I'd be there to take the place of the daughter he lost."

"I should never have listened to you," Daniel shouts, shifting lanes and going faster. "You told me nothing but lies. You had me so confused so I'd go along with whatever you wanted me to do. You used me."

"Slow down," I shout. "Please, Daniel, I do love you. That's real. It was all for our family."

With one hand on the wheel, Daniel turns his beet-red face back to me. "You're a fucking liar. You're a—"

"Watch out," I scream.

A second later, we crash. As the air bags inflate, I instinctively throw my arms and body over my son to protect him. The car careens across the road, slamming into a low concrete wall, and flips over. The last thing I hear before I pass out is the sound of shattering glass and my baby's haunting cry.

CHAPTER FIFTY-SIX

THE WIFE

Three Months Later

After months of moping, this morning I've decided to open all the blinds in the house and let the sunshine in. There will be no more time spent wondering how things could have been different. It's time to move on.

I walk down the hall to the nursery, stopping in Jonah's empty room filled with his toys and books. The house feels eerily quiet now. I've grappled with whether to stay here or move out to get away from all the bad memories. I've decided not to leave. This is my house, the one I grew up in and it's home, no matter how crazy things got.

Wearing a new blue silk dress, I walk down the stairs and go into the kitchen.

"Lucy? You in here?" I call out as I walk into the room. My new nanny, Lucy, a middle-aged woman from London, is sitting in front of Jonah feeding him his breakfast. As usual, my son's food is everywhere — the floor, the highchair, there's even a splatter of something on the refrigerator.

"Jonah, what a mess you've made again," I say with a laugh. "How's it going, Lucy? Did he eat all his breakfast?"

"He's a good little eater. Don't worry about him. He won't ever starve."

My son holds out his sticky hands, covered with what looks like bananas and yogurt. He's beckoning for me to pick him up. "Ma-ma."

I love it when he says my name, but I'm already dressed for work.

"Not a chance, sweetie," I say to my son's hopeful grinning face. "Sorry, Buddy. Mommy has a meeting this afternoon with a very important new artist." I lean over and kiss him on the top of his head, making sure I don't get too close to his messy hands.

While Lucy cleans him up, I go back upstairs to the guest room to retrieve my bag. That's where I sleep now, the guest room. After everything that happened, I can't stay in my old room, the one Daniel and I shared.

When I return to the bottom of the stairs, Lucy has Jonah all dressed for our outing. He's wearing the cute little red hat my father gave him. Jonah smiles as Lucy transfers him from her arms to mine.

"Your Uber's here," she says.

I nod. "I'll drop Jonah off here around noon before I go into work."

Jonah and I climb into the waiting car for our thirty-minute drive up to Westchester County. When the car stops in front of the entrance to the building, I unbuckle my son, thank the driver and get out of the car.

After I sign in to the guest book, I walk down the long corridor to Room 1011. The door to the room is ajar. When I push it open, the first thing I notice is that the curtains are open, as I had requested. The room is sunny. A small woman wearing light-blue scrubs sits in a chair near the bed reading *Little Women* out loud. I hired her after the accident. She's been sitting by the bed for months.

"How's our patient today?" I say.

"Awake," says the nurse.

"Any response?"

She shakes her head. "Like the doctors told you, Ms. Fowler, people with severe traumatic brain injuries can seem awake, but they're not really with us."

I look over at my sister in the bed, pillows stuffed behind her head. She looks tiny and her icy-blue eyes are like flat pools of water next to her pale white skin. Her strawberry-blonde hair falls in waves to her shoulders. At first glance, she looks perfectly fine until you notice the blankness in her stare.

We're not sure how much she understands, if anything. She never speaks. The doctors say as more time goes by it's less likely that she ever will. Still, every now and then I think I see a glimmer of understanding in her eyes.

I tell the nurse to take a break and ask her to close the door on her way out. Pulling a chair close to the bed, I sit with Jonah on my lap.

"How are you feeling today, Sasha?" I say brightly. "Isn't Jonah getting big? Each day he looks more and more like our father, don't you think? Even my mother noticed the resemblance the other day. It's great for me because I look like our father. People naturally assume Jonah's my biological son."

My sister blinks and I wonder if that means she understands. We put the TV on for her every day, but her face never changes. They've tried to get her to write, but she doesn't seem to know how to hold a pencil or even what writing is. After all this time, the doctors have little hope she'll improve. But she is my little sister, so I'll always provide her with a safe place to be. She'll be well cared for in this private hospital for as long as she needs. That way, I can also keep an eye on her.

After the accident, our car was totaled. It took seven emergency workers over an hour to get them out. Daniel went through the windshield but was still alive. He held on for a day but in the end, it was better that he died. His handsome face was completely destroyed. I know him, he wouldn't have wanted to live like that. His appearance was so important to him.

"I can't stay long this morning. I have to get to work and Jonah has his gymnastics class at noon. You should see him tumbling, Sasha, he's quite athletic. He must get that from Daniel." I shift in my seat as I prepare to deliver some bad news. "I also wanted to tell you that Daniel didn't make it. Only you and Jonah survived the crash."

Her pale-blue eyes remain fixed on my face. No emotion of any kind is evident.

"So we're clear," I say my voice moving into a loud whisper, "I found out everything you and my husband were up to before the crash. After all that's happened, knowing you and he were trying to kill me still hurts. Thank God for baby monitors."

I shift Jonah to my other thigh and get him settled. "I only found out about you and I being sisters *after* Daniel died. While you were in the ICU, I was so angry with you. I wanted anything of yours out of my house. I went into your room and started throwing everything away. As I tossed all your things into a large garbage bag, I found your sketch book under your bed. I flipped through the book again and on the last few pages, I found two beautiful charcoal portraits of my father. It struck me as extremely odd that he was your subject because you hardly knew him. After that, I tore the room apart but found nothing else to explain those drawings."

Sasha blinks. I carefully examine her face. Unable to tell if she understands me or if it's just an involuntary movement, I keep talking.

"After the police finished their investigation of the accident, everything they recovered from the car was sent to me. That's when I found your journals. I learned then about all the things you and Daniel did to torture me — the missing watch, the threatening notes, the flowers and a whole bunch of little things like Jonah's eardrops. All your gaslighting was specifically designed to make me look and feel vulnerable and unstable. You were setting me up. It almost worked. Given my erratic behavior, it wouldn't have been a stretch if I accidently killed myself, would it?"

Sasha closes her eyes.

Does she understand?

"But without question, the most shocking thing I learned from your diaries was the truth about us. Why didn't you just come to me? I would have welcomed you. I always wanted a sister. We could have figured things out."

Sasha opens her eyes and blinks twice.

"It doesn't matter now. It's all behind us. I'm in charge of your care. Don't worry, there will always be a place for you here at Twin Oaks," I whisper while holding Jonah close to me. "Unfortunately, I won't be able to share your real identity with anyone, especially not our father or our son. It would kill Dad and ultimately destroy our beautiful little boy. I know you'll agree that no child should have to grow up with this kind of sordid tale hanging over him. I'm afraid your identity will have to remain our secret. It's the right thing for Jonah. I'm sure you only want the best for him."

Sasha blinks again. At this point, I've told her all she needs to know. What I haven't said is that keeping her here isn't totally altruistic on my part. Everyone has an agenda and so do I. I won't be encouraging the nurses to help dredge up any of Sasha's hidden memories. If my sister ever starts to regain her speech, the hospital will let me know. I can't have someone stepping forward claiming to be Jonah's mother. That would be too traumatizing for my son. This private hospital is the right place for her. They'll keep me informed.

Holding my son on my shoulder, I stand and walk halfway across the room before turning to face my sister.

"The emergency technicians at the accident told me you draped yourself around Jonah before the crash. They said your body took the brunt of the impact, leaving him unscathed. You saved his life and prevented him from getting hurt. For that, I'll always be grateful."

My sister's eyes follow me as I move towards the door.

"They say a mother could singlehandedly lift a car off of her child. I believe that's true. I know there's nothing I wouldn't do to protect mine."

THE END

ACKNOWLEDGEMENTS

In this book, I wanted to explore one of the strongest human emotions — the bond between a mother and child and how that connectedness impacts their lives. I have always believed a mother would do just about anything to protect her child and that's what drives this narrative. From the beginning, I had a very clear idea of what this story should be. But it was my literary muse, Peter Black (aka my husband), who helped me shape the plot and characters so that it all worked seamlessly. He, along with my other first readers, Diane McGarvey and Marlene Pedersen, gave me invaluable input that plugged the holes and made the story move fast. So, huge thank you to all. Couldn't do it without you.

I was feeling pretty good about the manuscript when I sent it to my editor, Publishing Director at Joffe Books, Kate Lyall Grant. She and I had worked on several books together and I knew she had a keen eye, and trusted her advice. Kate picked up on a personality trait in the main character that she felt needed to change. As soon as she said it, I knew she was one hundred percent right. (It didn't even require too much rewriting!) This subtle change in the mindset of the main character made all the difference in the world. From there, everything fell neatly into place. Thank you, Kate. You made it so much better.

On the second round of edits, I'd like to give a shout out to Anna Harrisson. She painstakingly picked through awkward sentences, timeline and plot holes and ultimately made the entire narrative stronger. On the third and final round of edits, I want to recognize Stephi Cham who went through the manuscript word for word, tightening it up. (Clearly, I do not know how to use a comma and hyphens are not in my writer's toolbox.) I'm very grateful you both were there to shine it up.

I'd also like to thank the team at Joffe Books who work diligently to make each book launch a success. The marketing, social media and general support is great. It would never happen without you.

Lastly, thank you to the readers. I've so appreciated all the nice comments, notes and supportive reviews I've received over the years when you like one of my books.

THE JOFFE BOOKS STORY

We began in 2014 when Jasper agreed to publish his mum's much-rejected romance novel and it became a bestseller.

Since then we've grown into the largest independent publisher in the UK. We're extremely proud to publish some of the very best writers in the world, including Joy Ellis, Faith Martin, Caro Ramsay, Helen Forrester, Simon Brett and Robert Goddard. Everyone at Joffe Books loves reading and we never forget that it all begins with the magic of an author telling a story.

We are proud to publish talented first-time authors, as well as established writers whose books we love introducing to a new generation of readers.

We won Trade Publisher of the Year at the Independent Publishing Awards in 2023. We have been shortlisted for Independent Publisher of the Year at the British Book Awards for the last four years, and were shortlisted for the Diversity and Inclusivity Award at the 2022 Independent Publishing Awards. In 2023 we were shortlisted for Publisher of the Year at the RNA Industry Awards.

We built this company with your help, and we love to hear from you, so please email us about absolutely anything bookish at: feedback@joffebooks.com.

If you want to receive free books every Friday and hear about all our new releases, join our mailing list: www.joffebooks.com/contact

And when you tell your friends about us, just remember: it's pronounced Joffe as in coffee or toffee!

ALSO BY MCGARVEY BLACK

TRUST ONLY ME
THE FIRST HUSBAND
MY SISTER'S KILLER
THE WOMAN UPSTAIRS
TWICE ON CHRISTMAS
THE BABY I STOLE

Milton Keynes UK
Ingram Content Group UK Ltd.
UKHW042257300924
449060UK00002B/2

9 781835 263471